CW01216340

E: rosiejonesauthor@gmail.com
F: www.facebook.com/rosiejonesauthor
Twitter: @RosieJonesBooks
Instagram: @rosiejonesauthor

For my wonderful brave, strong and beautiful nieces, Sharn and Ruby.

CHAPTER ONE

Rumbling along the rough, dusty track, the vehicle left a plume of sand in its wake. Inside, the soldiers could feel the hum of the engine in their stomachs as it bounced over dips in the dirt track, crawling at its steady pace. Corporal Jake Parsons wet his lips with his tongue. He could taste the desert, dry and arid in his mouth.

Four more months.

That was it. Four more months, and he would be out of this desert nightmare, back with his wife and the rest of his family. By the end of the year, Britain was due to withdraw all of its troops from Afghanistan - and that meant he would never have to return again.

Hitting a particularly large pothole, the vehicle lurched forwards, throwing the soldiers forward in their seats. Tired and forlorn, they barely even noticed. Jake imagined the damp English air hitting his tanned face as he jumped down from the C-17; he could almost feel the softness of his wife's skin against his and the knot of the cotton bedsheets beneath them. Knowing that they would be handing the base over to the Afghan soldiers within the next two months was a relief. After that, they just had tidying up to do, then they could go home, for good. He was almost there. The next four months should be a breeze.

Closing his eyes while relaxing against the hot metal body of the vehicle, Jake thought about the last time he saw her. Her face a picture of pride and love, she had waved him off, her golden hair billowing around her face in the cold winter breeze. But her eyes contained an unmistakeable sadness he couldn't ignore. This will be the last time, he had silently promised her. The last time I put you through this. When I get back, things will be different.

Bang. His eyes snapped open. He lifted his weapon. Bang. Bang. Suddenly the troops sprang to life, shots ricocheting from the vehicle's armoured body. A mayday call came over the radio; one of the other vehicles in the convoy was under ambush, the driver having been shot - they were struggling to resist. Hold your positions. *But, the gunfire growing heavier, Jake could hear desperation in their voices. They needed help.*

"I said hold your position, Corporal Parsons!"

Not again. He had promised himself that. Squeezing his eyes shut, he desperately tried to block out the urge to react, to do what he hadn't last time.

"Follow your orders, Corporal Parsons."

But he couldn't, could he?

Not when lives were at stake.

Unclipping his belt, he leapt up, forcing his way past the other soldiers to the rear of the vehicle, away from his Commanding Officer. He bellowed at him to sit tight and wait for back up, but the intensity of the shots seemed to increase by the second; the thought of not acting when he had the chance to do something *this time was too much to bear.*

Within seconds he had left the vehicle and was firing back at the insurgents.

Adrenaline pumping through his veins, he did what he was trained to do. He was quicker than them; within seconds he had taken out three men. But he was outnumbered - vastly outnumbered. Undeterred, frenzied, he drove forwards, low to the ground, shooting back at the insurgents who were firing hard at the convoy. He felt a shot fly past his right shoulder - here they came, his guys, following him out into the desert cloud.

Eventually, the shots began to slow and within a couple of minutes, they had petered out completely. Carefully and watchfully, the soldiers ungrouped from defensive positions. The front vehicle had been almost completely obliterated by the gunfire. There were no survivors. Reeling from the discovery of so many soldiers dead, mostly Afghan but a few of their own, it took the remaining section a few minutes to realise that nobody had eyes on Corporal Parsons.

He had vanished, right before their eyes.

***

The shop door greeted its cheery ding as Charlotte pushed it open to enter the shop. The sickly sweet aroma of fondant icing filled her nostrils and she took a deep breath, trying to ignore the nagging nausea deep inside her.

"Hello, Amber," she called with a smile, approaching the desk while gazing at the ornate cakes, displayed proudly on the shelves. "Izzy, don't touch anything!"

"I won't, Mummy."

Izzy licked her lips, wondering how sweet the icing would be on her tongue. Actually, she didn't need to wonder - she had tasted Amber Patterson's cakes before, and they were delicious. Her mum always came to this cake shop, every time it was someone's birthday. She reached up and pulled the straw hat from her head, holding it gingerly in her hands as though it might blow off and knock down one of the cakes any second.

A rummaging sound behind the desk caught their attention. Charlotte peered into the cupboard at the back of the shop. "Amber?"

Suddenly, Amber appeared, a smear of chocolate frosting across her pink apron and a faint dusting of icing sugar on her nose. "Charlotte! Izzy!" She stepped out from behind the desk to embrace them.

"Izzy, don't you look grown up in your uniform! I can't believe how old you're getting!"

"Daddy says I'll be as tall as Mummy, soon," Izzy beamed proudly.

"So you will!" Amber gently patted her head. "Are you ready for the big reveal?"

"Of course," Charlotte's voice was barely audible over her daughter's ecstatic squeals.

Amber grinned, ducking back into the cupboard. Seconds later, she emerged with a large white box, which she placed carefully on the counter. "Three layers, one chocolate, two sponge and buttercream, no jam, as requested."

Her nimble hands made neat work of the box, gently unfolding it to reveal the work of art inside. Charlotte loved the cake as soon as she saw it. Amber's cakes were always impeccable, but this had to be one of her best yet.

"It's amazing!" She beamed, studying the cake in amazement. "Honestly, Amber. It's truly incredible. You are so talented."

"Thank you," Amber stood back to admire her handiwork. "I hope it'll make the perfect centrepiece."

"Oh, it will!" Charlotte sighed with relief. "Thank you so much. How much do I owe you?"

After carefully reassembling the box, Amber ripped off a paper slip, hanging from a nail in the work surface. "It's two hundred and eighty, please."

Charlotte withdrew her credit card from her purse and pushed it into the card machine without so much as a flinch. After punching her pin number into the keypad, she pushed the card back into her purse safely.

"Izzy, can you take my keys, please?"

Izzy reached for the keys as asked.

"Thank you so much again," Charlotte smiled, wrapping her arms around the box.

"Hold it from the bottom," Amber instructed, hovering around the cake nervously - it was, after all, her latest baby. "I'll get the door for you."

Izzy trailed behind her mum, back through the shop, towards the front door. They said goodbye to Amber; once the cake was safely down the front step and on its way to their luxury SUV, parked six or seven metres away in front of the neighbouring newsagent, Amber closed the shop door and went back to work.

"Amber's done a good job, hasn't she, Mummy?"

"Yes. Daddy is going to *love* this cake! Can you open the boot, please?"

Izzy lifted the fob and pointed it at the car, jabbing the button with her stubby little thumb. The tail lights flashed and, as the boot swung open ready to receive the cake, the car sang its welcome bleep. Charlotte was only metres from the car when Izzy suddenly squawked. She turned abruptly, almost dropping the cake in surprise.

"My hat!" Izzy squealed, running after her hat which danced through the air towards a stand of newspapers.

"Izzy!" Charlotte sighed, exasperated. "I almost dropped the cake! I thought you were hurt!"

"I can't lose my hat, I need it for school!" Izzy cried, grabbing it just as it reached the door of the newsagent, the tartan pattern of her uniform glowing in the early morning sun. "Mrs Cross said that I must always wear my hat."

"Alright. Come on now, quickly. You don't want to be late."

Charlotte was about to return to the car when her eyes caught on the front of the newspapers. She rarely concerned herself with the news these days, it fed her anxiety. But today, she couldn't take her eyes off it. Recognising the piercing emerald eyes on the front page, her mouth dropped open and her stomach lurched. Her heart pounded in her chest. Her chest felt so tight, she could barely breathe.

Thump.

She dropped the cake.

"Mummy!"

Within seconds, Izzy was at her feet, her hat now securely in her hands, her mouth open in a perfect 'O', staring in shock at the stricken cake.

"Mummy! Mummy!"

Charlotte gulped. Her eyes fell on the box, her hands trembling violently. She glanced in the direction of the cake shop. To her relief, there was no sign of Amber. She bent down and scooped up the box as quickly as she could, then rushed to the car and placed it in the boot, closing it with a thump.

"Mummy, did you break the cake?"

"Get in the car," she ordered, her voice barely a whisper.

"But Mummy," Izzy protested, "what about the cake? What will we do now? What will Daddy say if we give him a broken cake?!"

"Get in the car!" Charlotte ordered more

firmly, her voice now raised. The corners of Izzy's mouth turned down and instantly, Charlotte regretted raising her voice - she hardly ever did, especially not to her daughter. "Come on, you don't want to be late for school."

To Charlotte's relief, Izzy climbed into the front seat and sat in silence for most of the short journey. Her mind suddenly swimming with thoughts, it was all she could do to hold herself together long enough to get there. Cruising through the large iron gates, she sighed with relief, glancing at her daughter who sat beside her solemnly, her hands in her lap.

Charlotte squeezed Izzy's right hand. "I'm sorry I shouted. I shouldn't have. I was just shocked, about the cake. But I was wrong to take it out on you."

"Will it be ok?" Izzy's bottom lip trembled.

"Of course," Charlotte forced a smile. "Of course it'll be ok. Don't worry about that."

"Why did you drop it?"

"I... I tripped," Charlotte lied. "And lost my balance."

Izzy nodded, contemplating that for a moment. Then, grabbing for her bag, she pulled it onto her lap and smiled innocently. "I'm sure Daddy won't mind, Mummy! It will still taste nice!"

Reaching the end of the long drive, Charlotte pulled to a stop in the car park. "Yes. I'm sure it will."

She walked Izzy to the doors as she always

did, waving a cheery goodbye. But once her daughter was out of sight, the weight of the world suddenly fell on her shoulders. Her eyes filled with tears and she had to bite her lip hard to keep it together long enough to get to the car. She climbed in as quickly as she could and left the carpark more hastily than she intended, spitting up a small cloud of gravel in her wake. She was so deep in thought that she barely noticed the other parents arriving for the morning drop off, waving from their cars.

Speeding down the road towards home, she blinked hard, trying to blot the image of the young man from her mind. His piercing eyes - although the newspaper print was black and white, she could still see them in piercing fresh green, burnt into her brain, a detail she could never erase. His strong jaw. His short, dark hair. The earthy green collar of his uniform. She could almost smell him now, the faint hint of tobacco on his clothes mixed with the sweetness of his peppermint breath. By the time she reached the automatic front gates and turned into her spotless resin driveway, tears were streaming down her cheeks and dripping onto the leather steering wheel in front of her. She couldn't open that box. Not again. It had been closed for so long; opening it, even just a crack, would be disastrous.

***

Her cheeks flushing deep scarlet, she frowned and roughly clenched her jaw, trying desperately to hold back the tears which filled her eyes.

"Nobody, nobody! Nobody, nobody!" They chanted, surrounding her in a crescent shaped human wall. Firmly, she fixed her eyes on the dirt, scuffing her almost worn-through shoe around in the mud, focusing on nothing else until she zoned out and could barely hear their voices anymore. She was used to being the one in the middle. The one everyone looked at, and turned on. The odd one out.

Still staring at the floor, she frustratedly picked at the frayed sleeve of her faded cardigan. The other children still surrounded her, chanting, in their brand-new uniforms, bright green and perfect, barely worn for a week. She had been to three schools in as many years, moving from place to place, passed from house to house, nobody really wanting her. Slipping out of one hand-me-down uniform, into the next.

Closing her eyes, she allowed her mind to wander where it always went when things were tough. Her mum. One day, her mum would come back, wanting her. Loving her. She'd be able to leave this school and start afresh, wearing a brand new jumper and shiny new shoes which had never before been worn. She would have friends. She would have different sandwiches in her lunch every day, a packet of crisps and a homemade slice of cake - carrot on Mondays, chocolate on Tuesdays and Fridays, fruit on Wednesdays and Thursdays. Someone to smile and wave when she ran from the classroom at the end of the day, someone to cook her dinner, admire the paintings she'd worked hard on at school. Someone to read her a story and tuck her in at night, in her own bedroom, under her own duvet. Someone to kiss her. Someone to hold her.

"I bet you were left in a dustbin!"

Then the chanting changed. "Dustbins! Dustbins! That's why her jumper's all shabby and her tights have ladders. Dustbins!"

She tried to leave the circle, but nobody would let her. Every time she got close, they shoved her back again and she sank to the floor, in the dirt, knowing that later on, she'd be scolded for getting her uniform so muddy. How do you get your uniform so muddy? Have you been rolling in the mud? You're supposed to be a young lady, you know! I don't have time to wash clothes all day. Don't you ever think of anyone else?

As the chanting intensified, she pushed her fingers in her ears, lifting her knees up to her chest and firmly pressing her eyelids against them, until everything went white and strange shapes taunted her. No matter how hard she tried, she could still hear them. Chanting. Over and over and over again. Dustbins! Dustbins! Nobody! Nobody!

The noise overwhelmed her. She started to sob. Shoulders shaking up and down, she cried, for the mum she so desperately wanted but never had, and the life she wished she could lead. She didn't want much. Just someone to love her - really love her, not because they were paid to - and school uniform that was the same as everyone else's. She didn't want to be the odd one out. She would keep her shoes spotless, her jumper and blouse immaculate. She would never ladder her tights.

Suddenly, her fingers still in her ears, she realised

that the chanting had stopped. With watering eyes she slowly peered up through her tears, her chin still close to her knees and her damp, thick fringe stuck to her forehead. To her relief, everyone had scarpered. Well, almost everyone. There was only one boy left, and he was kneeling right in front of her. She narrowed her eyes suspiciously through the salty strands of her fringe.

"Do you want to play?"

Slowly, she shook her head, sinking her face back down to her knees, waiting for him to leave. But when she finally stopped crying and looked up two minutes later, he was still beside her, cross legged, his arms firmly around his knees. Waiting.

"What do you want?"

He shrugged. "We could play tag? Or stuck in the mud? Or just run around?"

She stared at him. He wasn't shabby like her, his uniform was freshly washed and ironed just like the others. His hair was neatly brushed and he didn't smell like he was in need of a wash.

"I mean, why do you want to play with me?"

After staring at her for a couple of seconds, he smiled, his eyes travelling across the playground. "Everyone needs someone to look out for them."

She followed his gaze over to Billy Kemp, the ringleader, who was scowling over at them, nursing a fat, bloody lip. Her eyes widened. "Did you do that?"

The boy - she didn't even know his name - smirked. "Yeah."

"Why would you do that?"

"He's a bully. He needed putting in his place."

She looked back at Billy, who was still scowling - he wasn't going to bother her again. Not now she had her - dare she allow herself to even think it it - friend - with her. She wiped her wet, hot cheeks on the back of her sleeve and took a deep, shaky breath."Tag?"

***

Leaning over the cool granite worktop, the bass of the music vibrated through Charlotte's body. She had been staring at the cake for about half an hour now, as though if she stared at it for long enough, it might knit itself back together.

It wasn't too bad, she supposed - the top two tiers weren't badly affected, the bottom having taken the brunt of the drop. Still, it wasn't perfect. She wanted it to be perfect, it needed to be perfect. Nervously, she tapped her hands on the worktop, the music uncomfortably loud, penetrating her eardrums. But she couldn't turn it off. She needed something - anything - to distract her from what she had seen.

Those eyes.

They were all she could see when she closed her own. Piercing into her as though they could slice her in half. She shivered, even though the tiles were warm under her feet, the underfloor heating on even though summer had barely finished. Charlotte didn't like being cold.

Taking a deep breath, she turned away from the cake, busying herself with the other preparations. Three large, unopened boxes of decorations sat in the hallway, having been delivered within the last hour. She only had a couple of hours until she needed to collect Izzy from school, and four hours before the caterer would arrive. She ran her soft hands gently along the top edge of the box, unable to think clearly for the music pulsating in her head. Maybe she should turn it off. She searched the room for her phone. Once she eventually found it, she turned the music off.

A sudden silence filled the air and she sighed with relief, closing her eyes. She needed to keep busy. As long as she kept busy, the pain would fade, the box could be closed again. This would fade away, just like before. She wasn't that person anymore. Reaching for the painkillers on the worktop, she punched two from their blisters, knocking them back with a glass of water. Then she stood for a moment, her eyes closed, wishing that the pain would simply go away.

After a minute or two, she'd had enough of feeling sorry for herself. Shaking her head, she pulled a sharp knife from their expansive selection and cut the top of the box, releasing a dozen helium balloons up towards the high ceiling. She admired the way they shone in the early afternoon sun for a moment, then examined the room around her, deciding where to place them. After spreading them evenly throughout the room, she opened the next box, which contained the tableware. Smoothing a luxurious gold tablecloth and a beautiful sequinned runner across their solid acacia dining table, she smiled, then covered the chairs with matching chair covers. Once the chairs had been covered and distributed around the room she looked around, admiring her handiwork. If there was one thing that Charlotte knew how to do better than anything else, it was throw a party. She had spent a lifetime dreaming up the most extravagant birthday celebrations, and now she had almost unlimited funds, she was able to put her plans into action.

She laid the table with charger plates and scattered sequins, perfectly placed. After hanging the personalised banner over the bifold doors, she stacked champagne flutes on the granite worktop. Finally, she heaved a tall coffee table into the corner of the room, before covering it with a table cloth and placing the cake on top, turning it until the worst part was at the back. Hopefully, nobody would notice too much. If she placed the chocolate fountain on the kitchen island, that would attract most of the guests' attention - they might not notice the slightly collapsed cake at all.

Once everything was in its place and she still had time to spare before collecting Izzy, she sat down to have a salad. It was the first thing she'd eaten all day, and she was actually hungry - her returning appetite was a relief. Maybe, she would watch some daytime TV to occupy her mind until it was time to leave. Holding the plate, she perched on the sofa, reaching for the remote. Waiting for the picture to load, she filled her fork with food and lifted it to her mouth. And there it was. The picture flashed up on the screen and she stopped suddenly, her mouth open, mesmerised. There they were again. Those green eyes.

The portrait disappeared from the screen and instead, she saw the front of Queen Elizabeth Hospital, reporters everywhere, cameras flashing, microphones held out in anticipation. Expectantly, the camera zoomed in on the doors, waiting for someone to emerge. Her hands trembling, Charlotte dropped the plate on the coffee table with a clatter, her eyes fixed on the screen. She'd lost her appetite. The cameras started flashing; two shadows appeared behind the glass doors then emerged, hand in hand, just like they had before.

Although they looked about fifteen years older than last time, she knew straight away that it was them. The shouts of reporters surrounding the entrance, and the click of cameras trying to catch the perfect shot almost drowned her and her eyes watered, her bottom lip trembling like Alana's hands, holding the piece of paper.

"Five years ago, our youngest son, Jake, was presumed dead after going missing in action in Afghanistan. It has been a long five years, but we never gave up hope that he would come back to us, alive. Now he has, and our dreams have come true. However, as you can appreciate our family is fragile, and our son has been through a lot, and we would respectfully ask for some privacy while he readjusts to life back on home soil. Ourselves and Jake would like to thank the public for their messages of support throughout this nightmare."

***

Eyes fixed straight on the whitewashed walls and sterile, plastic floor, Jake's skinny legs dangled over the edge of the bed. He could hear the doctor talking to him, but his mind was swimming; he couldn't find the words to respond. Anything he wanted to say seemed futile. Dropping his eyes down to his pale, scarred arms, protruding from the bottom of the oversized hospital gown which hung off his emaciated frame, he closed them, drifting back to happier times when he felt whole again.

Questions. So many questions. He was tired. All he wanted to do was curl up in the quiet, in the dark, and go to sleep. Eat a proper meal and sleep. For hours. Days. Weeks even. He had not slept properly for longer than he could remember, always slightly conscious just in case he needed to defend himself, hunger pains and thirst keeping him awake anyway. Slowly, he edged off the bed and moved to the corner of the room, sliding his back down the wall and eventually settling with his arms around his knees, allowing his eyelids to droop again. He felt safe with the hard walls behind him, surrounding him.

He had wanted to escape for so long, to return home. But it had hit him, when lying in bed on the large aircraft heading back to the UK, that he no longer knew what home meant. At some point in the last five years his memory had dissolved along with the flesh on his body, the people and places he once longed for had fizzed away, replaced with all he knew now. The dry sand, the rancid smell, the constant sense of weightlessness he had felt for the past five years, being high on constant adrenaline and delirious through lack of water and nutrition.

"Jake?"

Instinctively, he threw his arm out, eyes snapping open as the hairs on his right arm stood on end, sensing a light touch.

"I'm sorry, I didn't mean to startle you..."

He gulped, blood pumping through his veins once more. He could barely focus, his eyes felt as though they were swimming. So, this was it. For five years, this was what he had longed for, wished for more than anything. This was it?

CHAPTER TWO

It was always them. The two of them, against the world. Since Jake had given Billy Kemp a fat lip, nobody had picked on Charlie, not even when they moved up to secondary school and the difference between Charlie in her hand-me-down trousers and scuffed up blazer, and the rest of the girls, in their brand new pleated skirts and immaculate blazers, would become instantly obvious.

On their first day, on the way to school, Jake slipped out of his brand new blazer and held it out to her. "Here. Have mine."

"Are you mad? Your mum will go mental!"

"She won't even notice. And I don't care. I'll say I was playing football and lost it."

Charlie said nothing, but quietly swapped blazers, infinitely grateful that Jake had taken the fall for her. With a brand new blazer, perhaps everything would be alright. Perhaps she could pretend that her mum had bought it for her. She could imagine her browsing the rows of uniform in the school shop, gently easing the blazer off its hanger and slipping it over her daughter's shoulders. Just right. Don't you look grown up!

On the evening of Charlie's fourteenth birthday, they lay on a picnic blanket by the lake, gazing up at the willow branches which waved above them in the warm summer breeze.

"One day, we'll leave this place," Jake declared, the corners of his lips curling up at the thought. "Together."

Charlie turned to face him, butterflies dancing in her stomach as she felt his little finger brush against hers on the itchy picnic blanket. "Where will we go?"

He shrugged. "Where do you want to go?"

Charlie had spent the last eleven years of her life, as long as she could think for herself, wishing that her mum would turn up and whisk her off to some faraway place. They would live by the sea, just the two of them, licking ice creams and riding donkeys, running through the fresh haze of the breakers as they hit the sand under their feet. No more foster care. No more residential homes. They wouldn't need anyone else. But with every birthday that passed, the likelihood of her mum turning up to whisk her away seemed to become more and more remote. Suddenly, lying on the picnic blanket with Jake by her side, she realised that she was wrong. It wasn't supposed to be her and her mum. Maybe there was someone else, someone who had been in her life ever since she was seven years old - maybe it was meant to be them against the world, after all?

She reached for him, running the back of her hand along his cheek. His skin was still baby soft, but other parts of him had changed in the past year. His voice was becoming deeper, his green eyes more intense. Sometimes, she caught him looking at her and she could tell that things were changing between them. For a moment neither of them said anything. Then, very slowly, he sat up and kissed her.

His lips were soft and gentle against hers, and her stomach lurched with excitement and anticipation. He tasted slightly minty and she could smell a hint of his parents' cigarette smoke in his hair as his body pressed against hers and his palm gently cupped around her cheek. She allowed herself to melt into him until eventually, he broke away and sat back, his eyes glittering adoringly.

"I think I love you, Charlie," he whispered nervously, his heart thumping in his chest like a war drum.

Charlie's pulse quickened and her heart seemed to skip a beat. It was the first time that anyone had ever told her that. "I think I love you too."

His fingers laced through hers and they lay on their backs, staring up at the blue sky scattered with wispy clouds above.

"I'm joining the army when I leave school," Jake announced eventually. "We'll get our own flat. I'll look after you."

"The army? Why the army?"

"I want a good job. I'll earn a good wage, I can support both of us. Nobody will ever tease you again. You'll have everything you need."

The wind whipped through the trees again and Charlie took a deep breath, imagining what it might be like to step through their own front door for the first time - their own space, which they wouldn't have to share with anyone. To have her own things in their own places - books on a book shelf - not pre-loved ones with ripped out pages or scribbles inside; brand new, tidy books which she had chosen for herself. Her own clothes in her wardrobe, furniture which matched. "I wish I could skip forwards a few years. Get out of that place."

Jake frowned. "I thought you said Marie was alright?"

"She is... but it's not my home. And she's not my mum. She never will be. None of them ever will be. I want to stand on my own two feet... have my own space. My own stuff. Somewhere permanent."

"I know," he squeezed her hand.

For a few minutes they lay in silence, enjoying the warmth of the sun on their skin. Then Charlie turned, her elbow on the blanket, resting her cheek on the palm of her hand. "I think I want to be a nurse."

He smiled. "Yeah?"

"Yeah. Do you think I'd be good at it?"

"Definitely. You're caring... loving... you're a warm person."

"I want to work with kids. Make them better. Give them hugs. Look after them when they don't have anyone else, when they're hurt and scared."

Her smile faded, one of her earliest memories fleetingly crossing her mind. It only lasted for a second. Sitting in her dirty nightie on the front step of the police station, clutching a threadbare teddy to her chest, shivering from cold and fear. Her eyes wide like saucers, silent tears running down her face while she waited for her mum to come back.

"You'll be amazing," Jake broke her from her thoughts. "We'll be amazing. Together."

***

Spinning around on the tiled floor in her sparkly tights, Izzy squealed with delight. Holding Myles's hands tightly, she spun all the way to the left, then all the way to the right. He lifted her, flying her around the room like a plane. When he dropped her gently back on the floor, she cried, "again, Daddy!"

Watching from a distance, Charlotte absent-mindedly lifted a pile of plastic plates with one hand and dropped them into the rubbish sack she held in her other. Getting into the party mood had turned out to be impossible. She'd been distracted when greeting the guests, almost missing Myles's grand entrance because her mind was completely elsewhere. She could barely look him in the eye when, her hands trembling, she'd lit the candles of his cake.

"Charlotte?"

Pressure on her shoulder caused her to jump with surprise, and she dropped the sack. It landed on the floor with a thump. For a couple of seconds, Charlotte felt dozens of pairs of eyes on her. She bent down and scrambled for the sack. By the time she stood up again, everyone had gone back to their conversations. Or maybe they'd never been staring in the first place. Maybe it was all in her head.

"Are you okay?"

It was her best friend, Effie. Could she really call her that? They'd only known each other for a few years, since being introduced by their husbands. But now, Effie was the only person besides Myles that Charlotte spoke to almost every day, and besides Izzy and Myles, the only person who seemed to really care for her; not just as Myles's wife, but as Charlotte herself.

Charlotte forced a smile. "Of course. Never better."

"It's just... you seem a bit... distant."

"I'm fine." Charlotte replied firmly, dropping the last of the used plates into the sack. "Glad that it all went to plan, that's all."

"It's a great party," Effie watched Myles and Connor on the makeshift dance floor, spinning their excited children around. Absent-mindedly, she held her palm against the swell of her stomach. "Do you ever think about giving Izzy a sibling?"

Charlotte swallowed hard. It seemed to be all she ever thought about these days. There was almost no escaping from it. "Sometimes."

Effie grinned, still holding her neat bump. "Oh, it would be so lovely if you did! They could grow up together, like Izzy and Callum. Connor was saying the other day how much Myles would love another child. What's stopping you?"

Charlotte narrowed her eyes ever so slightly, but kept them on her daughter. Sometimes, Effie could overstep the mark. She was outspoken, opinionated, sometimes interfering. But they were some of the reasons that Charlotte liked her. She had always been more of an introvert, reserved, always thinking before she spoke in case she upset someone. She'd felt almost like she was treading on eggshells her whole life, desperate to make people happy so they wouldn't shut her out. On the other hand, Effie said what she thought, whenever she thought it. She walked around with her head high, and if anyone didn't like it, then too bad. Charlotte quite liked that about her. Sometimes, she wished she could be more like Effie. When they were out together, she could hide behind Effie, use her like a sort of human mask. It was easier to pretend that the real her, hidden deep inside, didn't exist, when she was with Effie.

"Excuse me, I just need to..." Charlotte didn't have the energy to finish her sentence. She lifted the bin bag and carried it through the kitchen to the utility room, then burst through the door into the fresh night air. Stepping out onto the sandstone paving, she quickly padded down the passageway which led to the bin store, in just her tights. Once she'd dropped the bag inside the chute, she leant against the brick wall of the house, tilting her head up towards the night sky and closing her eyes.

The fresh air in her lungs was a relief. Their home was hardly small and they had plenty of space for their guests, but it had seemed unusually claustrophobic inside. Almost as though there was an unwelcome presence, filling half the room, staring at her... with those piercing green eyes. Gasping, Charlotte's eyes snapped open, the smell of tobacco forcing its way into her lungs. She turned, wild-eyed, to find Connor metres away from her.

Although she would have preferred to be on her own, the realisation that it was only Connor was a relief.

"Charlotte?" He frowned curiously, wondering what she was doing standing outside by herself, her face tear-stained. "What's wrong?"

Embarrassed, Charlotte furiously wiped at her eyes with the back of her hand, instantly regretting it - her face would be even more of a mess, now.

"Do you want me to get Myles? Or Effie?"

"No, no, I'm fine," Charlotte shook her head. "Please don't. I don't want to make a fuss and spoil the party. I'm fine."

"You don't look fine." He took a drag of his cigarette, still peering at her. "Are you upset about the cake? Because if you are, you don't need to be - it looks fine! Nobody even noticed, not really. I only know because Effie told me..."

"I'm not upset about the cake."

"Then, what is it?"

Charlotte had to think fast. Connor was Myles's business partner and they worked together every single day, they were almost as close as a married couple.

"I er... it's a bit embarrassing," she muttered. "I'm just a bit emotional. Hormones, I think."

"Oh." Connor shifted awkwardly, then his eyes widened. "Oh! Myles said you were trying... are you..."

Charlotte's eyes fell to the floor. "No. No, I'm not."

"Oh..." he smiled sympathetically, gently squeeze her upper arm through the lace of her dress. Charlotte had to suppress a sudden urge to flinch at his touch. "I'm sorry. Effie and I had to try for months, too. It's tough, especially when the first one came easy. I'm sure it will happen for you again soon. Don't worry!"

Charlotte forced a weak smile.

"Maybe when it happens, this one will be a mini-me for you, eh? Seeing as Izzy is the spit of her dad!"

Taking a deep breath, Charlotte wiped the last of the tears from her eyes. She had to pull herself together. The last thing she wanted to do was put a downer on Myles's birthday.

"Please don't say anything to Myles. I don't want to ruin his birthday."

"Of course I won't. My lips are sealed."

"Thank you. I'd better get back inside. They'll be wondering where I am."

***

Side by side, Alana and John watched through the glass as their son, curled up in a ball in the corner of the room, raised his gaze to the psychiatrist. Although he'd had a much needed shower and was now clean, his eyes were vacant and glassy, and the gown hung off him like he was a small boy wearing his dad's shirt. His hair and beard so long and matted, he was barely recognisable. He had always had neat, short hair, and a clean-shaven face. Fighting the lump in her throat, which was growing by the second, Alana tightened her grip on the small black holdall which she had brought to the hospital.

"He needs to come home."

She jumped slightly at the sound of her own voice; she hadn't intended to speak out loud. "Wear his own clothes. Sleep in his own bed."

John said nothing. He had hoped and prayed for this day for so long, the day that his son would come back to them. When Jake first went missing, John had kept his mobile in his hand or his pocket at all times, believing that it would only be a matter of time before they called to say they'd found him. He never stopped believing that his son was alive, not when the days dragged on and the news reports dwindled, not when army officials had told them that Jake was highly unlikely to be alive; not even when he had opened the local newspaper barely a year and a half after his son had gone missing to find notice of the court application. He still believed, deep in his gut, that Jake was still alive when, in his best shirt and trousers, he attended the hearing in which the Judge ruled that Jake was most likely dead, and issued the certificate of presumed death.

The certificate was only a piece of paper to

John. He would never stop believing that his son was still alive, not until he had evidence - not circumstantial evidence, or presumed evidence, but cold, hard evidence. Jake's body had never been recovered. None of Jake's belongings had ever been recovered, not a drop of his blood had been found. It was like he had simply disappeared off the face of the earth. People didn't just disappear. Not even in a war zone like Afghanistan - if he was truly dead, someone would have found something, or claimed responsibility - surely. But milestones started to pass. The first birthday Jake hadn't called. The first Christmas. Two years since he went missing. More birthdays, more Christmases. Three years became four.

When it finally came, the phone call had sent shockwaves through their lives, just like the first one. A couple of months ago, John had finally resigned himself to the fact that he would never see his son again. Whether he was dead or alive. He had to stop fighting it, because it was eating him and Alana up inside. Worst of all, their all-consuming grief had driven their other son away, who had started a new life on the other side of the world, desperate to live out of his brother's shadow. They still had their lives to lead, and Jake would have wanted them to live them. So, after clearing his old room of most of his possessions and packing them in boxes in the loft, they booked a holiday, somewhere they had always wanted to go. They hadn't been on holiday for six years, worried that they might miss the call, when it came. What if they were away, and uncontactable, and Jake thought that they didn't care?

"We have to move on," John had told Alana one evening over dinner. "We can't keep our lives on hold indefinitely. He wouldn't want us to stop living too."

Alana had said nothing at first, but continued to eat, her eyes on her plate. She didn't know what to say. John had always been the strong one, her rock, the one who never gave up hope even when she felt as though they were trying desperately to swim against the strongest current, and losing. How could they give up on their son?

Silently, John stood and crossed the room to his jacket which was hanging on a hook in the corner. He reached into his pocket and pulled out a rolled up brochure. Alana hadn't even noticed it there. Then he smoothed it flat and place it on the table, the weight of what it represented thick and heavy between them.

They never got to go on the holiday. Their bags were packed, ready in the hallway, and John had been carrying out one last sweep of the house before they left. Windows... automatic lights... keys... curtains... then the phone rang. Alana hovered in the hallway at the bottom of the stairs, staring at it.

"Let it ring... we don't have time," John had called from the top of the stairs, closing the bedroom door with a thump behind him. "It's probably someone selling something. Nobody important ever calls the house phone these days."

But Alana couldn't ignore it. Something deep inside her was telling her - no, screaming at her - to answer it. To lift the phone, and answer it. So she did. One sentence. That was all it took to knock her legs from under her; she had collapsed into a crumpled heap on the floor, barely able to talk for the primal cries of relief that escaped from deep inside her. The shock meant that she could barely remember that moment now, only what the caller had said. The words kept playing on loop in her head, over and over and over again. *Mrs Parsons? We've found your son. Jake is alive.*

CHAPTER THREE

Watching the big hand judder its way around the clock face, Charlie's stomach lurched violently. The steady tick vibrated in her head ominously; she could feel her pulse beating in her temples, in perfect time. Get a grip. *That's what Jake would be saying if he could see her now. He would be laughing at her.* Why are you even worried? You'll get straight As, you always do.

And he wouldn't be wrong. She did always get As. But sometimes, she thought that the pressure that came with that was almost worse than it would have been if she was failing in everything. Everyone expected her to do well. Her teachers, her classmates, her key workers. She couldn't bear the thought of letting people down. Couldn't bear the thought of letting herself down. Throughout her life, her grades had been the one thing she had control over - not even her third or fourth-hand uniform or books could take them away from her. Besides Jake, she had nothing else, so she threw herself into her schoolwork, dreaming of the day when she could set off to university and be brilliant, starting the next stage of her life. She never wanted to rely on anyone. She would have her own career, her own money, and perhaps in the future she and Jake would have children. They would be so loved, and they'd have everything that she hadn't. Two parents. Lunch boxes full of treats. A holiday somewhere hot and sunny every summer. A big birthday party every year, with a posh cake and crisply wrapped presents in brand new boxes and thick wrapping paper, the sort you really had to tug at to get to the present inside. A house with a garden.

It didn't have to be big - just warm and safe, and she would let her children pick their own paint for the walls, their own curtains and their own bedspreads. They would each have their own wardrobe, with their own clothes. Clothes which came with tags on, perfect and unworn, not bobbled and shrunken and slightly stained from their previous owners. They would have brand new toys in boxes for Christmas, which Charlie and Jake would spend hours assembling, before perfectly attaching the stickers. They wouldn't have to sneak an extra piece of fruit up their sleeve at snack time, just in case it was all they'd have to eat for the rest of the day. They wouldn't have to dive into the lost property bin whenever there was nobody around, searching for uniform items that looked a bit less tired than the ones they were wearing. They wouldn't have to make a card in class that they knew nobody would ever open when it was Mothers' Day.

"You have ten minutes left."

Charlie jumped slightly at the invigilator's warn-

ing, dropping her gaze back to the biology paper in front of her. How long had she been sitting there? She shook her head, frustrated at herself for wasting valuable time. She still hadn't finished, let alone read through her paper. Pupils around her were casually reading through theirs, even closing them, placing their pens triumphantly in a neat line in front of them on their desks. She had *to finish this. She couldn't be a nurse if she didn't do well in biology. Suddenly, the stakes felt impossibly high.*

Tightening her grip, she started to scribble again. She wrote and wrote until her hand was stiff and she had a hot, squidgy blister on the side of her finger. Just as she finished her final sentence, the invigilator's voice rang out across the hall, "time's up! Please close your papers."

Dropping the pen on the desk with a clatter, Charlie mentally swore. She'd not had time to proof read anything. If she had read any of the questions wrong, or gone off on a tangent, or made an embarrassing spelling error, there was no opportunity to fix it. Nervously biting her lip, she closed the paper, hoping that the extensive preparation she'd done for the exam would shine through. She had tried her very best.

Once the papers had been safely collected, the students filed out of the hall in a line. Reaching the courtyard outside, they broke into conversations. Oh my God, what did you put for question 6?! *Charlie pushed her pen in the pocket of her hoodie and exhaled heavily, resigning herself to the fact that there was nothing she could do now except wait until August. She pushed her way through the others, who were now congregating in small groups, and started her journey home. She was so deep in thought that she almost missed him, sitting on his bike at the end of the school driveway. "Charlie!"*

She looked up, a smile spreading across her face. He had come to meet her. He cycled over and stopped right in front of her, leaning sideways to kiss her. "How did it go?"

"I don't know... I ran out of time."

"You'll have done amazingly. You always do."

"I keep thinking about things I should have written... but I didn't..."

"Stop worrying, there's nothing you can do about it now!"

They walked away from school, away from the others who were starting to trickle out of the school gates behind them.

"One more to go," Jake steadied the bike with one hand, snaking his other arm around her waist. "Then we'll be free. For the whole summer."

"Yeah," Charlie breathed, although the thought of almost three months without school wasn't quite the celebration for her that it was for him.

"I got an interview," he announced, out of the blue.

Stopping in her tracks, Charlie's eyes widened. "An interview? When? For what?"

Jake grinned, and she didn't even need him to answer. His eyes lit up, full of ambition. He wanted to do well, too. He'd been planning this for years. These exams were the first step towards the rest of his life.

"Next week. I went to the career centre in town last week. They've set my assessment up for next Tuesday and Wednesday."

Charlie threw her arms around him, almost knocking him off-balance. "That's amazing. Well done."

"Well, I haven't got in yet! And even if I do, I'll have to pass phase one."

Releasing him, Charlie held him at arms length. "You'll pass, there's no doubt about it."

Suddenly, the realisation that she was about to lose another person close to her hit her like a smack in the face. Jake had been the biggest constant in her life for so many years, and now things were changing so quickly she almost wished that time would stop. She knew that, long term, it would be good for them - they wouldn't be apart forever, once he had finished his training she'd be able to see him again. If they wanted the careers they had planned for the last few years, they had to knuckle down and work hard, setting things up for their rest of their lives.

That wouldn't make it any easier to say goodbye, though.

***

Leaning over the stone sink in her scant, lacy nightdress, Charlotte stared at her reflection in the mirror. What if he could tell? Had her appearance changed? Lifting one hand from the sink, she watched it shake in front of her. Was she losing it?

Every time she closed her eyes, she could see them again - those eyes. His eyes.

The door clicked open behind her and she froze for a second, then grabbed her toothbrush and began to brush her teeth. Myles approached from behind and wrapped his arms around her. She concentrated on brushing each tooth, forcing herself not to flinch under his touch.

"Thank you," he breathed against her neck, causing the hairs at the base of her hairline to stand on end. "It was a great party."

She spat her toothpaste in the sink, watching it swirl away down the plughole before she replied. "You're welcome. I'm glad you enjoyed it."

"I did."

His lips continued to graze against her neck and she swallowed hard. It took every ounce of her self-control not to wriggle out of his arms. Suddenly, his alcohol-tinged breath on her skin and the clammy warmth of his body against hers felt somehow wrong; dirty and disgusting, as though he wasn't her husband at all, but a stranger. She gritted her teeth and tried to keep her breathing level, disgust bubbling away inside her.

He felt her flinch. And he stopped. "What's wrong?"

"Nothing," she replied breezily, placing the toothbrush back in its holder, before reaching for a hand towel. "I'm exhausted, that's all. It's been a busy day."

"Mmm..." he mumbled, his hands now roaming their way up the bottom of her nightdress. Charlotte wished that she was wearing her pyjamas. She didn't even like nightdresses - she only wore them because Myles bought them for her, and she didn't want to seem ungrateful. "Maybe you need to... unwind."

To her relief, before she was forced to protest, his hands migrated to her shoulders and began to massage. She could cope with that. She watched him in the mirror, his face looming behind hers. His fingers continued to work the knots out of her shoulders, and she started to relax, some of her anxiety evaporating through her skin as he worked it away.

"Are you sure it's only exhaustion? You don't seem quite yourself."

Charlotte gulped, her eyes back on the sink. "Yeah. I'm just tired, honestly."

"You wouldn't lie to me, would you?"

She shook her head. "Of course not."

Eventually, she managed to slip out of his grip and leave the bathroom, sliding down between the crisp cotton sheets of their super king bed. She reached for the book on her bedside table, opened it and pretended to scan through. Not that she actually read a single word. Her mind was too busy, swimming with thoughts and memories, flooded with 'what ifs'. What was she going to do?

Her mind was so busy, she almost didn't notice Myles slip into bed beside her. His hands began to roam again, and she clenched her jaw, swallowing hard.

"I er… not tonight, Myles."

"But it's my birthday…" he mumbled against her skin.

"I… I can't…"

A thick silence fell between them. She placed her book down on the bedside table, waiting for his response. But to her relief, his face softened.

"Oh, darling. Are you…"

She shook her head. "Not this month. I'm sorry, Myles."

"What have you got to be sorry for?!" He asked, pulling her into his arms. "It's one of those things. I'm sure next month will be our month!"

"Mmm," she forced a smile, the guilt of her lie weighing heavily between them.

***

The snap of the lock echoed through Jake's head, as though there was an empty space between his ears. Sometimes, he wondered whether they had stolen part of his brain when he was locked up. Put him to sleep. Operated without him knowing. Cut part of it away. Everything seemed so jumbled. Although the house felt familiar as he stepped across the threshold, he felt strangely uneasy. It didn't feel like his home anymore. He didn't belong here.

His eyes fell on the suitcases, stacked precariously in the hallway. His parents looked too, then Alana turned to John. "We need to put those away."

"Did you go somewhere?" Jake heard himself say. He felt disjointed. As though the words were being spoken by someone else, but coming out of his own mouth, like he was just the messenger.

Shifting awkwardly, they exchanged glances, before his dad shook his head. "Nowhere, son. You go and take a seat in the living room. Are you hungry?"

"No," Jake said, but he immediately did as he was told, because that's what he was used to.

After slipping his shoes off (not that they really felt like his shoes - his mum had arrived with a holdall of clothes a couple of days before, which he barely recognised as his), he padded into the living room and took in his environment. It was clean, fresh and calm. Everything was in its place. He took a deep breath; the homely smell of the room was familiar, and slightly comforting. In front of him was a wooden sideboard, littered with photo frames. Taking a few steps forward, he picked up the first. It contained a photograph of him, in his uniform. He looked young. Presumably, it was taken at his passing out ceremony, which he could barely remember.

Chewing his lip, he placed the frame back on the wooden top and picked up the next. It was an old, faded photo, presumably his parents on their wedding day. Quickly, he put that photo down and moved onto the next. His stomach lurched, his heart suddenly aching. Besides his parents, she was the first thing he truly recognised since arriving back in the UK.

The sound of footsteps behind him caused him to spin around suddenly, dropping the frame as he did so. It smashed on the wooden floor by his feet and, upon seeing that it was only his mum with a cup of tea, he bent down to pick up the pieces, loathing himself for not being able to pull himself together.

"Don't worry about that," Alana fussed, placing the tea quickly on the coffee table and bending down to pick up the broken glass. "It's fine, I'll sort it."

"No, I'll do it," Jake replied, hastily pushing the glass into a pile.

"Jake, stop, you're going to-"

One of the shards sliced through Jake's palm. He held it up to the light, staring at the blood which was now dripping onto the photograph below. The wound was deep, but he was unable to feel anything. He had been in agony for so long that his body had grown used to it; he barely registered normal pain now. His hands shaking, he wiped the blood splattering off the photograph, then held it up. "Where is she?"

Alana cupped her son's hands in hers, holding them still. Her thumbs brushed his as she looked up at him, grateful that he finally seemed to remember something of his old life.

"Bee's fine, Jake. She's with Sally."

"Sally?"

"You remember Sally, the lady who always looks after Bee when we go away?"

Jake couldn't remember. He looked down at the photo in his hand and traced his thumb over her furry ears, remembering how soft they used to feel against his fingers, how her tail used to beat hard against the wall every time he walked in the door. That must be why the house feels so strange, he thought with relief. Once Bee's back, everything will be alright. "Can you get her back? I want her here."

Alana nodded, a relieved smile breaking across her face; for the first time since her son had gone missing, she could finally do something to help him. Something that would make a difference. "Yes. Yes, I can. Now, come with me. Let's get that cut sorted."

Again, without protest, he did as instructed. His hands were already scarred with cross-cross marks, each one telling the solemn story of a day in captivity. Dropping down onto one of the kitchen chairs, he held his fingers over his palm, stemming the bleeding so as not to make a mess.

"Here," Alana approached the table with a little red bag.

Suddenly, a memory popped into Jake's mind. He remembered sitting at the table, his foot up on one of the other chairs, blood running down his leg from his knee to his ankle. Grimacing when Alana wiped it with an anti-septic wipe and secured a large plaster over his wound, patting it and saying...

"There you are, as good as new."

She patted his now dressed hand and zipped up the first aid kit. He wished that were really true.

"Mum..." he muttered, as she returned the first aid kit to its cupboard. She returned to him, taking a seat opposite. "I can't really remember anything."

"I know," she patted his hand. "The doctor said that's quite normal, when you've been through severe trauma like you have. I'm sure your memories will come back in time."

Keen to stop them trembling, he pressed his lips together. "I er... I'm glad I'm home. I don't want you to think that I'm upset or... disappointed. I'm not. I just can't remember what it's like to be happy... I think I've forgotten how to show it ..."

Alana's eyes clouded with tears and she cleared her throat, trying to force them back. She had to be strong for him, like she had when he was a little boy, crying because he'd hurt himself or because someone had upset him.

"You will," she forced a smile. "Soon enough. Once you've settled back in. In time, you'll feel happy again."

Padding back into the living room, she collected up the broken glass, swallowing the lump in her throat. She had never seen Jake like this. Empty and broken, a shell of the young man she'd said goodbye to last time he went on tour. If she was honest with herself, she was petrified. Petrified that he'd never be that man again. All she wanted was for him to be happy, yet the weight of what she knew she was going to have to tell him, sooner or later, pressed down on her shoulders, heavy like a lump of lead. How could she possibly tell him? What if it tipped him over the edge? Yet, she hated lying to him. Maybe his memory would come back, and she wouldn't have to?

She scraped the broken glass into the swing bin. "Would you like to come with me? To collect Bee? Perhaps getting out and about would help you remember? Sally's house is right by your old school. We could drive past if you like?"

Jake shivered. He longed to collect Bee, but the thought of going out into the world, just the two of them, unprotected, filled him with dread. Anyone could be waiting outside. If they were seen together... she could be in jeopardy, too. "I think I'll wait here... if that's ok?"

"Of course. Why don't you go upstairs, to your room? Dad's putting the cases away, he'll have finished shortly. He'll stay here with you."

Jake glanced out of the kitchen window. The house was so open. The rear fences were low, anyone could climb them within seconds. He stood up and checked the back door - it was unlocked. Hastily, he clicked the lock shut. "You should leave this locked, at all times."

Alana watched him, sadly. "Of course. We must have forgotten to lock it, we were in a rush to get to the hospital..."

"You must never forget. Do you hear? Never."

She nodded, slightly taken aback by the

brusqueness of his voice. "Ok. I won't. But you are safe here, Jake, I promise. Nothing ever happens here."

"You can never be sure..." he muttered, tucking his chair back under the table carefully, his hand wandering absent-mindedly to his chest, where he used to keep his weapon.

Alana retrieved her keys from the peg on the wall, then pulled her jacket on and reached for Bee's lead. "I'll be back in half an hour, ok? Go upstairs, take a shower. Make yourself at home. Maybe get some rest?"

Jake did as he was told. He padded upstairs, his skinny ankles clicking with every step. Moving was painful. The soles of his feet were blistered from walking barefoot on the sweltering sand. Despite the fact that they'd been dressed, they were excruciating to walk on. Reaching the landing, he instinctively opened the door next to the bathroom. Immediately, the room felt familiar and comforting. Although it was sparse and bare now, devoid of any of his possessions, his old bed was still in the corner, his old wardrobe next to the door. This was definitely his room.

After gently closing the door behind him, he stared into the mirror above his bed. His reflection shocked him; it felt as though he was staring at someone else. His cheeks were gaunt and pale, almost lifeless. His eyes looked sunken and bruised, and his beard was wiry and sun bleached. When he couldn't look at himself anymore, he checked that the windows were locked and then pushed a chair in front of the door, so that the back was underneath the door handle. Then, he peeled his clothes off down to his underwear and slid into bed, closing his eyes, allowing his mind to rest properly for the first time since he'd been captured.

CHAPTER FOUR

Turning the key in the lock, Jake could barely contain his excitement. They had waited a long time for this day. The lock released with a satisfying click and he pushed the door open, filling his lungs with the scent of their new home.

It was tiny, but perfect for the two of them. One room, with a bed and some furniture at one end, a small kitchen area at the other, and a small sofa in between. In the corner was a door to the shower room. He dropped his bergen and another large bag a metre from the doorway and clicked the door shut behind him. He had a lot of work to do before Charlie finished college. At the moment everything was soulless; plain and beige, empty apart from the furniture which was scattered throughout the room. He desperately wanted it to feel like a home to her. It would be the first real home she'd ever had. And she knew nothing about it yet.

It was no secret that Charlie was desperate to move out of her sheltered accommodation, and into a place of her own. They had been planning it for years, and she had been counting down the days until the summer when she would be free from college, and they would be able to afford to rent somewhere. One lunchtime, a week after his eighteenth birthday, Jake had seen the advert for the studio flat in the window of the corner shop near the barracks. The realisation that he'd be able to afford the rent and bills on just his wage had turned his stomach with excitement. Charlie was planning to go to university twenty minutes from the flat, which made it the perfect base for both of them. Jake would be able to come back at weekends when he wasn't deployed, and Charlie would be able to travel to and from her classes and placements every day. The more he thought about it, the more he was convinced that it was meant to be theirs.

Unsurprisingly, his parents weren't keen. They couldn't understand why Jake would waste his money on rent, when he could stay at the barracks during the week and go home to them at the weekend. They were of the opinion that as soon as Jake was deployed and Charlie started her own life at university, their relationship would probably fizzle out and then Jake would be left paying for a flat he wasn't even living in until the tenancy ended. Why don't you wait and see, *they'd said.* See how you feel once Charlie's settled at university - she might not even get a place! *But Jake knew. This was meant to be. They were meant to be. He wanted to be with Charlie for the rest of his life. It didn't matter that they were young - he had never been so certain about anything in his life.*

Jake hung some of his clothes in the wardrobe in

the corner of the room. He folded his t-shirts and placed them carefully in the drawer unit to one side of the bed. After unwrapping the new duvet cover he had bought, he threw the plastic covering in the bin and made the bed, straightening the duvet until it was perfect. He placed his toothbrush in the holder in the bathroom - it all felt quite surreal, as though he was spreading his possessions inside a hotel room rather than his own home. He looked at himself in the mirror. The responsibility of having his own home weighed heavily on his shoulders - it was a responsibility he took incredibly seriously. All of the lads at the barracks thought he was mad. Why would he want to get tied down, have to pay rent and bills when he could be having the time of his life? The truth was, there was nothing he would rather do than spend the rest of his life with Charlie.

Once the flat was ready, he got in his car and drove to her college. It was half an hour's drive. Charlie would have to take the train for the next few months until she finished there, but he knew she wouldn't mind. It was a small price to pay for their own freedom and their own home, and once her exams were done she would be able to start making a life here, maybe find a job until her university course started in September. Jake grinned to himself, contemplating all the lazy weekends they could spend in bed, with nobody to disturb them and nobody to tell them what they could and couldn't do. Money would be extremely tight for a while, but he didn't care. They didn't need to spend money to have fun. Simply being together was enough.

Arriving early, he sat in his car for a while until

students began to wander out of the college gates and down the road. His eyes scanned the crowd; he didn't have to wait long. Within a couple of minutes, there she was, her long blonde hair blowing in the wind around her face as she looked up, saw his car and smiled. Within a few more seconds, she opened the door and slid into the passenger seat.

"Hey," she smiled, leaning over to kiss him. "What are you doing here?"

"I thought I'd surprise you. I had a day off."

Charlie squeezed his hands. "Ah, you never said!"

"Yeah, well... it wouldn't have been a surprise if I told you, would it?"

He pulled away from the kerb and started to drive back towards the flat. Assuming they were going back to Jake's parents' house, Charlie didn't question where they were going

"Ugh, Kelly was being such a cow this morning," she rolled her eyes. "She hogs the bathroom all morning! I literally can't wait to leave."

Jake smirked. "It won't be long now."

"Two months too long..." she muttered, rummaging in her bag as he continued to drive.

Engrossed in one of the textbooks she retrieved from her bag, Charlie didn't notice where they were going for a while. Out of the corner of his eye, Jake saw her look up, her face falling into a confused frown as she tried to focus on the scenery outside.

"Where are we going?"

Jake grinned - he couldn't help it. "It's a sur-

prise."

Curiously, she peered at him. "What?"

"It's a surprise," he repeated, braking for the approaching roundabout. "You'll see."

He enjoyed the anticipation on her face as they edged ever closer to the flat. She pressed him to tell her where they were going, but he wouldn't.

Finally, they arrived. Charlie looked around them, confused. "What are we doing here?"

"I just need to pick up something from a mate."

"Oh. Shall I wait here?"

"Nah, come with me. I might be a while."

Unquestioningly, she reached for the door handle and climbed out of the car. Jake headed towards the front door, his hand clasped firmly around the key in his pocket. His stomach was turning with excitement; he had to clench his jaw to stop himself from beaming. When they reached the door he knocked, but of course there was no answer. Finally, he produced the key from his pocket.

"You have a key?"

"Yeah."

"Why?"

In silence, he turned the key in the lock and opened the door, allowing her to enter their new home for the first time. He bit his lip, hiding his delight as she looked around her in confusion at the cosy studio flat.

"Welcome home," he breathed, a beaming smile breaking out across his face.

Her eyes widened, taking it all in - the fresh, crisp bedding on the bed, the empty holdall scrunched up in the corner of the room."Home?"

"Do you want to look around first, or shall we go straight to get your things?"

Flinging her arms around him, tears streamed down her face. She had waited so long for this moment; the moment of freedom, when she finally had somewhere of her own to call home. And, as always, Jake had been the one to come to her rescue.

***

"Quick!" Charlotte hissed as they sprinted across the car park, Izzy's swimming bag swinging from the crook of her arm like a pendulum.

"I'm trying, Mummy!" Izzy cried, her polished leather shoes slapping across the tarmac.

They made it into the swimming pool four minutes late. Charlotte ushered Izzy towards her class, who were already in the water and beginning their warm up. Running her fingertips through her hair to push her fringe off her dewy forehead, Charlotte's skin burned under the glare of the other parents who weren't used to such a commotion at the start of the lesson. Charlotte was never late.

"Where've you been?" Effie hissed.

"I lost track of time..." Charlotte's voice trailed off as she waved back at Izzy, who had now entered the water and joined her class. Panic over. They had made it.

"That's not like you."

Charlotte didn't reply. She watched Izzy

swim like a fish through the water, her body working in perfect tandem with her arms and legs in a neat front crawl. Watching Izzy swim was one of the highlights of Charlotte's week. Swimming lessons were available at school, but Charlotte liked to take her instead. Izzy was a natural swimmer, and she found it mesmerising to watch her own daughter glide through the water, her technique better than Charlotte's would ever be. She hadn't even learnt to swim until she was twelve, when she was forced to do swimming lessons at school. As one of only three children in the year that couldn't swim, Charlotte had been so embarrassed. It gave the other kids even more ammunition to use against her, especially as all she had was a faded, bobbly swimming costume which was a size too small and clung in all the wrong places. Determined never to force her own daughter through that, Charlotte had signed Izzy up for lessons as soon as she was old enough.

"Is everything alright?"

Effie's voice broke Charlotte out of her daydream. She looked up, her eyes wide and her expression blank.

Curiously, Effie peered at her. "Talk to me, Charlotte. What's up?"

Dismissively, Charlotte shook her head, her eyes back on her daughter. "Nothing. I'm fine."

"You don't seem fine."

Charlotte bristled in her seat, forcing a small smile as Izzy looked over between lengths, and waved.

"You've been weird all week. Since the party. Forgetting things, turning up late, barely hanging around to chat."

"Well, I've been busy," Charlotte replied curtly, her heart thumping a little harder in her chest.

"I'm not the only one who's noticed," Effie continued. She lowered her voice, her face softening. "Was it what I said at the party? About giving Izzy a sibling? I'm sorry if I upset you. I didn't realise you were trying... Connor said..."

Exasperated, Charlotte sighed. "No, you didn't upset me. I'm finding everything a bit tough at the moment, that's all."

Effie placed her hand on her knee supportively. "Why didn't you talk to me? I'm always here for you, you know that!"

"Yeah, I know," Charlotte smiled weakly. "I'm sorry. I didn't mean to shut you out."

"It was insensitive of me to press you about giving Izzy a sibling, especially when I'm..." Effie gestured at her bump. "So, I'm sorry. I am."

"No, its not your fault," Charlotte placed her hand on Effie's and squeezed it. "Honestly. I'm sorry, I've been a rubbish friend lately. I haven't even asked you how you're feeling for weeks!"

Effie grinned. "Except for having ankles the size of tennis balls, and not being able to reach down to tie my laces up, I'm grand!"

Charlotte laughed. "You still look glam though. I was a mess when I was pregnant with Izzy."

"I doubt that. You're never a mess," Effie's gaze returned to their children in the pool.

Charlotte's smile faded, memories of the hardest time in her life clouding her mind, like an oil spill spreading across the surface of the pool.

***

Jake's eyes travelled down the lead to his old dog, who was plodding along as though they had all the time in the world. Bee was sixteen now, and her whole snout was grey. Jake still thought of her as she was before, the bouncy, excitable pup she had been when they first brought her home. Old memories were coming back to him every day, but he still couldn't remember what she had been like when he left for Afghanistan. She hadn't forgotten him though. A rare smile crept onto his face as he remembered how she had jumped at him when she returned, finding him in the house for the first time in five years. She had licked him all over, as though trying to erase all his wounds, inside and out. It had worked, a little.

"Time to go home, girl?" He asked softly.

She turned her head, staring at him adoringly. Bee was the only thing that had kept him going for the past week, giving him purpose, a sense of normality. His parents tiptoed around him like strangers, constantly second guessing themselves and overthinking everything before they spoke. For the first few days, cameras had been set up yards from the front door, desperate to snap a shot of the soldier who had seemingly risen from the dead. It was a relief now that they had lost interest and gone. Every day, Jake got up and got dressed, ready to take Bee for her morning walk. Being out in the fresh air, just the two of them, accompanied only by the sound of the wind whipping through the trees and the pad of Bee's paws on the ground was a relief. He didn't have to say anything, didn't have to force a smile, didn't have to pretend that he was happy to be home all the time when all he really wanted to do was bury himself in his duvet, and never come out. It had been so long since he'd had freewill that he had almost forgotten how to live.

The mind was a strange thing. His brain had almost erased all his memories for the past five years and beyond. The psychiatrist said it was his body's way of trying to protect him from the horrendous things he had experienced and seen during his captivity. He could barely remember anything of his life before, although sometimes the odd memory came back to him. He could remember some of his time at the barracks now, and wondered whether the soldiers he could see in his memories had been the ones on his last tour. The only people who had visited were army officials, and Jake couldn't deny that it was a relief. What would he do if someone turned up claiming to be his friend, and he didn't even recognise them? What if they asked him questions about what had happened, ones he couldn't answer?

Upon arriving home, Jake double-locked the front door behind him and slipped Bee's lead off. She trotted into the kitchen for a drink, before lying down on her favourite mat by the kitchen door. After hanging the lead on its hook, Jake collapsed into the sofa, closing his eyes. The house was quiet; his parents had gone out shopping, and it was a relief to be alone.

The distant sound of Bee stretching and grumbling as she fell asleep startled Jake, and his eyes snapped open. He hated feeling so edgy. He could never relax. All it took was the slightest sound, and he was back on guard again. Hypervigilance - that was how the psychiatrist had described it. His foot briskly tapped up and down on the wooden floor, causing his whole body to shake. He needed something to keep him busy. But what? The dog was too old for another walk.

Climbing the stairs, his eyes fell on the loft hatch in the landing above. Maybe he could find something up there to help him remember who he was before? He unclipped the trap door, reaching for the ladder. Once extended he climbed it carefully, step by step, until he was plunged into darkness. Being in such a confined space felt strangely comforting. There was only one way into the loft, and it had been locked from the outside, so he knew that nobody else would be up here. And if anyone joined him, he would see them coming.

Grappling around in the dark, he managed to find a light switch. The loft was full of old, dusty boxes, most of them looked as though they hadn't been touched for years. Slowly, he edged along the boards, reading the labels on the boxes. *Kitchen.* Why did his parents still have a box of kitchen utensils in the loft? They'd lived in this house for over a decade. Jake's lips curled into a small smile. A memory. He could remember lifting some of the boxes up towards the hatch for his dad, his muscles trembling under the weight of the box. *That's it, Jake. We'll keep these up here for now, until we've replaced the kitchen.* And yet they were still in the loft, collecting dust. *Camilla.* Jake tried hard, but he had no idea who Camilla was. Maybe he'd go back to that one later. *Jake school reports.* He smirked - they would be amusing. Yet he did have some vague memories of school - what he really wanted to remember was the life he had in the few years before he went to Afghanistan - who and what he had left behind. Why this house still didn't feel like home, even though his bedroom was starting to feel more familiar and he did have some memories of the house.

Crouching at the far end of the loft, he studied a cluster of smaller boxes. *Photos.* That was exactly what he needed. Boxes of photos - maybe seeing places and people would trigger more memories? Carefully, he ripped the brown tape from the top of the first one. The photos were old and musty, they felt unloved and forgotten in his hands. Most of the photos in the box were old, some even black and white. He leafed through photos of babies, toddlers, adults he didn't recognise. Their clothes were old fashioned as were the items in the background; old cars, sixties style decor. He assumed that the younger people in the photos were his parents and their siblings.

The box wasn't what he was looking for, so he stuffed the photographs back inside and moved the box to one side, giving access to the next. This box looked a little newer than the last, the tape was stronger and it took more effort to rip it off. The box contained several albums, including a silky white one which look fairly new. Optimistically, he opened the album and began to leaf through. It was a wedding album. There were his parents, together in their outfits, his mum wearing a silly fascinator which made him laugh. He rarely saw his dad in a suit - he scrubbed up well. He recognised his brother, James, and his girlfriend Kelly. Who was now his wife - his parents had told him that they'd got married since Jake had gone missing, and were now living together in New Zealand. So whose wedding album was this? Jake turned the page again.

Then it hit him, like a slap in the face.

His heart thumped in his chest, his cheeks flushed hot. As soon as he saw her in her simple white dress, her blonde hair tied up in a sophisticated style and a beaming smile on her face, memories came flooding back to him. His mind was filled with her - she was all he could see. Charlie - his wife. Where was she?

CHAPTER FIVE

Fidgeting from one foot to the other like the platform was made of lava, Charlie glanced up at the board. It was five forty-three, and the train was late. Anxiously, she glanced around her at the other people waiting to board, many of them looking weary and fed up. On the other hand, she could barely contain her excitement. Two minutes, and she would hold him in her arms for the first time in three months.

The tannoy announced the train's imminent arrival. Charlie smoothed her hair, her eyes widening hopefully as she scanned the distant tracks for the train. She wanted to be the first one to see it. Her stomach bubbling with excited anticipation, she reached into her bag for a packet of mints, popping one into her mouth and chewing it to calm her nerves.

And then she saw it. The train appeared around the corner, and suddenly she felt like she was going to cry. She couldn't articulate it exactly - it felt like her longing for him had built up more and more every day since he had left, and now he was back she could finally let it all out. She caught the woman next to her peering curiously, and she quickly wiped a rogue tear from her cheek, feeling a little foolish. But what did it matter? He was home now, and that was all she really cared about, not the opinions of strangers.

The hiss of electricity through the tracks heightened her anticipation. She bit her lip hopefully, peering into every passing train window, hoping to catch a glimpse of him. Eventually, it slowed to a stop and there was a loud bleep as the doors opened. The passengers disembarked. Her eyes scanned every inch of the platform, waiting for him. Within thirty seconds, the platform was emptying as all the waiting passengers had boarded the train, and the stream of people leaving the train had dwindled. Her heart continued its drumroll in her chest. Where was he?

Just as she was about to grab her phone and call him, she saw him - he was one of the last passengers off, jumping from the far end of the train with his heavy bergen on his back and his beret on his head.

"Jake!"

She heard herself scream his name, sprinting along the platform towards him, tears of relief streaming down her face. Beaming, he saw her coming, and dropped his bergen just in time to receive her in his arms. She flung herself at him so hard that he almost fell over, but he fastened his arms around her and spun her around, holding her tightly, as if he would never let her go.

"I love you," she beamed, pulling away briefly so that she could reach his lips. He kissed her long and

hard, making up for all the time they'd lost, and would never get back.

"I love you, too," he mumbled against her lips, his mouth hungry for hers. "God, I've missed you."

Eventually he released her, and they walked hand in hand out of the station, back towards home.

***

Charlotte thought she would feel better as the days ticked past, but she was wrong. Instead, it felt like her anxiety increased every day. The news reports on Jake had dwindled, but he was the first thing on her mind when she opened her eyes, and the last thing she saw when she gave into sleep at night. She kept trying to remind herself that she had a new life now, that everything had changed - and it wasn't her fault. How could anyone say that she should have made a different choice? Yet still, she couldn't shake the feeling of guilt deep inside her.

And she was petrified of her new life crashing down around her. She had tried so hard to build a good life for Izzy. She had the best education money could buy, she barely wore clothes more than a few times before she grew out of them, and she always had home cooked food in her belly. She had scores of friends who adored her. She had hobbies - swimming, ballet, tap dancing, music lessons. She had two parents who loved her, and she lived in an enviable home. Every night, when Charlotte tucked her in and switched off her bedroom light before leaving the room, she almost had to pinch herself that this was the life she was able to give her daughter. It was the polar opposite of the sort of life she'd had, growing up. And it was all down to Myles. Charlotte was scared. If Jake turned up, what would Myles do? What sort of life would they have then?

The weight of her secret kept Charlotte up at night. She saw him everywhere. She dropped a whole box of eggs at the supermarket when, out of the corner of her eye, she thought she saw him standing at the end of the aisle. She almost smashed into the car in front of her at a red light, when she was certain she saw him driving past her on the opposite side of the road. She found herself crouching under the bay window one morning, convinced that he was standing at the door with a parcel. She found herself looking over her shoulder every second of the day, and even Izzy was starting to notice.

Eventually, one Monday morning, when Myles was away for a few days at a business meeting in New York, Charlotte decided that she had to conquer her fear once and for all. She realised that she didn't even know what he looked like now. Perhaps if she could catch sight of him, she would be able to rest easy. And despite her fear of bumping into him, she wanted to know that he was ok. Her heart ached when she thought about the years that they had spent together. The warmth of his fingers interlaced with hers, the way his gaze made her feel entirely perfect on their wedding day, even though her wedding dress had been second hand and slightly too tight, bought from a charity shop. She just needed to see him. Just once.

She hadn't kept in touch with his parents for long after he went missing. She didn't even know whether they lived in the same place, but she figured that she had six hours before she had to pick Izzy up, and nothing else to do. She had nothing to lose.

The journey took almost an hour and a half. When she pulled up in their street, far enough from their front door that they wouldn't notice her, she instantly knew that it was their house. It looked exactly the same, they even had the same car on the drive, and the same flower pots under the front window. Her mind wandering to the first time they had slept together in his bedroom, shy and awkward at sixteen, she swallowed the lump forming in her throat. She had kept that box shut for so long, she had learned to get through every day without thinking about him much. It was only on the significant days, like his birthday or their wedding anniversary, that she allowed herself to think of him, and only for five minutes. But now, he was consuming her again. She felt out of control.

Suddenly, there was movement. Charlotte froze. Her eyes widened, watching the front door swing open - there was Bee. The knowledge that the old dog was still around brought Charlotte a strange sense of comfort - she had sat with her so many times as a teenager, poured her heart out to her sometimes. Charlotte wondered how old she was now - she was surprised to see that she was still around. Perhaps the dog had waited out, trusting that one day, her favourite person in the world would return.

Perhaps if Charlotte herself had waited a little longer...

Then her heart almost juddered to a halt. It was him. He emerged from the house, holding Bee's lead, and for a moment Charlotte thought he was going to look right at her. As soon as she saw him, she knew that she had been wrong. Seeing him, right there, in real life, deeply intensified her heartache. All she wanted was to climb out of the car and shout for him, like she used to when he got off the train and came home to her. She found her hand on the door handle, every fibre of her body longing for her to go to him.

Quickly, she mentally shook herself.

Her own feelings didn't matter - nothing was more important than Izzy. Charlotte knew what it was like to grow up with nothing, and she didn't want that life for her daughter. Izzy didn't deserve that.

Quickly, she pressed the start button and turned in the road, her heart pounding in her chest, praying that he wouldn't see her. She swung the car around quickly and pulled away faster than she intended, throwing herself back in the seat as she sped away. She could never come back here. Not ever. She had to find a way of closing the box, sealing it shut. Her own feelings didn't matter. All that mattered now, was Izzy.

***

Jake was fed up of being afraid. He was fed up of being on edge. Fed up of jumping every time he heard an engine start up, fed up of having to spend thirty seconds scanning the area before he could set foot outside his front door. Fed up of harrowing memories coming back to him night after night, flooding his mind with pain he thought he'd locked away. Fed up of waking wrapped in his sweat-drenched bedsheets, fed up of his mind running over and over as he lay in the dark, wondering where she was.

He had no idea how to find her. He couldn't find her on social media, her old mobile number had been disconnected, and emails he sent to her old account bounced back. She had seemingly disappeared shortly after he had, not even contacting his parents or any of their old friends. He had spent days trying to find her, but to no avail. It was as though Charlie Parsons had died when he had.

And then he saw the car. He had eyes on it the second he opened the front door, because it wasn't the sort of car he would expect to see on their street, and he was absolutely certain that he'd not seen it before. It was sleek, sporty, matt black and practically brand new, with tinted windows and huge alloy wheels, and it practically screamed money. It had one occupant, although he couldn't see who it was - the car turned on the spot within a few seconds of him opening the door, speeding off in the opposite direction. He ran the personalised registration plate over and over in his mind, then pulled his mobile out of his pocket and tapped it into his notes. M2 BOND.

Upon their return, Bee settled in her favourite spot by the back door, and Jake padded up the stairs to his room. He typed the registration plate of the car into his old laptop and scrolled through the results, but he couldn't find anything. If only he had a friend in the police force. Casting his mind back, he thought about the unusual matt finish. The car had to be a limited edition, he had never seen one like it. He searched for the make and model and matt black, but nothing came up. He tried a few more search terms, but still nothing.

Frustrated, he reclined on his bed with a sigh, the laptop still perched on his lap. But then, before giving up, he searched one more time. And there it was, the car. The exact car, although the registration plate wasn't shown, with the headline, *Businessman apologises and receives heavy fine after being caught driving 20mph over the limit in brand new car.* But what sort of businessman would be interested in him? He clicked through the link, scanning through the details of the article until he found a name. Bond. Just like the numberplate.

"Myles Bond," Jake turned the name over on his lips.

Who was Myles Bond? He'd never heard of

the man before.

Typing the name into the search engine, Jake's foot tapped impatiently on the carpet. Who was this man, and what did he want from him? The more he thought about the way the car sped away, the more it unnerved him. The driver had *definitely* been watching him. And it couldn't be a journalist, not in a car like that. Whoever was driving had serious money. And money meant power.

He gulped.

Scrolling through the results, he found numerous articles about Myles Bond. He quickly learnt that he was a multi-millionaire, he lived in a huge, fancy house with the sort of big, iron gates that Jake could only dream of ever owning. He liked cars, fast ones. He went to private school, he took over a family business when he was twenty-one years old and had evolved it, joining with one of his childhood friends to turn the business multi-national within the last five years. Jake narrowed his eyes. He *still* didn't know what Myles Bond could possibly want with him. What was the connection?

And then he saw her, just a glimpse, in the background of a photo. Standing next to Myles Bond, her now dark hair styled in casual waves and a full face of make up, wearing the sort of designer dress he could never have imagined her wearing. She looked so different that he might not even have recognised her at first glance, if they crossed paths in the street. She had her arm around him and her head leant against his shoulder, behind the scenes at some sort of event. Charlotte Bond. Myles Bond's wife.

***

"You look beautiful!" Alana smiled, straightening the white flower in Charlie's hair. "Perfect! Just perfect."

Charlie smiled nervously. Her soon-to-be mother-in-law was kind, and she had welcomed her as part of their family since Jake and Charlie had announced their engagement, a few short months before. But she wasn't a substitute for her own mum. Charlie ached for her, now more than ever. She had dreamed about this day for months, imagined what it would be like if, for the first time in her life, her mum was actually there for her.

What would she wear, what would she say? What would she do when she saw her little girl walking down the aisle in a wedding dress, even if it was second-hand? It was the best dream, satisfying a longing trapped deep inside Charlie for her entire life. But, whenever she woke up, it hit her twice as hard. Her mum wasn't there; of course she wouldn't be at her wedding. She didn't even know where Charlie lived, nor that she was a nurse now. Charlie's smile faded. She hadn't been there for her graduation, either.

"Are you ready?"

Charlie turned towards the registrar's voice, floating in from the doorway. She smoothed her dress down and gulped, forcing all thoughts of her mum to the back of her mind. She had spent enough of her life longing for her mum, she was a grown up now - getting married to the man she loved more than anyone else. She wouldn't let thoughts of her mum spoil her special day.

"Yes," she nodded, shakily. "Yes, I am."

The registrar smiled kindly. "I'll go back in, we'll pop the music on. You can come in whenever you're ready."

"Thank you."

The registrar ducked back through the doorway, pulling it closed behind her with a small clunk. Charlie turned back to Alana. "I don't know why I'm so nervous! I've been waiting for this day for so long..."

"Every woman is nervous on her wedding day," Alana smiled. "It's a big deal!"

"Yeah. It is."

She heard their song playing the other side of the door. She took a deep breath, her eyes on Alana's hand which was poised on the door knob. Alana turned it. Before she knew it, Charlie was walking down the aisle, towards the love of her life. The beaming grin on his face reassured her that everything was going to be alright. She loved him, he loved her, and nothing else mattered - nothing else in the world.

***

Sensing eyes on him, Jake glanced up to find an old man in the corner, scowling in his direction. He returned his gaze to his foot, which was tapping impatiently on the floor. Forcing himself to sit still, he placed his elbow on his knee, pinching the dewy bridge of his nose between his fingers. Why was it so *hot* in here? Two hundred and eighty pounds an hour, and they had never heard of air conditioning?

"Mr Parsons?"

He shot out of his seat, standing to greet the woman who stood before him. He frowned. He had asked for a lawyer; he needed someone who was going to fix things, as quickly as possible. Someone who knew their stuff. This woman barely looked older than him.

"Nice to meet you, I'm Ruhi."

Taking her extended hand, Jake shook it in his clammy palm. "Jake."

"Would you like to come this way? I can get you a tea, or a coffee?"

He cleared his dry throat. "No, thank you."

They reached the door of a meeting room and she opened it, gesturing to an empty seat. Jake walked inside. The room was clean, sterile. Devoid of emotion. The only signs of life were a sad looking pot plant in the corner of the room, and a half empty box of tissues on the table.

"Take a seat, Mr Parsons."

"It's Jake," he corrected, mildly agitated. He took a seat anyway, side on so that he could still see anyone coming through the door.

"Jake," Ruhi echoed. She placed a fresh file on the table and took a seat in the chair opposite. "How can I help?"

Jake gulped. "I er... I said I needed to see a

solicitor..."

"That's me."

He felt his cheeks flush. "Oh... I'm sorry. I assumed... you don't look old enough to be a solicitor, that's all."

"I'll take that as a compliment," she smiled, opening the file to reveal one solitary piece of paper. "Let's start from the beginning. When you called, you said you needed some advice on a matrimonial matter. Is that right?"

Jake nodded. "Yeah. It's er... my wife. She's married someone else while she's still married to me."

"Right."

Ruhi didn't say anything else, so Jake continued. "I er... I went missing. For a few years. But I'm back now... and she's married to someone else. And I need to know what I have to do to overturn that... fill in a form or something... because she can't be married to him, you see, because she's still married to me."

He found himself turning his wedding band absent-mindedly around his finger. He had only been wearing it for a week since his parents had returned it to him, but already it felt like part of him again. Like he had never taken it off in the first place.

Ruhi scribbled something down. "When did you get married?"

"August 2013."

"When did you go missing?"

"March 2014."

"And you're sure that she's married to someone else, now? Not just cohabiting?"

Jake nodded, reaching into his rucksack for the file of papers his parents had given him. He pulled out a manila folder and emptied the contents, pushing a copy of the decree towards her. He could barely look at it. The smell of the dusty, unloved piece of paper made him feel sick. Ruhi lifted it from the table carefully, her eyes scanning over the document.

"It's a decree of presumption of death and dissolution of marriage," Jake muttered, although he knew that he didn't need to explain it. "I went missing in Afghanistan. I was held captive until I was rescued by Allied forces a few weeks ago. When I came back, I found out that my wife, the *one* person I could trust more than anyone else in the world, has ended our marriage and got married to someone else. But it can't be valid, you see... it can't be legal... because I wasn't dead. I'm not. I'm alive. As you can obviously see. So now, I need this overturned, so I can get on with my life, with Charlie. That's my wife's name."

Ruhi nodded sympathetically, slipping the paper back down on the table. "Have you spoken to Charlie about it? About what she wants?"

"I haven't managed to track her down yet. But I know she'll want to be with me, I *know* she will. We went through a lot together you see, when we were kids. It was always us. She wouldn't have done this if she didn't really think I was dead... but now I'm back, things can go back to normal."

The sympathetic expression on her face antagonised him further. He didn't need sympathy, he needed a good lawyer. Someone who could get to work, quickly. Pressing his lips together, Jake's nostrils flared as he took a deep breath, then another, and then another, until he felt his temper subside.

"Look, I know you think I'm crazy. But her marriage now… it's not legal… it can't be. Because I was never dead. So this…" he picked up the piece of paper and waved it in the air, "is wrong."

"Jake… I'm really sorry to hear what you've been through. I've seen your story on the news, I can't imagine what that must have been like for you. But I'm afraid, it's not as simple as Charlie's new marriage being null and void because you've turned up. When the Judge made that order, they would only have done so because they were satisfied that there were reasonable grounds to believe that you had passed away. And the effect of that order would have been to dissolve your marriage, so that Charlie was free to marry again. And because she was free to do so, her second marriage remains legal and valid - the fact that you've been found doesn't change that, I'm afraid."

"But…"

Jake didn't know what to say. He felt deflated, like a balloon which had been prodded with a large pin. His high hopes for this meeting were all that had kept him going for these past few days; given him something to focus on - the first day of his new life, the life where he'd sort everything out and could live - *really* live - again.

"What we can do though, is deal with ancillary relief."

Jake peered at her, his eyes hot with angry tears that he wouldn't allow to spill.

"Now that you've been found, we can deal with the division of your marital assets. So any property and money you had when you were married... we can make sure that it's split fairly."

Jake felt a laugh of irony escape from his throat. "Well, that won't be necessary. We didn't have anything. Not a bean."

"Are you sure?" Ruhi asked. "Charlie might have received a financial settlement when you went missing..."

"I don't care about money," Jake replied roughly. "All I want, is to have her back. I've never been as happy as I was then, when she was my wife. Money means nothing if I don't have her. Please, you have to help me. I need to get that order overturned."

Ruhi slipped the decree back in its folder. Sympathetically, she pressed her lips together. "I can look into it, but I have to be honest with you - the chances of us being able to do that are slim. You need to be prepared for the fact that Charlie has a new life, with a new family. She may even have children. Your best chance is to find and talk to her. Find out what she wants. Sort things out together."

"I don't understand how this can be legal.

I can't get my head around it. They never found a body, because I wasn't *dead.* And if it's not bad enough that I missed out on five years of my life in that desert hellhole, I can't sleep for nightmares and I can't concentrate during the day because my mind is buzzing with images I can't get out of my head. Awful, *awful* images that I can still see when I close my eyes. My career's probably finished because I can't be a soldier if I can't stop these damn *voices in my head.*" He slammed his fist on the table, making Ruhi jump. "And the one person… the *one* person who I know could help me get through this… is married to someone else. And there's nothing I can do about it! I wish they'd shot me dead five years ago, I've lost everything anyway. It would have been for the best."

Unexpectedly, Ruhi reached for his hand, squeezing it supportively for a few seconds. Then she lifted the tissue box gingerly. Jake ripped a tissue out of it, wiping at his face furiously. He hadn't even realised that he was crying.

"I'm sorry, Jake. I wish I could do more. I really do."

Crumpling the tissue firmly in his fist, Jake cleared his throat again, standing so abruptly that he almost knocked his chair backwards.

"Sorry," he sniffed, steadying it before tucking it under the table gently.

Ruhi closed his file and returned it to him. "Not at all. I do understand that this will be a huge shock."

He followed her back down the corridor, the fresh feeling of defeat deep in his gut. What was he going to do now? He had worked himself up to this meeting, determined that the lawyer would be able to help him get Charlie back. But she couldn't. And he couldn't fight the feeling, deep inside, that perhaps Charlie didn't want him after all. Perhaps she was happier now, married to a rich businessman, enjoying the life she'd never had before? She must have seen him on the news - pretty much everyone had, Ruhi had recognised him straight away, and she didn't even know him. She had even driven to his house that day - well, he was sure that it must have been her - and she had driven off. So clearly, she didn't care about him as much as he thought she did?

"Oh," as they reached reception, he dug in his pocket and shakily pulled out his wallet, a solitary card in his dad's name inside, lent to him the day after he got home from hospital, until he had his own again. Pathetic, Jake thought every time he looked at it.

Ruhi rested her palm on his forearm. "It's on the house, Jake."

"Oh... thanks."

"And if you do change your mind about ancillary relief, let me know, ok? I'll get that sorted for you."

"Ok," he nodded. "Thanks."

"Take care of yourself, ok?"

***

"Wow, Mummy!"

Charlotte smiled, extending her arms to receive her daughter.

"You look sooooo pretty!"

"Just like you." Charlotte leant down and planted a kiss on her forehead. "Even in your pyjamas, with your hair all over the place! Are you all ready for bed?"

Izzy sighed theatrically. "Yes. I want to stay up late though, show Sophie my new tea set that Daddy bought me! Please?!"

Charlotte opened her mouth to reply, but before she got the chance, Myles clicked out of the kitchen and into the hallway in his shiny new shoes, adjusting his cufflinks.

"Half an hour, ok? But then you must go to bed."

"Yay! Thanks, Daddy!"

It was his turn for a hug then, and he spun Izzy around before planting her back down. As her feet touched the floor, the doorbell rang.

"Sophie! Sophie!" Izzy jumped up and down with excitement. "Can I answer the door?"

"You shouldn't answer-"

"Go on, then!" Myles grinned.

Charlotte glanced at him as Izzy skipped down the hallway. "I don't really want her answering the door, what if-"

"Oh, don't be so daft. It's only Sophie, I opened the gate for her! And there's CCTV all over the front of the house."

"Yes, right now it is, but what if she answers the door another day, and..."

"You worry too much," Myles cut in with a grin. She used to love that grin, but recently it had become more of an irritant. It seemed like the more she tried to keep Izzy safe and impose rules, the more he undermined her. He always liked to be the hero. Why did she always have to be the bad guy?

"Sophieeee!" Izzy squealed, jumping into her young babysitter's arms.

"Hey, Izzy-bee!" Sophie grinned, hugging her tightly. "How are you?"

The pure delight in her daughter's face helped Charlotte to relax a little. It was going to be fine. Sophie had looked after Izzy a dozen times, they always had a great time. She knew that they would return later to find Izzy happily tucked up in bed, her hair brushed and her teeth scrubbed clean. They were lucky to have such a reliable babysitter.

"Right," Myles gently pulled his freshly dry-cleaned jacket from one of the hooks. "There are some drinks and snacks in the fridge, help yourself, Sophie. Bedtime in half an hour, ok?"

"Sure," Sophie smiled through her braces. "Thanks, Mr Bond."

"Myles," he rolled his eyes theatrically. "You don't need me to call me that, Sophie. You make me sound old!"

"You *are* old, Daddy!" Izzy grinned, then laughed when Sophie tickled her.

"Thanks," Myles clenched his chiseled jaw, admiring his face in the mirror. "I don't think I look *that* old though, thanks very much!"

Reaching for her own jacket, Charlotte sighed. She wasn't at all in the mood for tonight. All she wanted was to tuck Izzy up in bed, under the glow of her nightlight, then lie next to her until she fell asleep. Check that all the windows and doors were locked for the five-hundredth time. Process her own thoughts in her overcrowded mind, without having to pretend that she was enjoying herself, or force her involvement in conversation.

"Are you alright?" Myles touched her shoulder once Izzy had dragged Sophie up the stairs to her bedroom. "You look a bit... peaky."

"I'm fine," Charlotte forced a smile, shrugging off his grip. "We better get going, or we'll be late."

"Charlotte..."

She had almost reached the door, but his hand on her forearm stopped her in her tracks. She swallowed the lump in her throat, taking a deep breath in an attempt to sink the panic that rose from within her. Suddenly, his voice sounded distant and distorted, as though he was at the end of a never-ending tunnel. White spots filled her vision and she stumbled against the wall, the back of her neck prickling with beads of sweat.

"Charlotte?"

Eventually, he came back into focus. Charlotte pulled her jacket tightly around her, trying to stop her body from shivering.

Myles felt her forehead with the back of his hand. "Charlotte, you're sweating. You don't look well."

"I'm fine," she croaked, then cleared her throat. "I'm fine. Sorry, I just felt a little dizzy."

"Shall I get you a glass of water?"

"No, let's get going. I don't want to keep Effie and Connor waiting."

"Are you sure?"

"Yes!"

She shrugged past him, swinging the door open so hard that she had to grab it before it hit the wall. She flinched, trying to ignore the ball of panic rising in her stomach. Every single thing she'd touched since that *damn* cake went wrong. It felt like everything was about to fall apart, and there was nothing she could do to stop it. Maybe this was her punishment. For all her lies.

Silently, she strode out of the porch and down the front steps towards the car. Tightening her grip on her bag, she pulled open the door and climbed into the passenger seat beside Myles, who fastened his seatbelt and started the engine. The car crawled down the drive and swung out of the gates, the house quickly disappearing from view behind them. Charlotte glanced back in the wing mirror, hoping that Izzy would be safe. Every bone in her body was screaming at her to stop, to turn around, but she couldn't. Myles already knew something was up, she didn't want to make this any worse. She wanted it all to go away.

The hairs on the back of her neck stood on end as Myles's hand settled on her thigh. Clenching her teeth, she fought back tears, forcing herself to look out of the window so that he wouldn't see.

CHAPTER SIX

She was working a night shift. Six until six. That's why she didn't hear her phone, tucked safely in her locker. She was so exhausted by the end of her shift that she barely even looked at it before starting her journey home across town, the sky still dark above the sleepy houses. It was cold on the bus and she tucked her chin into the top of her jacket, allowing her eyes to close for most of the journey home.

Charlie thought about Jake. What she wouldn't give to pull back the duvet and find him there, warm and cosy under the sheets, waiting for her - keeping the bed warm, that's what he would say. A smile crept to her lips. She just wanted him back. She loved being a nurse, and it kept her really busy; she'd barely had time to miss him for days. But it was always the journey home that got her, when she was exhausted and needed a hug, someone to share the burden of her day (or night). The story of the tired old man whose hand she had held, whom she had sung to during his final moments. The relative she had held in her arms for a minute while he com-

posed himself, after finding out that his mother's cancer had spread, and the doctor had broken the news that she probably only had two weeks at best. The little spark of happiness when she was able to wave goodbye to a patient she had nursed for the past six weeks, as he was finally well enough to go home.

Jake called sometimes. Every few days, but it wasn't the same. She knew how bad things were out there, how battle tired he was already, even though he'd been gone little more than eight weeks. She couldn't add to that burden - it was her job, as a nurse, to make people feel better. And that applied to her husband too. Still, he was a third of the way through, and that brought them both some comfort. And hopefully this would be the last time, the last time he ever had to set foot in that country.

The scuffle of footsteps from behind roused her from her doze and she jolted upright, her eyes wild for a moment - had she missed her stop? Luckily not - it was the next one. She gathered up her bag and slung it over her shoulder, reaching forwards to press the stop button. The bus slowed and came to a standstill beside the bus shelter.

"Thank you," she smiled weakly, nodding at the bus driver before leaving the bus.

"Bye, love," he replied, but she had already jumped down and was walking briskly towards home. It was only a couple of minutes walk - she was so close now, she could almost feel the softness of her duvet around her.

Catching the light from a dingy street lamp, her breath smoked around her face in the cold morning air.

It wouldn't be long before it was light again on her journey home. The world seemed less hostile when the sun came up and she could feel the warmth of the sun on her face. And once spring came, and summer... well, Jake would be home, and all would be well.

Reaching the front door of their flat, she turned the key in the lock and shoved the door hard. It was sticking more than ever lately - she supposed that she'd better get it sorted. If she left it until he got back, it would probably be impossible to open.

Exhausted, she slipped her clothes from her body and dropped them in a heap on the floor around her. She'd pick them up later. After brushing her teeth and scrubbing her hands, she climbed into bed and wrapped the duvet around her, sighing with relief as her whole body relaxed and she gave into sleep.

When she opened her eyes again, the room was bathed in early morning light and she yawned, glancing over at her alarm clock. It was only eight thirty, she had barely been asleep an hour! She closed her eyes and was drifting off again when the buzz of her mobile on the floor woke her. She lay there, wondering whether to bother getting up, until eventually the buzz quietened and she closed her eyes again. Jake knew not to call her this early. Whoever was calling could wait.

She could see his eyes, the soft folds of skin around them as he looked up at her desperately. It's ok, *she had promised him.* It's going to be ok. *And then, because she didn't know what else to say, she started singing. His breathing was shallow and his skin was grey, she knew from the emptiness in his eyes that it was al-*

most time. She found a store of bravery she didn't even know she had deep inside her, and she forced herself to keep singing, her voice not faltering once. She held his papery hand in hers and she stroked his skin gently, letting him know that she was still there when his eyelids drooped and his breaths slowed. Eventually there was a rattle from deep inside him, and his chest rose and fell one last time. Then, once she was sure he was gone, she placed his hand back gently on top of the sheets. It was only then that she allowed herself to cry.

Suddenly, she awoke with a jolt.

Was that a knock on the door? She was sure that she'd heard it.

Rubbing her eyes, she sat up in bed, squinting at the slight gap between the window and the blind. It was no use, she couldn't see anything, it was too sunny outside. There it was again - an unmistakeable knocking, this time harder, tap tap tap. She sighed, flung the covers back and reached for her dressing gown. It was probably a delivery again, for the neighbours. They were a nightmare, always ordering things even though they both worked full time, leaving early in the morning and coming back late. She had been woken up about three times in the last two weeks by delivery drivers.

"Alright!" She grumbled as they knocked again. She was beginning to get really frustrated now - she was going to give the delivery driver a piece of her mind. No more parcels. Not when she had been working all night, all she wanted was a good sleep before she had to go back for her next shift! It wasn't so much to ask.

She flung the door open, her brow knitted in a

frown. Instantly, her face softened. "Oh. Alana, I wasn't expecting you - sorry, I just got back from a night shift..." she pulled her dressing gown tighter around her body at the sight of her father-in-law behind.

"Sorry to wake you." Alana grabbed her hands. It wasn't like her and Charlie's face fell. Something was up, she could sense it.

"What's going on?"

Alana gulped, glancing back at John, whose face was ashen. "Can we come in?"

"Of course..." Charlie stepped back to let them enter. John closed the door behind him with a definitive clunk.

Suddenly, Charlie felt embarrassed. She hadn't washed last night's dishes nor those from the night before that, and her dirty uniform was still in a pile on the floor, exactly where she had left it. She'd been working back to back nightshifts for a week, and hadn't even had enough time or energy to run the vacuum around.

"Sorry, I would have tidied up..."

She crouched, scooping up her clothes quickly, although she could tell from their faces that the clothes were the last thing they would be concerned about. In all honesty, she wanted to delay the inevitable, because she knew they must be here for a reason - they had never turned up out of the blue like this - and so she knew that something must be very wrong. She just didn't know if she had the strength to hear it.

"Charlie..." Alana grabbed Charlie's elbow, stopping her in her tracks.

Charlie looked down at the pile of clothes in her

arms, shaking her head. "I don't think I'm ready to hear it..." she whispered, a lump forming in her throat.

"I know..." Alana whispered, her voice faltering.

Wriggling away, Charlie dumped her uniform in the washing basket in the corner of the room, then smoothed her duvet over neatly so that she could sit on top of it. She gestured to the sofa.

"You can sit down, if you like. Would you like a cup of tea?"

Alana's eyes filled with tears as John firmly put his arm around her. Charlie's eyes travelled from his arm around his wife's waist, to the scruffy slippers he was wearing on his feet. She had never seen him show affection to Alana like that, nor had she ever seen him go out without proper shoes on.

"Charlie." His voice was a lot firmer than his wife's. "Charlie, look at me."

She didn't want to. She closed her eyes. Deep in her heart, she knew why they were here, and she couldn't do this - not now. Only four more months. Four more months and Jake would be back, and all would be well.

"I'm sorry, love," Alana sniffed, moving out of her husband's grip to sit beside Charlie on the bed, taking her hand and squeezing it. "We've had some... terrible news. It's Jake."

Charlie said nothing. She perched, still and silent, on the edge of the bed. Maybe if she didn't acknowledge it, it wouldn't be true? It couldn't be - she was his wife. If something had happened to him, surely they'd have called her first? There had to be some mistake. They must have called the wrong soldier's relatives, got Jake's parents confused with someone else's. Yes, she sighed with relief, that had to be it.

"Jake's been missing for three days. He went missing when his patrol came under enemy fire. And they've found no trace of him. So they think... well, they're pretty certain... that he's dead."

***

Bathed in the dim glow of the moon, Jake perched on the window sill, the laptop precariously balanced on his lap. His eyes travelled to his uniform, hanging from the top of his wardrobe door. He knew that he ought to be asleep, getting some rest - he had an early start the next day. But, no matter how hard he tried, his mind refused to rest. It was as though he had necked ten espressos one after the other; his brain wouldn't switch off. All he could think about was her, and when he closed his eyes his mind came alive with plans and ideas; what it would be like to feel her skin on his again, how soft her hair would feel entwined with his fingers. Whether her lips would taste the same as they always had.

Since his meeting with Ruhi, Jake had pulled himself together. He knew what he had to do now. If the law wouldn't help him, he would have to help himself. She couldn't be that hard to find, she was married to a millionaire.

It had always been them. Once she saw him,

she wouldn't be able to ignore it - the force that had always pulled them together, the spark that shot between them whenever they were close enough to feel it. He *still* felt that pull, the invisible tug that drew him towards her. And now, he knew what he had to do. He was going to sort himself out. Tomorrow, he had a meeting with his commanding officer, and he hoped that he'd be able to get back to the barracks, get on with his job. Get some purpose back into his life. And then, he would find Charlie. Prove to her that he was still the man he was before he left, that he was still all the things she loved about him. She wouldn't be able to ignore him then.

The full moon freed itself from behind a cloud, bathing the windowsill in bright moonlight. Jake gulped. Suddenly he was back there again, slumped in the corner of his desert cell, staring up at the moon outside. It was whole and still and beautiful. If he focused hard enough, he could blur out everything around him and imagine that he was lying in paradise, on a beach somewhere, staring up at the moon and the stars. Dampening his cracked lips slightly with his parched tongue, he coughed a dry lump from his throat. Pain shot through his chest and he clamped a hand to his ribs, as though he was trying to hold himself together. How he wished that this would end. They threatened him all the time, beat him until he was black and blue. Sometimes the beatings lasted so long that his mind blocked out the pain and his body became warm and fuzzy, his mind disconnected from reality. Sometimes he willed them to finish him off. Bring an end to the nightmare.

Slamming the laptop shut, Jake furiously wiped a tear from his cheek. He had promised himself not to let what had happened define him, having finally escaped their clutches after five years - he didn't want to spend another five years letting them ruin any chance of happiness he had now. He had to be strong. Block it out, and move on. He was a soldier, he needed to compartmentalise. Close the door, and never open it again.

***

"She's fast asleep, absolutely fine," Charlotte sighed with relief, slipping inside the bedroom and closing the heavy oak door behind her.

"Of course she is," Myles peered at her strangely. "Sophie's been looking after her."

"I know."

Perched on the side of the bed, she unfastened her earrings, placing them carefully in the leather jewellery box on her bedside table. "I worry, that's all. You know I do."

Next was her necklace. Busying herself, she tucked it safely in the box, next to the earrings. His hot gaze was on her back, analysing her. She didn't like it.

"Charlotte, I think you ought to visit the doctor."

She frowned, briefly glancing behind her before turning her attention back to the jewellery box, desperate not to let him see the guilt spreading across her face. "Why would you say that? I'm fine."

"Are you?"

She said nothing for a few seconds, her heart pounding so hard in her chest that it felt as though it might burst through her ribcage. "Yes," she forced, managing to keep her voice level. "Absolutely."

"You have to admit, you've not been yourself lately. Anxious. Scatty. Clumsy. Earlier, before we left, you almost fainted! It's not like you at all. I think it would be best if you get checked out."

"There's no need. I told you, I just felt a bit dizzy. It was hunger, because we ate later than normal. You know how I get, with my blood sugar."

"Even so. It doesn't hurt to have a check up and a chat, does it? I'll come with you. And we can discuss the next steps, you know, with our baby plans… it's taking a lot longer than I thought it would, maybe there are some tests we can have done? Maybe it's linked to how you've been feeling lately?"

Now, her pulse was raging in her temples. She fastened her grip on the bedsheets beneath her, the weight of her secret pressing down so hard that she could barely breathe.

"I'll call the doctor tomorrow, make you an appointment."

"No!"

"What? Why?"

"I er... I'll do it. You're so busy, it will take me five minutes to make an appointment. I'll call in the middle of the day, when it's quiet."

"I don't mind calling... I'm here to help you, remember? I know what you need."

His hand caressed her shoulder blades and she bit her lip hard, bringing tears to her eyes, desperately trying not to flinch under his touch.

"Myles, I can organise my own doctor's appointment. Izzy needs a check up, I'll ask about that at the same time."

Feeling his eyes boring into her back again, she pressed her lips together, her eyes focused on a little scuff on the skirting board down by her feet. She'd have to speak to the cleaner about that. After what felt like a lifetime, he finally replied.

"Ok. If you're sure. But I would like to come with you, so let me know when it is, please?"

"Mmm," she nodded, forcing a smile as she climbed under the duvet. "Of course."

Then he flicked the lights out and she lay in the dark, wondering how on earth she could get herself out of this one.

***

"Corporal Parsons!"

Jake stood to attention before his commanding officer.

"What a pleasure it is to see you looking so well."

"Thank you, Sir."

"At ease. Take a seat."

Jake relaxed, taking a seat in the chair in front of Captain Williams's desk. Clenching a hand in his lap, he glanced around at the familiar medals and certificates which adorned the walls. It felt strange to sit in this office again, after all this time.

"How are you doing?"

"I'm good, Sir. I just want to come back. Get back to normal."

Williams nodded, his smile uncharacteristically kind. "I understand that."

Jake's eyes fell on the dull looking folder on the desk between them. He inhaled sharply, his mind flashing back to the manila folder on the desk in Ruhi's office. Not today. He had to hold himself together, just for today. "Is that my psych report?"

"Yes."

Jake nodded, leaning harshly on his upper leg to stop it from tapping up and down. He still couldn't sit still. Sometimes it drove him mad, his body's need to constantly move.

"I'm fine, Sir. I'm ready to come back."

Williams nodded, his face now blank and difficult to read. "The report says you suffered from some amnesia when you returned to the UK."

"My memory's fine, Sir. Yes, I did struggle a little bit when I first came back. But it's all come back to me now."

"What I'm worried about... and Major Oliver agrees with me... is that you've only had your memory back for a relatively short period of time. What you went through in Afghan was awful. Those memories are going to stay with you for a lifetime, and you need to develop coping strategies and ways of getting through them when they resurface. Because they will. And a few short weeks isn't enough time."

"Sir, I'm fine..."

Williams interjected silently, holding his hand up until Jake fell silent. "You're a brilliant soldier, Parsons. And I want nothing more than to have you back in my section. But I have a duty of care, to protect you, and everyone in the company. We have to be sure as to your state of mind, before you come back. And after all you've been through, you deserve a rest, time to recuperate. You're on full pay, make the most of it. We'll have you back when you're ready."

"With respect, I'm not a danger to anyone, Sir," Jake frowned. "And my state of mind is fine."

"I'm sure that's true. But we need to allow time for you to process what you've been through, and adjust to life back in the UK before you return to full duty. So what Major Oliver has suggested, and I support his recommendation, is that once you feel ready, you spend some time at a facility where you can work through your experiences, and deal with anything you've buried. And then, once you've done that, we can reassess."

Jake opened his mouth and then shut it, forcing himself to keep quiet. Shooting his mouth off wasn't going to do him any favours. Arguing with his captain would simply concrete his belief that Jake had lost his mind. "I'm not mad, Sir."

"I never said you were. But the mind is complicated, Corporal Parsons. You went through five years of hell. And you can't expect to spring back to normal now you're back. So, we'll transfer you to the unit once you're ready, you can spend some time there and once they're satisfied that you've processed what you went through properly, we can discuss your reintegration into the platoon."

Jake inhaled sharply. "Yes, Sir. I'm ready now."

"Excellent. If you're sure, I will enquire as to you starting there next week."

Williams stood, and Jake rose up from his chair, raising his hand into a salute. "Sir."

"Thank you, Corporal Parsons," Williams replied.

Jake nodded, turned and marched out of the door.

CHAPTER SEVEN

Her hands trembling, Charlie held the stick up to the light. Two unmistakeable red lines stared back at her, raw against the stark white background. She dropped the test. It bounced off the grey rubber floor and landed, face down, on the floor in front of her.

She couldn't move. Couldn't think. It wasn't supposed to be like this. They were supposed to settle down in a house with a garden, several years from now, Jake settled back in the UK. They were supposed to have fun trying for a baby, share the excitement and anticipation of this moment together. She wasn't supposed to be on her own, perched on the tired plastic toilet seat in the staff toilets, exhausted because she hadn't slept properly since Jake had gone missing a month before, hungry because it took all her energy to find the strength to get up and go to work in the morning, let alone plan her next meal. What was she going to do?

Maybe she should tell someone.

Suddenly, it struck her that she didn't have anyone to tell. She had no family, and barely any friends.

The only friend she had left from school was Jake; he had a few friends who they sometimes saw, but she didn't know them well enough to talk to alone. The handful of friends she had were work colleagues, and she could hardly confide in them - her nurse's uniform was the only thing that was holding her together right now, what if they decided she had to take some leave? She had only managed to keep working after Jake had gone missing by the skin of her teeth, promising that she wouldn't let her home life interfere with the work she did. She had thrown herself into work, taking every extra shift she could, not only because she needed the money now more than ever, but also because she needed something - anything - to keep her mind off her missing husband. She desperately needed something to help her pass the time. He was still out there, she could feel it deep inside her gut. She just kept having to believe it, wait out. He would come back for her. He always did.

The slam of the heavy door outside the cubicle made her jump. She reached down, scrambling for the test which was lying dangerously close to the edge of the cubicle. After stuffing it in the front pocket of her bag, she wiped her eyes on some toilet roll and stood up, smoothing down the front of her scrubs. Taking a deep breath, she flushed the toilet and forced herself to smile. Everything was going to be alright. He was going to come home, there was no way that he would let her do this on her own. Everything would be alright.

***

Charlotte waved to Sophie and Izzy, who walked off hand in hand, towards the park. Once they were out of sight, she walked into the surgery, breathing a sigh of relief.

Luck had been on her side. After Myles insisted that she make an appointment and she had failed to do so, he booked one himself for the following week. She'd tried to think of a way she could get out of it, petrified that if he came along it would be game over - he would insist on coming inside with her, and what would she say to the doctor then?! And what would she do if he glanced at the computer screen and saw her notes?

But, the day before, he'd been called away on urgent business. She had to pretend to be disappointed when he announced his last minute trip, and apologised profusely for not being there for the appointment. Panic evaporating from her body, she'd reassured him that she would be fine, suggesting that Sophie could come with them so that Izzy wouldn't have to be there while she spoke to the doctor. He promised that they'd book an appointment with a fertility specialist when he got back - hopefully, she'd be able to put that off for a bit longer.

The automatic door allowed her entry, then closed behind her with a clunk. Charlotte smiled at the receptionist, booking herself in on the touch screen. She took a seat on one of the waiting chairs and relaxed, enjoying the peace and quiet of being on her own.

"Charlotte Bond?"

She grabbed her handbag and followed the corridor from the waiting area to the familiar examination room.

"Hello, Charlotte," Doctor Kent smiled. "It's good to see you again."

"You too," Charlotte replied, closing the door behind her and taking a seat.

"How can I help?"

Charlotte swallowed. "I've been feeling a little... anxious recently. And I've had a bit of dizziness, too."

"Ok. When did it start? Was there anything specific which you think might have triggered it?"

"A few weeks ago..." she paused. "No... nothing in particular."

"Alright. Let's check you over, and see what we can do. Can you pop up on the bed for me, and slide your cardigan off your arm?"

"Yes."

Charlotte rose from the chair and slipped her cardigan off, before reclining on the bed. She stared at the white ceiling tiles while the doctor inflated the blood pressure cuff and then released it.

"Hmm... your blood pressure is a little high. Have you been under any stress lately?"

"I suppose so... a little."

The doctor placed the stethoscope on her chest and listened, before returning it to her neck and glancing at her computer screen. "Ok. And we put you on a new contraceptive a couple of months ago..."

"Yes."

"It's possible that your body may be reacting negatively to the type of pill you've been prescribed. We could try switching them over. On a level of one to ten, ten being the most, how anxious have you been feeling on a day to day basis?"

"I'd say... maybe a six... maybe an eight on bad days."

"Right. We could also try some medication for that, it shouldn't interfere with the contraceptive although I'd recommend that you use other precautions for the time being."

Charlotte nodded. "Ok."

"Is there anything in particular that you think might be causing your anxiety? Anything you'd like to discuss? As we discussed previously, it's quite common to feel confused and upset... bereaved even, after..."

"No, it's not that," Charlotte interjected, then she opened her mouth to continue, but promptly closed it. It felt like everything was closing in on her; her old life was catching her up, ready to collide with, and smash up her new one. It was like standing in the middle of a train track blindfolded, waiting for a train to hit. But how could she possibly put that into words in a ten minute appointment?

"I think I'm just struggling with everyday life, to be honest," she lied. "I've got a lot going on."

"Ok," the doctor smiled kindly. "Well, make

sure you get plenty of rest, and try to set aside some you time. I know it's difficult when you have a young family, but even if it's half an hour for a short walk in the evening on your own to reflect, or sitting in the garden with a book for ten minutes once dinner's done and everyone's happy, I'm sure it would do you the world of good."

"Thank you, I'll try that."

"And how are things at home - has your husband been supportive?"

"Yes, of course. He's busy - he works away a lot."

"Are you keeping lines of communication open?"

Charlotte pressed her lips together, folding her hands in her lap. "I'm not sure he would understand... he's the one who goes out to work, he thinks I relax all day. He doesn't understand what it's like, being on call for a small child twenty-four hours of the day."

"Well, when he's away working, I'm sure he gets a good night of uninterrupted sleep, and a sit down breakfast, cooked especially for him. *And* a lunch break. It's important that you find time for you too, Charlotte. Not just everyone else."

"I used to be a nurse," Charlotte explained. "And actually, I sometimes think that being at home is harder. I never get time just to be me... I'm Izzy's mummy all the time... I can go days without being called by my name sometimes."

The doctor reached forwards and placed her

hand on Charlotte's arm supportively. "Like I said. Make some time for you. Treat yourself with respect, or nobody else will."

***

Despite his initial reluctance, Jake settled into his new unit well. He did everything that was asked of him, worked through his sessions with the psychiatrist, took on board their suggestions and practiced the exercises he was given at every opportunity. Spending every spare minute in the gym, he built up his muscles and strength until finally, he felt good again. His uniform no longer swamped him like a child; he could finally see muscle definition and not simply skin and bones when he looked in the mirror. The colour was back in his face, and he finally felt like some form of himself.

And he was making progress in other areas too. He had spent hours meticulously scouring the internet for anything he could find about Myles and Charlotte Bond. Myles's head office was in central London, but he lived with his wife on a private estate, in a commuter town he'd never heard of. They had a child. A girl. He didn't know anything else about her - it seemed that the Bond family were quite secretive about their private lives.

Myles and Charlotte were married in November 2016. That piece of information hurt Jake the most. He had imagined Charlie waiting for him, never giving up hope that he would be found alive. Yet here it was in black and white - the cold realisation that Charlie had married another man only two and a half years after he went missing.

After that revelation, Jake had given up on his research for a few days, torn between his desire to find his wife and bring her home, and the realisation that she had a new life now, and a new husband - and her new marriage had lasted significantly longer than theirs had. Maybe she loved Myles more? Maybe she thought of her marriage to Jake as a mistake, a blip, a stepping stone to the life she had now. Nice house, fast cars, more money than she ever could have dreamt of when she was young, moving from one foster family to the next with a bin bag, half full of the few belongings she had. And they had a child together. Was it fair for Jake to barge back into her life, turn her whole world upside down?

But, after a few days, his desire to find her and at least find out the truth got the better of him. He had to hear the words from her mouth - if she wanted to stay with Myles, continue to live the life she had now, then he would respect that. Or at least try to. But he had to hear it from her first - he had to know what she wanted. Otherwise he'd always be wondering what if, and he knew he would never be able to move on with his life.

He had a day of leave, and decided to spend it doing his first piece of field research. He needed to find out where Myles Bond lived, because he had drawn a blank trying to find out anything about

Charlotte which might help him find her. He got up early, rented a car and travelled to Myles's office. He got there before it was even light, because he knew that the traffic would be gridlocked long before rush hour, and he needed to catch sight of Myles when he arrived - *if* he arrived. Jake knew it was a long shot. He had no idea if Myles even worked in the head office. But he needed something to go on, and this was the only chance he had.

After his third bottle of energy drink, Jake relaxed against the headrest with a sigh. It was light now; he had already topped up the parking ticket on his car twice, and he was beginning to get restless. The street was busy with people travelling to work; Jake was reasonably confident that if he got out of the car and walked up and down a few times, taking a closer peek at the office, nobody would notice.

Stretching his legs, he inhaled deeply. The air was cool, but thick with the scent of exhaust fumes and recycled breath. Attempting to blend in, he zipped up his jacket and tucked his hands in his pockets, walking down the street past the office. It looked empty, he couldn't see any signs of life inside except for the bored receptionist sitting at the front desk.

Once Jake had walked for ten minutes, he became tired of walking past the same buildings. There had to be a better way of using his time - he couldn't sit here all day waiting. He didn't even know whether Myles would drive to the office or get a taxi or a train - perhaps he wouldn't even use the front entrance! Suddenly, Jake felt hopeless - it was as though he was looking for a needle in a haystack. Who was he kidding, of course he wasn't going to be able to find Myles and follow him back to his house. What had he been thinking?

Fed up, he fell back into the car and leant back against the headrest, sighing deeply. It had been a mistake to come here. A complete waste of time and money. He started the car and, resigning himself to a couple of hours of sitting in gridlocked traffic, he started the journey towards home.

***

"Your hair looks amazing!" Effie exclaimed, brushing a copper lock away from Charlotte's face. "I love the colour! It suits you!"

"Thanks," Charlotte smiled. "I fancied a change."

Her eyes travelled over to Izzy, leaping up and down on the trampoline next to Callum, shrieking with excitement. Charlotte found herself smiling. For the first time in weeks, she felt like she wasn't suffocating. She still felt anxious, but with Myles away on business and still no contact at all from Jake, she was beginning to feel like things might be alright.

"Callum's been so excited to come here. He's loving it!"

Effie waved at her son. He waved back, bouncing joyously into the foam pit with Izzy.

"And it's good to see you too. Where've you been?!"

Charlotte bristled in her seat. "What do you mean?"

"I've been trying to catch up with you for weeks! Nobody's seen you. I was getting worried."

"I've been busy, that's all."

"Doing what?"

Charlotte opened her mouth, then promptly closed it. She didn't know what to say. How could she explain her incessant web searching for the last few weeks, the shopping trips which had taken twice as long as usual because she was too afraid to get out of her car in case she bumped into him? The days where she'd pretty much locked herself in at home, because she was scared of who she might find the other side of the front door?

"Getting your hair and nails done, clearly!" Effie laughed.

Charlotte bit her lip, then forced a smile. "Yeah. Something like that."

"Well, as long as you're ok. I've been worried about you, since Myles's party. And then at dinner... you weren't yourself."

"I wasn't feeling well."

"I know. Myles said, when you left. I was wondering... you're not pregnant, are you?"

"No. I'm not."

"Are you sure? He said you came over all dizzy! And I wondered if that's why you've been hiding away the past few weeks..."

"I haven't been hiding away!" Charlotte protested. "And I'm not pregnant! Can you drop it, please, Effie? It's hard enough without you keep going on about it!"

Turning away, Effie puffed like a disappointed child. "Sorry. I didn't mean to upset you. It was only a question."

"Well I'm fed up of everyone going on about it! I just want to be left alone!"

"Charlotte-"

They were interrupted by a crunch and a high pitched scream, followed by two young children wailing. Charlotte turned to see a couple of adults in bright orange t-shirts jump into the foam pit, one of them lifting a bawling Callum up onto the mats, and the other crouching down in the pit, talking to someone.

"Izzy!" Charlotte whispered.

She leapt from her seat and rushed over, in time to see her daughter being carried from the pit, her red cheeks hot with tears, one arm bent the wrong way. Charlotte's stomach lurched. She opened her mouth to talk, but no words would come out.

"Mummy!" Izzy screamed. "Mummyyy!"

Charlotte opened her arms for her. The woman in the orange t-shirt handed her over carefully, making sure to avoid her arm which was now dangling precariously down by her side.

"She needs to go to hospital," she announced, even though that was quite obvious to everyone who could see what had happened. “Are you her mum?”

“Yes,” Charlotte choked. “Izzy darling, keep still, ok? It’s going to be ok.”

“It hurts!” Izzy bawled, her eyes filled with tears. “Make it stop, Mummy!”

“I’m here.” Charlotte said, holding her carefully like a baby.

“Bring her through to the office while we wait for the ambulance.”

“Oh, I’ll take her…”

“She needs to go in an ambulance. That arm needs immobilising, and she can’t wear a seatbelt like that!”

“Oh…” Charlotte looked down at her daughter, her heart physically aching every time she saw a rip of pain tear through her little body.

“Charlotte!”

She could hear someone calling her name from across the room, but at that moment in time, she didn’t care. All that mattered was her four year old daughter, who was screaming in her arms, the blood draining from her face every time a wave of pain ripped through her little body.

“Shall I call Myles?”

Now Effie was beside her, Callum holding her hand. For once, she was speechless - she didn’t know what to say.

“No. What can he do, anyway? He’s in New York. We’ll be fine, I’ll call him when we get there.”

Walking away, Charlotte heard Effie say

something else, but she wasn't listening. Her hearing was tuned into her daughter, she couldn't process anything else. For the first time since she'd walked past the newsagent and seen the front of that newspaper, the only thing on her mind was her daughter.

***

Shaking with frustration, Jake fastened his grip tightly on the steering wheel. What a waste of six hours. What a waste of fifty quid to hire a stupid car that he hadn't even needed. He had achieved nothing. His first rest day in what seemed like ages, and he had wasted it driving to London, sitting outside a dirty old building for two hours, and then crawling in a traffic jam on the M3. Still, finally he was making progress.

Even the flashing signs overhead irritated him. Smart motorway. It hadn't seemed so smart when he was crawling along it at sloth speed, over an hour ago. He jabbed the radio button, filling the car with the ear-splitting shriek of music he didn't recognise. Quickly, he hit the volume button, turning it down until it was manageable. Then, looking up at the road every couple of seconds at the fast-moving traffic in front of him, he flicked through the stations.

On the fifth press, a familiar sound filled the car. It was their wedding song. The irony made him laugh. Fastening his grip on the steering wheel again, he began to hum along. Suddenly, it struck him that he hadn't actually enjoyed music for longer than he could remember, let alone allowed himself to join in. Humming louder and louder, he began to feel the stress dissipate from his body, and his grip loosened. He could see her beside him in the passenger seat, her hair glowing in the afternoon sunshine and her white dress perfectly complementing her tanned skin. His lips turned into a smile. What he wouldn't give, to have her sitting beside him right now.

Brake lights in front brought him back to the present and he slammed his foot on the brake pedal just in time. Clearing his throat, he opened the window a crack, allowing fresh air into the car. He took a deep breath. He needed to pull himself together.

After deciding to turn off the motorway and find a more scenic route, something in the distance caught Jake's eye. He quickly recognised a figure standing on the edge of the pedestrian bridge, hoisting themselves high over the top of the metal bars. Jake swore, his stomach turning upside down when, for a split second, he thought they were going to topple right over the top of the bars, onto his bonnet. Instinct took over. Quickly, he indicated and swung the car into an emergency rest area by the side of the motorway, then climbed over the barrier and sprinted along the grass verge the other side. The long, itchy grass was strewn with litter, but he kept going. He reached the iron bridge and began to climb, scaling the rungs until he was able to hoist himself up onto the bridge and run along it, towards the figure who was still standing there, the wind blowing in her hair. It was long and blonde, like Charlie's. She was wearing an oversized hoodie, but Jake could see that she was short and had a medium build, like Charlie. He gulped.

"Charlie?"

He was within metres of her when she turned. Relief flooded his body when he saw her tear-stained face and could instantly tell that it wasn't her. It wasn't Charlie. However, clearly the girl was terribly distressed. She had a river of black makeup running down her cheeks, and her eyes were bloodshot and red from crying.

"Stay back!" She yelled. "I mean it... if you come too close, I'll jump."

"Ok." Jake held his hands up, coming to a standstill about five metres away. "I'm not coming any closer. Please don't jump."

"Why would you care?" She sniffed, fastening her grip on the top of the metal railings.

"Because I do."

"Nobody cares!" She climbed up a rung. Now, there was only one between her and the tarmac below.

Jake couldn't stand it. It took every ounce of strength he had to fight his instinct to reach forwards and grab her, pull her to safety. But he knew that one wrong move would see her toppling down onto the cars below.

"Can we talk?" Jake asked. "Please?"

"I don't want to talk."

"Well, can I then? Talk to you?"

He saw her hesitate - it worked, breaking her out of her little bubble long enough for him to catch her attention. Lowering himself to the floor, he brought his knees up to his chest, wrapping his arms around them, a sign that he wasn't going anywhere. He would sit here for as long as it took. He had sat this way beside Charlie once, that day in the playground. And he had saved her. Maybe he could save this girl too? "I'm Jake."

Her bottom lip trembled. "Bella."

"Nice to meet you, Bella."

She frowned slightly, then let out an awkward laugh. "That's a weird thing to say... when you come across someone who's about to jump off a bridge."

Jake shrugged. "What's the right thing to say in that situation?"

She opened her mouth, lost for words. Then she sniffed. At least she had stopped crying. Jake wasn't sure if it was his imagination, but she looked a little better, as though having someone to talk to had lifted some of the weight on her shoulders already.

"Can I tell you something?"

She shrugged.

"I'm having a tough time at the moment, too."

Turning in his direction, she blinked at him.

"I er... you've probably seen me on the news."

Her face looked blank.

"I'm a soldier. I went missing in Afghanistan five years ago. And now I'm back. Only, it doesn't really feel like I'm home. Everything's changed, and I don't know what to do to fix it."

Bella's eyes widened. "Oh, I have seen you on the news! You're that missing guy, Corporal Parsons!"

"Yep, that's me."

Gobsmacked, she stared at him in silence.

"I thought when I got home, everything would go back to normal... I dreamed about escaping and coming home for so long, you know. Even when I started to lose my mind and forget everything that came before, I still knew that I had to get home... that I had people waiting for me. But... coming home's almost been harder than being stuck out there. Because I've lost the person I love more than life itself. And I don't know if I'll ever get her back."

"Who?"

"My wife. Turns out, she didn't wait out for me. She's married to someone else now."

"Wow! I'm sorry."

"Yeah. So am I."

Bella gulped, a strong gust of wind blowing her hair off her face. Her cheeks were dry now. Quietly, she muttered, "I lost someone I love too."

Jake sat patiently, waiting for her to continue.

"My mum..."

She didn't say anything else, but blinked back fresh tears, returning her attention to the cars whizzing past underneath.

"I'm sorry."

"She died four years ago now. I thought it was supposed to get easier in time. But it's got harder. I think about her *all* the time. I just want to be with her. More than anything. I can't see any other way."

"There's always another way," Jake mumbled, eyes on her loosening grip on the metal railings. "I think your mum would want you to be happy. She wouldn't want this for you, would she?"

"I don't know how to be happy," she sobbed. "And I'm so, so tired of having to pretend. I want to close my eyes, and for it all to be over."

"I felt like that. When I got back… I genuinely wished that I could have died out there. It seemed too hard… managing, pretending to be happy when all I wanted was to rewind time, go back to the day when it all kicked off… get my old life back. But you can't turn back time. You can only look forwards."

She was silent, wobbling slightly when reaching up with one hand to wipe tears from her scarlet cheeks. Jake clenched his fist, again resisting the urge to lunge forwards and grab her. He had to trust her to make the right decision.

"It's not been long. And there are good days and bad days. But I lost friends out there, in Afghanistan. My best friend, actually. He didn't get to choose. And I kind of think… I owe it to him, to make the most of my own life. There must be a reason why I survived. Maybe it's him looking out for me. And what sort of a friend would I be, if I didn't make the most of that chance? What would he say?"

Bella sniffed. "You think I'm being selfish?"

"No. Not at all. I think you're hurting. And you're struggling to see a way out at the moment. And that's ok. But this is a bad day, Bella. You'll have good days. And eventually, the good days will start to outnumber the bad, and you'll start to enjoy life again."

"Do you? Enjoy life?"

Jake shrugged. "Occasionally. When I'm cuddled up on the sofa with the dog. Or tasting steak which has been freshly cooked on the barbecue. Or having a laugh with the lads at the unit." He smiled slightly. "I still miss her, and I miss my friends. It still hurts. But we only get one chance at this, and I've already had more than my fair share, so..." he shrugged, "I guess I need to make the most of it."

He scuffed the toe of his trainer in the dust in front of him. "I'm sure there are lots of people who love you. And if they lose you, they'll feel a hole in their lives just like you feel a hole from losing your mum."

She cleared her throat. "My dad."

"There you go then. I bet he loves you."

"Yeah. He does. And he tries his best, but... it's not the same. I see all the other girls... going shopping and getting their nails done with their mums... and dad gives me a wad of cash and tells me to go and buy what I need. But I can't *buy* what I need."

"I get it. And I know there's nothing I can say to make it better. Life just sucks sometimes. It's unfair."

She smiled weakly, mulling over his words. Jake said nothing else. He sat patiently, waiting for her. He had all the time in the world. Life had a funny way of turning things around. An hour ago he had been driving down the motorway, seething because he'd wasted a day, desperate to get home. And now here he was, sitting at the top of a pedestrian bridge as though he had nowhere else to be, and nothing else was more important than helping this girl here, right now. Maybe this was all meant to be, after all.

The distant sound of a car door closing startled Jake, and he turned to see the fluorescent glow of a police car, parked at the end of the bridge. A police officer began to jog towards them. Bella shook her head, her face suddenly a picture of panic again.

"Did you call them?" Her body wobbled on the railings with such magnitude that Jake's stomach flipped upside down.

"No. I promise, I didn't."

"Don't come any closer," she yelled. "Or I'll jump!"

"Stay back!" Jake yelled at the police officer, who stopped in his tracks as instructed. Then he turned back to Bella. "Please don't do that, Bella."

"I can't do this anymore," she whispered. "I almost believed you for a minute there. But it's not going to go away."

"Bella..." Jake pleaded, his voice wobbling as he stood up and put his hand out, offering her a lifeline. Perhaps he should run forwards and tackle her, drag her down to the ground. But he knew what it was like to have your choice taken away, and he knew that she would hate him for it. But could he trust her to make the right decision?

"Thank you, for listening to me."

She stopped then, looking at him again with her tear stained face, her hair sticking to her cheeks.

"Talking to you has made a huge difference to me. It's been a long time since someone listened, and didn't judge me, or tell me what to do. Or analyse what I'm saying. I'm really grateful."

She stood still, her eyes wide, focused on him.

"I'd love to talk to you again, sometime."

She bit her lip, glancing over the railings at the cold, hard reality below.

"Now please, let me help you too? We can help each other get better?"

He took a couple of steps forwards, extending his hand. He was barely a metre from her now; it took all his self-control not to lunge forwards and grab her. She hesitated for a couple of seconds, her eyes travelling back to the cars whizzing past below, and then to his relief she stepped down, reaching for his hand, before flinging herself into his arms. He wrapped his arms around her and they stood on the bridge, enveloped in each others' arms, stunned at how someone can suddenly appear in your life and make such a difference, simply by being there at the right moment.

CHAPTER EIGHT

Captain Williams marched across the tarmac, wearily straightening his beret on his head. This was the last thing he needed; he could already see the flash of cameras in the distance, beyond the armed guards who stood at the gates.

"Sir!" They stood to attention as he approached.

"Thank you," he muttered, his eyes softening at the sight of her, huddled up in an oversized hooded jacket, her hair a mess and the skin around her eyes red raw. As much as he wished she wasn't here, he understood why she was. Things had been difficult enough for the men in the platoon, but their suffering was nothing compared to hers. He knew that she had been through hell and back over the past few weeks.

"Mrs Parsons," he smiled weakly. "What are you doing here?"

"I need to talk to you," she pleaded, her bottom lip quivering as she shifted from one foot to the other in front of him. "Please. I know you're busy, but this is urgent."

"I still haven't heard anything, I'm sorry."

"I know. But I still need to talk to you. Please."

She looked as though she hadn't slept for weeks. Perhaps she hadn't. "Now's not really a good time..."

The cameras flashed away behind her. He sighed, clenching his jaw. The last thing he needed was a PR disaster. There had been reporters at the gate for weeks, every day since the news of Parsons's disappearance had broken.

"Alright," he gave in. At least if he got her somewhere quiet, the cameras would stop flashing. "Come with me."

The guardsmen let her through the gates and she followed him towards the building, her hands stuffed deep inside her hoodie. She followed him through the door and up the stairs to his office, where he told her to take a seat and closed the door gently behind him.

Charlie looked around her. How many times had Jake stood to attention in this office? Suddenly, she felt out of place. Maybe she wasn't being formal enough, perhaps she wasn't showing him enough respect? He was Jake's boss, after all.

"I'm sorry, I don't know if I should be calling you Sir, or..."

"Leo's fine, Mrs Parsons."

She nodded, picking the raw skin around her nails off in her lap. "Ok. You can call me Charlie, by the way. You don't need to call me Mrs Parsons."

"I'm sorry I don't have more news. We're doing everything we can to find him, I can promise you that. Special Forces are assisting."

"Thank you," she inhaled shakily. "I er… I really need you to find him, bring him home."

"I know."

"When do you think he'll be home? Do you think it will be in the next month or two? Or a few months? Or maybe six?"

"Charlie…" Leo exhaled, peering at her over the top of his desk. "I need you to understand something. We're trying to find Jake, but we don't know where he is. And you need to prepare yourself for the fact that Afghanistan is… a very hostile country. It's not like it is here. I will do everything in my power to find Jake, but I can't promise you that we will. And if we do find him, it's very likely that he won't be alive."

She blinked at him, the realisation that she might never hold him in her arms again hitting her like a tonne of bricks. She knew - of course she did. She had thought of nothing else since he had gone missing. But hearing it from someone else, someone who was close to the action, almost made it even harder. Especially now that she wasn't the only one who was going to lose out if he never came home. Doing this all by herself was incomprehensible.

"I need him back…" she whispered, tears falling from her swollen eyes. "Please, bring him home to me."

Silently, he leant forwards with a tissue. Charlie took it and dabbed at her eyes gingerly. The skin around them was so sore, it was like awful sunburn.

"I'm pregnant," she blurted out, watching as the Captain's kind smile disappeared, replaced with one of regret. "I don't want my baby to grow up without a dad. I *don't think I'll be enough... on my own."*

His kind smile returned, and he gently placed his hand on hers. "Of course you will be."

***

The clock on the wall nearby ticked in perfect time with the steady thump of Charlotte's heart. She watched over her sleeping daughter, her arm set in a cast between her upper arm and her wrist, suspended upright in a brace.

A nurse peeped her head around the cubicle curtain. "Why don't you go and get something to eat? You've not left her bedside in hours!"

Charlotte smiled weakly. "I'm fine, thank you. I don't want to leave her..."

"Izzy's sedated. She won't wake for a few hours yet, at least. You need to look after yourself, too!"

Charlotte traced her little finger down Izzy's warm cheek. She looked so peaceful.

"She's absolutely fine. Go on, the canteen's down the hall."

Charlotte's stomach grumbled at the thought of food. Perhaps the nurse was right. "You have my mobile number, in case there's any change?"

"Of course," she smiled kindly. "I'll call straight away. But like I said, she'll be under sedation for a good few hours yet."

Charlotte hated leaving Izzy, but she couldn't deny that she was starving. She'd not eaten since breakfast, and it was past dinnertime now. After peeling her cardigan from the back of the chair, she planted a kiss on the top of Izzy's head. "I'll be back as soon as I can. I love you."

She stopped by the curtain and watched Izzy sleeping for a few seconds, before gently drawing it around the cubicle. It felt strange walking away. She knew that her daughter was in good hands, and she wouldn't have a clue that her mum had left, but Charlotte still felt guilty. Walking down the corridor towards the canteen, her stomach groaned. She clutched her bag to her shoulder and carried on putting one foot in front of the other, until she reached the lift and travelled down to the ground floor.

The air felt fresher as she walked towards reception and the canteen and she took a deep breath, grateful not to be breathing in regurgitated air. Once in the canteen, she chose a sandwich and a drink from the chiller cabinet, then out of habit reached for a packet of chocolate buttons for Izzy - her favourite. She wanted to make her smile when she woke up.

"That's six pounds thirty, please."

Charlotte dug into her purse and touched her card on the card reader, then picked up her tray. "Thank you."

Choosing a table near the full length windows, she sat down, admiring the first signs of sunset across the darkening sky above the buildings outside. She was exhausted. What a day. Be careful what you wish for, she thought - she had wished for a distraction, and this certainly was one.

After practically inhaling her sandwich, Charlotte dug out her phone. Noticing that she had three missed calls from Myles, she immediately called him back. It barely rung before he picked up.

"Charlotte? Thank God! Why didn't you call me sooner? I've been trying you for ages!"

She fiddled with the edge of the sandwich carton. "I'm sorry, I didn't have any signal upstairs. I've been with Izzy."

"Is she ok?"

"Yes, she's fine. The operation went well. She's sedated, it will probably be another few hours until she wakes up. But it all went well. They think she should make a full recovery. No lasting damage."

"Oh, thank God," he sighed. "Are you ok?"

"Yes. I'm fine," Charlotte paused. "Just a bit... shaken. She was having fun one minute, and then the next... I can't bear to think about it." She shivered.

"How did it happen?"

"She jumped into the foam pit at the trampoline park with Callum, and landed on her arm."

There was silence on the other end of the line. "She's a little young to be visiting those places, don't you think? I see stories about children breaking limbs on bouncy castles all the time."

"It's a trampoline park, not a bouncy castle," Charlotte frowned. "And it's suitable from the age of three. The slot is especially for pre-schoolers..."

"Well, obviously it isn't," he interrupted.

Charlotte bit her lip. "She was having fun, Myles. It was an accident. Accidents happen. I didn't mean for this to happen, obviously I wouldn't have taken her there if I'd have known..."

"Of course you wouldn't!" His voice lifted again. "You know that's not what I meant, Charlotte. I'm worried about her, that's all."

"So am I."

"Are you sure you don't want me to fly back?"

"No, no... it's fine. We're ok. We're being looked after. By the time you get back, she should be ready to come home. That's when the fun begins, six weeks of no running around and no getting the plaster wet!"

"Well, *that's* going to be a challenge!"

"Yeah. Well, I'd better go. Get back to her."

"Sure. I love you."

"You too."

Feeling more alone then ever, she slid her phone back inside her bag, taking the last few sips of her drink. Then she crushed the can, slipped it inside the sandwich carton and stood with her tray, still facing the window.

And there he was.

Right in front of her.

Charlotte stopped, perfectly still, as though she was frozen in time. On the other side of the glass he stood, rooted to the spot, his eyes wide, unable to take his gaze off her. If she had left a minute earlier, or the nurse hadn't persuaded her to get something to eat, they'd have missed each other entirely. They had ended up at the same place at the same time, opposite sides of the glass, simply by chance.

She had imagined this moment so many times - but never like this. For the past couple of months, she had thought of almost nothing else, terrified that he was going to appear, turning the life she had built upside down. But now that he was here right in front of her, with the same slight smile and the same piercing green eyes, she no longer felt terrified.

In a blink, he disappeared. Charlotte stood closer to the glass, looking up the pathway, but there was no sign of him. Maybe she had imagined him after all?

"Charlie?"

Maybe not.

She turned; he was there. Right in front of her, within touching distance. She opened her mouth to speak, but the words got caught in her throat and she could barely breathe. Her limbs were heavy and she couldn't move.

"Sit down."

Gently, his warm hands on her upper arms led her to the table. Her legs gave way and she blinked hard, trying to clear the swirling white spots which blurred her vision. This couldn't be real - he couldn't be here, right in front of her.

"Are you ok?"

It was him alright. Butterflies came alive in her stomach, at the brush of his thumbs on her elbows. Suddenly, every bone in her body ached for him. The feelings she'd had for him five years ago and for as long as she could remember before that flooded back, forcing tears from her eyes.

"Hey, it's ok," he wiped them away with his thumbs. "It's ok."

Instinctively, she flung her arms around his muscular frame. Held tightly in his arms, she closed her eyes, inhaling deeply, her nostrils searching for that familiar scent of mint and tobacco. For a few minutes they just sat in silence, their bodies pressed together, senses exploring each other again for the first time in years.

"I thought you were dead," she whispered eventually when he withdrew, his hand still covering her upper arm protectively.

"I know."

Raising her gaze from her lap, her eyes met his. Instantly, it felt as though a spark of electricity passed between them, waking up all the feelings they'd ever had for each other. Charlotte's eyes fell to her wedding ring, sparkling in the artificial light. He followed her gaze. She opened her mouth to say something, but no words would come out.

"I know. You don't need to tell me."

She gulped. "I didn't know you were coming back."

"I know."

"What are you doing here? Are you hurt?"

"No. I came in with a girl who was in a bad way. I came with her in the ambulance, waited with her until her dad arrived."

"Your girlfriend?"

He raised an eyebrow, shocked that she could even ask such a question. "Really? Of course not. What are you doing here?"

"My daughter broke her arm."

Expectantly, she waited for his reaction, but he didn't flinch. "Is she alright?"

"Yes, she'll be fine. She's had surgery, it went well. She's still sedated."

"Is Myles here?"

Charlotte frowned curiously. "How did you..."

"I saw your car. Outside my house. I wanted to know who was watching me, so I searched online. I found his details first, then yours."

Slowly, she nodded, her lips pressed together nervously. This wasn't the reaction she had been expecting. She didn't even need to explain herself - he already knew all about her life, yet he hadn't turned up out of the blue at her house, nor had he exposed her to anyone. And he could have done.

Withdrawing his hand from her arm, he leant back in the chair next to her. "You knew that I was back?"

She nodded. "I saw your parents on the news."

"Why didn't you get in touch? Why did you drive away?"

She shifted in her chair. “I… I was scared.”

“Scared? Of what?”

Nervously, Charlotte chewed her lip. “I’m not the person I was, when you disappeared.”

“That doesn’t mean I don’t want to see you.”

“I was worried you’d be… angry…”

“Angry? Why would I be angry?”

Charlotte glanced down at her ring again. “Because I remarried… it wasn’t because I gave up on you, you know. Or stopped loving you. I was in a really dark place, after you left. I just wanted to be happy again.”

“I understand.”

“You do?”

“Yeah. I can’t imagine what it would have been like for you, waiting and waiting, struggling on your own. So you found a way out..."

“It wasn’t really like that…”

"No?"

"What do you mean?"

“Well... he’s a millionaire..."

She frowned. “Spit it out, Jake.”

He shook his head. “Come on… don’t make me say it…”

Charlotte stood abruptly, knocking the chair back. “When I said I’m not the person I was, that’s not what I meant. I would never have gone after Myles for his money. I didn’t even know about his business when I met him.”

“Charlie, wait…”

She picked up the chair and pushed it back

under the table firmly. "It sounds like you've made your mind up about me. But you don't know anything about me now, Jake!"

Picking up her bag, she turned to leave, but he grabbed her wrist hard, turning her to face him. For a second, she looked petrified. He dropped her, staring at his own palm, mortified that he might have hurt her, even if only for a second.

"I'm sorry. Please don't go."

"I need to get back to Izzy..."

"Izzy... that's your daughter?"

Her face softened slightly. "Yes."

"I'd like to hear all about her. Is she like you? Do you have a photo?"

Her stomach turned upside down. "No."

"Not on your phone?"

"It's dead."

"Ok... maybe I could come with you? To see her?"

"*No*, Jake!"

Her voice was a lot more forceful than she intended, and he stepped back as though she had physically shoved him away. He looked upset, and she knew that she had hurt him. But maybe it was for the best...

"This isn't a good idea. I'm glad you're ok, I really am. And it was good to see you. But I have a husband, and we have a daughter... and I need to think about her."

"Charlie... come on! I only wanted to see what she looks like, she's a big part of your life..."

"Will you stop calling me that?! Nobody ever calls me that, not anymore."

"I'm sorry..."

"I have to go. Goodbye, Jake."

"Charlie, please... I mean, Charlotte... please, don't go..."

"Goodbye, Jake."

Firmly, she turned and walked away, her footsteps echoing around the empty corridor, desperately holding herself together until she turned the corner, and he was out of sight. Then she let herself fall apart.

CHAPTER NINE

She tried not to lose hope, but with every day that passed, the possibility of seeing Jake alive again seemed more and more remote. She jumped out of her skin at every knock on the door, and could barely breathe every time her phone rang. She saw him everywhere. Standing right in front of her in a cubicle when she pulled the curtain open. Lying white and lifeless under a sheet when she carefully pulled it down to clean the patient's body underneath. Leaning against her locker, his piercing green eyes staring at her when she opened the door to the staffroom.

Charlie thought it might get easier in time, but it didn't - it got worse. As the tiny life grew inside her, she felt more and more alone. She was distant from her work colleagues, and from Jake's family, who tried their best to keep in touch with her. Drowning in sorrow and grief, she convinced herself that they had never really liked her - the only reason they were making an effort was because they hoped that Jake might be found alive. But Charlie knew, deep down. She knew that she would be bringing up this baby alone, because he wasn't coming home to her. He had never let her down. If he was alive, he would have found a way to contact her by now, whatever his situation.

Her nurse's uniform was the only thing holding her together, but even that was stretched to bursting. She could see her bump now when she looked down, the little part of Jake that she would always carry growing fiercely in her belly. Although she was petrified of going through it alone, she owed their unborn child a lot. If it wasn't for him or her, Charlie didn't think she could have lasted this long - she was certain that she would have given up hope on life altogether. But she couldn't, not while she had a piece of Jake inside her. She owed it to him to keep going.

Once her work colleagues found out about the baby, life became even harder. They asked all the wrong questions - if one more person asked if she was excited, she thought she might go out of her mind. They all knew about Jake, and nobody knew what to say, not really. She knew that they were only being polite, trying to make conversation, but every time someone said the wrong thing, the distance grew between them, and she shut them out even more.

The decision to leave, in the end, was an easy one. Her hand was forced. A patient almost died when, completely distracted, she administered the wrong medication to a patient with an allergy. She realised her mistake almost immediately and called a doctor, who was fortunately able to save the patient. But it was too late for Charlie. Overwrought with guilt and unable to trust herself, she accepted her superiors' offer to go on extended leave, until after the baby was born. Handing over her ID card before she left, she knew that she would never go back. It was over. All the dreams she'd ever had, for herself and for Jake, had broken into a million pieces the day he had gone missing. And now she had a baby, someone who was relying on her, someone she couldn't provide for.

How was she going to manage looking after someone else, when she couldn't even look after herself? Every time she saw the midwife she rattled on about her blood pressure, her iron levels, and protein in her urine. Had she been eating? Had she been sleeping? Had she support at home? Charlie nodded in response to all of her questions, unable to so much as begin to explain how she was feeling, and why. The love of her life had been ripped from her. She was pregnant and alone, watching her whole world collapse right in front of her. How could she explain how she was feeling in just a ten minute appointment?

She wanted to close her eyes, go to sleep, and never open them again.

Although her body was exhausted, her mind wouldn't let her rest. The second she closed her eyes, her mind was swimming with thoughts of Jake. Not only memories, but awful thoughts, things she never wanted to imagine. She could see him tied up, starving and thirsty, being beaten to within an inch of his life. She woke up screaming and crying in the night, then had to wrap her arms around his pillow and hold it tightly to her body. If she closed her eyes and breathed deeply, she could still smell the slight scent of him deep inside the pillow - if she forced herself hard enough, she could almost imagine that he was there, holding her; stroking her hair, promising that everything was going to be alright.

She went days on end without seeing anyone, or doing anything. She lay in the dark, the curtains closed, watching the time tick by on the wall clock above the fridge. Days turned into weeks, weeks into months. Her work colleagues stopped texting, having still not heard from her after several attempts. She ignored calls from Jake's parents, even managed to stay hidden when they turned up at the flat one day, concerned. Worried that they might call the police, she text them and told them that she had gone away, to stay with a friend for a while, and not to worry - she'd be in touch when she got back.

But months passed and, wrapped up in their own bubble of grief, they stopped trying to contact her. It was a relief, in a way. Charlie didn't know how to tell them about the baby. It was too painful seeing them, the similarities between themselves and Jake all she could see. She just couldn't do it.

***

Yawning, Charlotte rose from the crinkly fold up mattress next to Izzy's bed, stretching the aches from her muscles. It hadn't exactly been a great night's sleep, but she would never complain. The nurses had been kind enough to find her somewhere to sleep, right by Izzy's side, so that was good enough for her.

Her eyes on her daughter, she stood and pressed her fingertips into her shoulders, massaging out the knots. Izzy was still sleeping peacefully, groggy from the sedatives. She had woken in the night once the sedation wore off, but the surgery had really taken it out of her and she had slipped back into slumber just after four in the morning. Charlotte glanced at her watch. It was seven thirty now. It wouldn't be long before the breakfast trolley came round.

"Izzy?" She whispered softly, taking her daughter's free hand as she perched on the edge of the bed. "Morning, sweetheart."

There was no change - she was fast asleep. After stroking the hair out of Izzy's eyes, Charlotte tucked the sheets up higher on her chest, before gathering her bag from the chair next to the bed. She would have to be quick.

After glancing back to make sure that Izzy was still asleep, she crept out of the cubicle, gently closing the curtain behind her. Then she padded across the ward, trying not to wake any of the other sleeping children, and out into the corridor where she sped up towards the toilets. Once she'd relieved herself she splashed her face with water, then looked up into the mirror above the sink.

She was surprised that Jake had even noticed her when he walked past the window. She had changed a lot since last time they had met; in fact, almost everything about her was different. Her hair, her nails, her build... she wore make up now, when she never had before. Her clothes, the lines around her eyes, even the expression on her face. The last five years had aged her way beyond her years, chewed her up and spat her out, put her back together as a completely different person. She had gone through more anguish than most people went through in their entire lives. And she'd had nobody by her side - absolutely nobody. That was, until Myles walked into her life. And he'd had hold of her ever since.

Leaving the toilet, Charlotte closed the door gently behind her. Already alive, the corridor was buzzing with medics going on their morning rounds, porters pushing trolleys full of toast and cereal. Passing one of the nurses who'd cared for Izzy the night before, she smiled weakly, heading back in the direction of her daughter's cubicle.

"Charlotte?" Another nurse stepped out from behind the nurse's station, a folded piece of paper in her hand. "Someone left this for you."

Hesitantly, Charlotte took it. "Oh. Thank you."

"You're welcome."

Firmly crunching the piece of paper in her closed fist, Charlotte entered the cubicle and closed the curtain behind her, her heart thumping in her chest. Suddenly, a strange sense of longing filled her body, causing her stomach to drop as though she'd driven over a humpback bridge. Loosening her fingers, she raised her palm, allowing the paper to uncrinkle slightly under the shine of the strip light above.

Izzy was still asleep, so she sank down on the seat beside her bed and smoothed the paper out on the thigh of her jeans. She recognised the handwriting from the first letter. Her stomach dropped again, causing a wave of nausea to wash over her.

~~Charlie~~ Charlotte,

I couldn't leave without saying a proper goodbye. Since I got back from Afghan and my memory returned, all I've thought about is finding you, looking after you and loving you again.

I don't want to mess things up for you, I've only ever wanted to give you the life you deserve. But someone else has given you that now. I can't deny that it hurts to know you love someone else the way you once loved me, but I want you to know that I'm happy for you.

Nothing hurt me more when I was in Afghan than thinking of you at home on your own, waiting for me. I'm glad you found love again, and I'm really happy that you get to live the life I always wanted to give you. A lovely home, a comfortable life and a family.

I can't imagine living the rest of my life without you in it. You've been my best friend for as long as I can remember, please don't give up on me now. We can be friends - if you're happy in your marriage and you don't want to unsettle your daughter, I understand. But that doesn't mean we can't stay in touch - I don't want to live a life without you in it.

My number is on the back. I'd love to speak properly, once your daughter's home and settled and you don't need to worry about her so much.

Love Jake

"Mummy?"

Her stomach lurching, Charlotte crushed the piece of paper in her hand and dropped it, before reaching to stroke Izzy's fringe off her forehead. "Sweetheart! I'm here."

Izzy smiled through heavy eyelids. "I'm tired, Mummy."

"I know you are. You've been such a brave girl! Does it hurt?"

Izzy turned to look at her arm, suspended in the brace above the bed. She looked surprised to see it there, set in a perfect right angle. "No, Mummy."

"Good."

Charlotte bent to pick up her jacket, which had slipped off the back of the chair. Her fingers brushed the crushed piece of paper which lay solemnly next to it. She picked it up, placing it on the table which sat over Izzy's bed. Maybe she would go back to it later. Right now, her daughter needed her.

"I'm hungry."

Charlotte peered out to the corridor. "Breakfast's on its way. I can hear the trolley now, just a few more minutes."

"Ok. Is Daddy here?"

Charlotte shook her head sadly. "No, baby, he's not. I'm sorry. He's going to come home as soon as he can, though."

Izzy's face fell. "Will he be cross with me?"

Charlotte frowned. "Why would he be cross?"

"Because... I made a big fuss. And I cried, Daddy doesn't like it when we cry."

"No, Izzy, of course he won't be cross!" Charlotte reached for her daughter, gently holding her in her arms. "He's so proud of you, for being really brave."

Once she released Izzy she sat back, studying her daughter's face carefully. Her momentary anxiety had been replaced with a happier, more carefree look again. The breakfast trolley clunked out in the corridor.

"Here it comes!"

"Morning! Would you like some breakfast? We have toast and cereal."

"Yes, please!" Charlotte smiled. "Izzy, what would you like?"

"Ummm, rice pops please! And some blackcurrant."

"We don't have blackcurrant on the trolley, but there's a bottle in the relative's kitchen area."

"Would you like me to get you some?" Charlotte asked.

"Yes please, Mummy!"

"Ok. I'll be back in a moment."

Charlotte could hear Izzy chattering away as she walked down the corridor to the kitchenette. It was good to hear her sounding more like herself. No doubt by the end of the day, she'd be bouncing off the walls. That would be the hard part - keeping her still enough for her arm to heal. Charlotte reached for a plastic cup and filled it with blackcurrant and water, then turned the tap off and padded back down the corridor.

"Thank you," she smiled at the porter, who was emerging from the room with the trolley. She slipped back inside and placed the blackcurrant down on the table.

And realised that the note was gone.

Quickly she glanced around, checking that it hadn't got knocked down onto the sheets or underneath the bed. "Izzy, did you see a piece of paper here?"

"The lady took some rubbish away," Izzy shrugged, taking her first mouthful of cereal.

Charlotte's stomach flipped. Swallowing hard, she glanced back into the hallway as the sound of the trolley trundling away got quieter and quieter. She opened her mouth to reassure Izzy that she'd be back, but before she got the chance there was a sudden squeal and a cry, and a clatter as the cereal bowl slid off the bed and onto the floor, splashing milk everywhere.

"Oh, no!" Izzy leapt up. She cried out, pulling

her arm.

"Oh, Izzy! Keep still!" Charlotte cried, settling Izzy back on the pillow first and then scooping up the cereal from the bed, stripping the sheets back before the milk soaked through to Izzy's gown.

Izzy's eyes filled with tears. "Sorry, Mummy!"

"It's ok! It was an accident! It's fine, see?"

"Daddy would be so cross if he saw what a mess I'd made."

Charlotte peered at her, her hands full of saturated tissues. "No, he wouldn't. And anyway, I've fixed it, it's absolutely fine. You don't need to worry."

Once the mess was cleared up and Izzy had calmed down, Charlotte remembered the note. She rushed back to the doorway, looking left and right for the porter with the trolley. But she was nowhere to be seen. The note was gone.

She looked back at Izzy, who still looked utterly miserable. This was her fault, for allowing herself, even for a moment, to be so selfish. So stupid to even think that she could make contact with Jake, have him in her life, and everything would still be fine. This was a sign. A sign that Izzy was her number one now, that she couldn't sacrifice her happiness for anything. If she had been concentrating on Izzy rather than looking for the note, the bowl wouldn't have fallen, and her little girl would have a full belly and a smile on her face now.

"I'll go find you some more cereal," Charlotte smiled shakily, her decision made.

***

Jake liked to think that he'd returned to the hospital purely because he wanted to check on Bella, but he couldn't deny that he had an ulterior motive. That morning he had walked past the window of the cafeteria before entering, checking the table where they'd sat the evening before. Unfortunately, when he arrived, there was no sign of Charlotte. But he knew that she had to be somewhere inside this hospital. So he'd come up with a plan. He'd asked at the desk, posed as a family friend, and although they wouldn't tell him where Charlotte was, he left a note with reception. He desperately hoped that it would find its way to her - that it wouldn't be forgotten all day in someone's pocket, until it was too late and Charlotte took Izzy home. He almost slipped up when asking after her, calling her Charlie Parsons. She hadn't been Charlie Parsons for a long time. He needed to remember that she was Charlotte Bond now.

Then, he waited. Visiting hours weren't for a while, so he found himself sitting outside the main entrance, watching people arrive and leave, ambulances whizz past to the unloading bays, taking people inside. The noise and constant rush was strangely reassuring. Sometimes, when he was sat at home, it seemed too... quiet. He didn't understand why, but he almost missed the hum and buzz of Afghanistan. He had hated the place when he was there, despised those who'd held him captive, and longed for home. But recently he had come to realise that it wasn't the quietness of home he missed. It was the people in it. And the person who meant the most to him was living another life now, his parents tiptoed around him as though he was broken beyond repair, and even his own brother was too busy with his wife and his new life abroad to make any time for Jake now. Home was quiet and lonely, and he found himself counting down the days until he was next at the barracks.

Losing track of time, he sat there for two hours. Finally, glancing at his watch, he realised that visiting hours had started and he went inside, following the signs to the ward where he knew Bella had been taken. He'd stayed with her yesterday until her dad arrived, and after his meeting with Charlotte he'd checked in on her again, before she was moved from A&E to an overnight ward.

"Hey," he smiled, opening the door of Bella's side room carefully.

She smiled back, looking a lot brighter today. Jake was relieved. She'd been in such a state the day before, it was hard to see someone else struggling like that. "How are you?"

"A little better today, thanks to you." She gestured at the empty chair next to her bed. "Take a seat, if you want."

"Thanks."

He lowered himself into the seat gently, his eyes falling on the fresh flowers and bars of chocolate that sat, untouched, on her side table.

"From my dad," she explained.

"Did you talk to him? Like I said? About how you've been feeling?"

She nodded quietly.

"Good. And?"

"You were right. I told him everything. I cried. He cried. And after that I felt much better. It was like some of the weight was lifted... I mean, I still can't shake it... that feeling... but I feel like he's there for me... he knows what I'm going through now."

"A problem shared is a problem halved, and all that," he shifted in his chair, clasping his hands together in his lap.

Bella stared at him. "And did you?"

"Did I what?"

"Speak to her again? Charlie?"

Jake clenched his jaw. "I couldn't find her. They wouldn't tell me where she is, on the desk."

"Oh." Bella looked as deflated as he felt.

"I wrote something down though... a note. With my number. I asked them to pass it on to her."

"And have you heard anything?"

"No."

"I'm sorry. I hope she gets in touch. I'm sure she will, once she's got over the shock, you know... maybe she didn't know you were alive?"

"She did. She definitely knew."

Bella smiled sympathetically, carefully placing her hand on Jake's. It was strange, he'd only met this girl yesterday, but he felt comfortable in her company - it was as though he'd known her for ages. Like she was some sort of long-lost, younger sister.

"You know, you should keep trying. Don't give up. I'll bet she's just scared, to leave her husband. Her new one, I mean. Not you, obviously."

Jake raised his eyebrows. "You mean the millionaire? I'm kidding myself, Bella, she'll never leave him for me. They have a daughter together."

"But you loved each other. And it sounds like you still do!"

"Of course I do. But I don't think she feels the same."

"Er, of course she does! What was the first thing she did when she saw you? Almost fainted and then threw her arms around you!"

"That was just shock. After that she walked away, and told me not to contact her again."

"Yeah, well. Sometimes I shut people out when I'm scared. Like my dad. Doesn't mean I don't love him."

"Mmm. But this is a bit different, isn't it? She's *married* to someone else, they have a child together. And if you knew Charlie's background, you'd know that she'll never do anything to risk upsetting her family life. She'll never leave him. I do love her Bella, but I might as well give up now. Move on with my life."

"You *can't* give up. I can see how much you love her, and I only met you yesterday!"

"Love isn't always enough, Bella. You'll find

that out when you're older."

"I disagree with you. And you might think I'm only a stupid kid, but I know what it's like to love someone more than life itself, and for them to be snatched away from you."

Jake scratched at his stubble awkwardly. "I'm sorry... I didn't mean to upset or patronise you."

Stubbornly, she stared at him. "You love her, Jake. More than anyone else in the world. And I bet she still loves you, too. But she's scared, can't see a way out because everything is so... messy. And she wants to put her daughter first, I get that. But you have to fight for her. Show her you're there for her, that you're not going to give up. Even if she doesn't want a relationship with you, show her that you're her friend, always. Someone to fight her corner."

Jake stared at her, then sighed. His lips curled up into a slight smile. "You're sixteen going on thirty seven, you know that?"

"That's what happens when you've been through as much shit as I have." She saw his expression and pulled a face. "Don't..."

"What?"

"Look at me like that. I don't want people feeling sorry for me."

Pulling his phone from his pocket, his heart sank at the sight of the empty screen.

"Go."

"Where?"

"Er, to find her, obviously!"

"But this hospital's massive..."

"Ugh!" Bella rolled her eyes. "Is she worth fighting for, or not? I know if it was my mum, and I had the chance to see her and speak to her, even for a second, I'd be searching every damn room in this hospital."

"Yeah... you're right."

"Of course I am."

Standing, he reached for Bella, holding her in his arms one last time. He knew he probably wouldn't see her again; she was going home soon, with her dad.

"Thank you."

"No, thank you," he croaked, a lump forming in his throat at the thought of saying goodbye. He'd met this plucky teenager less than twenty-four hours ago, yet he felt quite attached. In a way, she reminded him of Charlie at that age - bolshy and brave, yet vulnerable and desperate for love all the same. He desperately wanted her to be alright. "Nobody else has listened to me the way you have... not since I got back."

"I'd have said that yesterday. But then I realised, it's me who shuts people out... they can't listen if I don't talk."

Silently, Jake stared at her. Suddenly, he felt foolish. He had more than a decade on Bella, yet she'd seemingly figured it all out for both of them while he sat there, feeling sorry for himself.

"Give me your phone," Bella sighed.

"What?"

"Give me your phone. So I can put my number

in it. Unless you never want to hear from me again?"

"Oh. Of course I do." He handed it over.

She keyed in her number, then glanced up at him. "I want to see the photos when you guys get back together."

He half-laughed. "You're more optimistic than I am."

"Here."

He took back the phone, slipped it back inside his pocket and reached for the door handle. "Good luck. Take care of yourself. And you can call me, if things get difficult, or you want to talk, ok?"

"You too," she nodded. "Don't give up, ok?"

CHAPTER TEN

Unable to contain the pain any longer, Charlie let out an agonised howl, tipping her head back as her body writhed in agony on top of the bed.

"Charlie... listen."

She felt the midwife's grip on her hand, but she didn't have the strength to look at her. Gritting her teeth, she squeezed her eyes shut, wishing that her heart would stop so that she wouldn't be in pain anymore.

"Charlie!"

"I can't do this," she managed once the pain subsided. "I can't! It's going to kill me!"

"Listen to me," the midwife said firmly, wiping a cool flannel over her forehead. "You can do this. Listen to me. Breathe... in, out. Long, slow, breaths. I'm right here with you, you're so close!"

"I can't even get through one more contraction. Please, make it stop!"

"Think of a happy time. Breathe in, and out, and think of a happy time."

Closing her eyes, Charlie sucked in a long breath,

then forced it out again through gritted teeth. She thought about the night this baby had been conceived, even though they hadn't known it at the time, when they had lay together, their bodies entwined, the whole night long. They had made love as though it was going to be the last time. Little had they known that it was. She gulped in another breath and tried to remember the strength and safety of his arms around her, holding her close, the warmth of his breath in her ear as he whispered how much he loved her. She tried to imagine that he was here now, he was the one holding her hand - whispering in her ear, telling her that she was going to be alright.

"I can see baby's hair, Charlie! Well done, love. You're so close now."

Once the contraction subsided, Charlie heavily exhaled, briefly opening her eyes to look around her. Upon seeing that they were alone in the room she closed her eyes again, trying to force that memory back, desperate to conjure that warmth around her again, that safety net that she'd missed ever since he went missing. This was supposed to be their moment, the moment they brought a new life into the world together. But she was all on her own.

"Ok, Charlie. This time, when I tell you to stop pushing, I need you to pant instead, ok?"

Charlie nodded. Her uterus contracted quickly and this time, instead of crying out in pain she channelled her fear into pushing, as hard as she possibly could.

"Ok, now pant!"

She did as she was told. Her eyes closed, she imagined Jake holding her hand tightly in one of his, while stroking her damp hair off her forehead with the other. Come on, Charlie! You can do it. *She smiled briefly as something shifted deep inside her, and she felt the burn of their baby's head as fresh air hit it for the first time.*

"Baby's here, Charlie! Now, breathe and listen to your body."

Jake was holding her hand so tightly, she knew that he was here - he wouldn't let her down. Proudly, he beamed, watching their baby's head slip out followed by her shoulders. With a gush, the rest of her body slid out into the midwife's hands.

"Well done, Charlie! You have a daughter!"

At the sound of the baby's high-pitched wail, Charlie opened her eyes, which filled with tears as soon as she saw the beautiful bundle between her legs.

"A girl!" She cried, tears streaming down her face.

"She's absolutely beautiful. Well done you."

There was a click as the midwife swiftly cut the cord, then she wrapped the baby in a blanket and placed her into Charlie's waiting arms.

"Hello," she whispered, taking in the soft curve of her baby's nose, and the pinkness of her brand new skin. She was the most beautiful thing Charlie had ever seen.

Her eyes full of tears, she looked up to where Jake had been standing just a moment ago, beaming proudly as their daughter made her entrance. But there was nobody there. He had vanished into thin air.

***

Standing in the courtyard, Charlotte enjoyed the warm autumn sun on her skin. It had been days since she'd stood outside, and she thought about nothing else just for a moment. Her eyes closed, she took a deep breath in, enjoying the clean, fresh air in her lungs.

Lifting the phone to her ear, she listened to the repetitive dial tone. She was just about to give up, when he answered. "Charlotte. How's Izzy?"

"She's fine. The doctor's going to check her over again later, but she should be able to go home tomorrow morning."

"Are you sure that's a good idea?"

"Yes, she's absolutely fine, Myles. She just wants to get home and sleep in her own bed. Play with her own toys."

There was a pause at the end of the line. Charlotte cleared her throat, waiting for him to respond.

"Perhaps it would be best if she stays in hospital a few more days, where she can be kept an eye on."

"Well, I'll be at home with her, keeping an eye on her. I know what to do, I used to do this for a living, remember!"

"That was a long time ago. And you were supposed to be keeping an eye on her when she broke her arm."

Charlotte bit her lip. "Children have accidents, Myles... it was an accident..."

"Which wouldn't have happened, if she wasn't at the trampoline park. She's *four,* Charlotte. I don't know what you were thinking."

Furious tears prickled in Charlotte's eyes and she pressed them closed, trying desperately not to let him hear how much he'd hurt her. "Myles, we went through this... the trampoline park is fine for her age. It was an accident, I..."

"We'll talk about it when I get home," he answered abruptly. "Don't make anymore stupid decisions, alright? Keep her safe."

"I will," Charlotte promised, and then he was gone.

She couldn't hold back the tears anymore. How could he think that of her? How could he blame her for what had been a simple accident? Children have accidents all the time, she thought to herself. She used to see little ones all the time when she worked her stint in A&E - they hurt themselves doing all sorts of everyday things. It was easy for him to say that, when he was never there. He was always at a meeting, or at the office, or jetting off to some faraway country for a business meeting. Charlotte could count on one hand the number of weeks this year where he'd been at home every night for an entire week. It was exhausting being in charge of a little person all the time. Especially one with as much energy as Izzy.

And it was already time to go back. She took a deep breath, wiped her tears away with the back of her hand, and turned. Right into Jake.

She gasped. "What are you doing?"

"Getting some fresh air," he peered at her curiously. "Are you alright? Is your daughter ok?"

"Izzy's fine," she sniffed. "I'm fine."

"Well, you don't look it."

As if reading her mind, he wrapped his arms around her and pulled her against his warm chest, closing his eyes as he breathed in the delicate scent of her posh perfume and shampoo. It wasn't the scent he remembered, but he loved it nonetheless.

Charlotte allowed herself to melt into him, closing her eyes. His arms still felt strong and welcoming, it was as though she could feel the frustration and exhaustion slipping out of her body and into his. Then suddenly, she came to her senses. "I need to get back to Izzy, she..."

"She'll be fine, for a bit. You need to take care of yourself, too."

She knew he was right, and she didn't want Izzy to know she was upset, so she didn't put up a fight. Once she felt better, she pulled out of his arms and they sat side by side on the bench, overlooking a small water fountain. Closing her eyes, the steady trickle of the water soothed Charlotte's mind and she took a inhaled slowly, allowing her shoulders to relax.

"I lost your note," she muttered, opening her eyes to find him peering at her all knowingly, as though he could read her mind.

"You got it, then. I wasn't sure if it would find

its way to you."

She nodded. "Yes. It did."

When she didn't volunteer anything else, he opened his mouth. "Did you read it?"

"Yes."

Subconsciously, his hand found its way to hers and slipped around it gently like a glove. His fingers interlaced with hers until they fit together perfectly, like puzzle pieces which had been lost for a long time, finally reunited. Charlotte didn't flinch.

"And?"

"I'm sorry I hurt you."

"I could say the same thing."

She frowned. "It wasn't your fault, though..."

"And it wasn't yours."

Her eyes scanned every inch of his face, analysing the thick stubble which now grew in place of the smooth chin she once knew. His emerald eyes contained the same sparkle, just with a few more lines around them. His pink lips, which she found herself wondering about before she could stop herself - would they feel as soft as the last time she kissed them?

She pressed her lips together, forcing the thought from her mind. "I did wait for you. For a long time. Long after most people had given up hope."

"I know you did."

"I didn't plan to meet Myles. We just bumped into each other, and something clicked."

Jake nodded, a pained expression fleeting

across his features for a second, but long enough for Charlotte to see it.

"If I knew you were alive, I would never have given up hope. But they said it was impossible... that you'd have been killed within hours of them capturing you. They said I had to get on with my life. And I was in such a dark place... I had to do something, or the not knowing... it would have killed me."

He squeezed her hand, swallowing back a lump that formed in his throat. "I'm glad you found happiness again. Someone to look after you. And look at the life you have now! You deserve it, more than anyone."

A sudden wave of nausea ran through her body and she realised that she hadn't eaten all day; too busy keeping an eye on Izzy, and trying to keep her entertained. It was even more exhausting doing it here, than at home.

"I never stopped thinking about you though," she whispered, smiling sadly. "About the life we could have had together. I was so, so happy back then."

"But you're happy now, right? And your daughter has an amazing life. And I could never have given you what you have now."

All Charlotte had wanted since finding out about her pregnancy was to give her baby a better life. She didn't want to be stuck in a tiny, cramped flat, working all hours while she paid a child-minder to watch her daughter's first steps, and hear her first word, and experience things for the first time together. And Myles had given her opportunities that she never had when she was on her own. A lovely home, the best education money could buy for their daughter... except... Izzy wasn't their daughter. She was Charlotte's. That hadn't mattered to Charlotte before now, because everyone thought she was Myles's, and so there was no reason for anyone to find out - ever. She had been careful to keep herself and Izzy out of the spotlight, so that nobody from their old lives might recognise her and spoil the perfect life that they had. A life full of security, and privilege, and safety; all the things Charlotte had never had growing up.

But now, she was sitting next to Jake, Izzy's dad, and the weight of the lie pressed down, almost crushing the breath out of her. Now there was someone else who might get hurt. And for the first time, she thought about what Izzy had to lose, if she was to find out the truth. How upset she'd be to find out that her whole life was a lie. She pulled her hand away quickly. "I need to get back to her."

"Did I say something wrong?"

Jake rose next to her as she stood, grabbing her elbow with his hand. Butterflies danced in Charlotte's stomach and she gulped, their eyes connecting as she was drawn towards him. His lips parted slightly and for a few seconds she found herself moving towards him, their bodies edging closer, desperate to be reunited after five years apart.

But then she remembered Izzy and something inside her snapped, closing the door on the what-ifs and the maybes inside her brain, and bringing her straight back down to the ground with a harsh bump.

"We can't..."

"I meant what I said in my letter, Charlotte. I don't want a life without you in it. But I won't stand in the way of your marriage. I won't lie, my first instinct when I found out about you and Myles was to look for a way to end your marriage and get you back. But I understand now. You have a family, a life together. I won't stand in the way of that. I promise you."

"Jake, I..."

"I'll always love you, Charlotte. But I understand that you love someone else now. I still want to be your friend. Support you, be there for you. Just like before. I know I'm an outsider in your world now... and you probably don't have any friends like me..."

"Stop it!" She shook her head, grabbing his hand again. "Having more money doesn't make me better than you. You're one of the most amazing people I've ever known."

His face softened then, and for the first time in her life, Charlotte thought he was going to cry. She'd never seen him cry before - not ever.

"I want to get to know you again. I want to laugh with you, have fun with you. And I'd love to get to know your family, but... if you want to keep that separate, I understand. We can keep in touch, the two of us. Talk sometimes… meet up occasionally, if you like. But the ball's in your court. It's up to you to decide. If I can have you in my life… whatever that involves… then I'll be made up."

She could tell by his expression that he was being sincere. Yet still, she felt torn. She had spent the past four years making a fresh life for herself, closing the door on her old life and desperately hoping that she would never be exposed. As far as her new friends and acquaintances knew, Charlotte had never been married before Myles, and Izzy was a child of their marriage. Nobody knew about her difficult past, nor the husband who had been ripped out of her life so suddenly. And she had let Izzy down miserably when she was on her own. Myles had picked her back up, given both of them a life that Charlotte could only have dreamed of. It wouldn't be fair for her to risk jeopardising that now.

But the pull she felt towards Jake was so strong. She was desperate to have him back in her life, even just as friends - have someone who really, truly understood her. For the past few months, and especially since finding out that he was still alive, she had felt so anxious and on edge all the time, upset and distant from those around her because she felt like she was living a lie, and it was all going to crash down around her. She couldn't remember the last time she had been truly honest.

Her stomach turned at the realisation that having Jake in her life now meant even more dishonesty. Dishonesty towards Myles, because she could never tell him that they were back in touch. He knew that Charlotte had been married before, but he thought that her ex-husband had abandoned her before Izzy was born. He assumed that her ex was the opposite of Jake - a waste of space, someone who had never supported her, and would only have been a hindrance in her life. And he told her that, all the time. How lucky they were to have found each other, how lucky she was that her life had got back on track when they met. If she told him, he might throw her out, and what would that do to Izzy? She shivered. Izzy would lose her home, her school, the whole life she knew. Charlotte could never cope on her own. She couldn't risk that.

And she would also be lying to Jake. She wanted to be honest with him, to tell him that Izzy was his daughter, but he was loyal and honourable, and she knew that he would want to tell Izzy the truth. That would turn Izzy's world upside down. She loved Myles.

"Please don't shut me out."

She gulped, running her fingertips along his palms. His skin was scarred, his nails bitten so short that they'd recently bled.

"I'll think about it. I need to get back to Izzy."

"Ok." He squeezed her hands again. "I promise I'm not going to mess this up for you, ok? When have I ever messed anything up for you before? Except when I went missing, obviously..."

She squeezed his hands back. "You never

have."

"And I never will. Give me your phone, and I'll put my number in it."

After hesitating, she pulled her phone from her pocket, unlocked it and handed it over. Within a couple of seconds he had keyed his number in, and handed back the phone. "There. Call me, ok? Or text... whatever you want. I just want to know you're ok. And I'm always here for you, no matter what."

***

"Jake! I thought you'd gone home."

Bella could tell by his jubilant expression that he had news. She swung her legs down from the bed and stood up, her eyes full of excitement. "Did she call?"

"No."

"Oh." Her face fell.

"I bumped into her again though."

Her eyes widened again.

Jake grinned. "It's good to see you looking perkier."

"Oh, shut up! You sounded proper old when you said that, you know!"

"Hey! Less of the old!"

He nudged her and then sat on the chair by her bed. "Are you feeling better though? I thought you were going home - I wasn't sure I'd catch you. But I wanted to fill you in."

"Yeah. I am, thank you. Dad's gone to pick up my little brother, then he's going to collect me. The consultant wants to see me one last time before I go."

"Ah, ok. Well, that's great."

"Yeah."

She looked nervous, and Jake sat forwards in the chair, his hands clasped between his legs. "Do you know what Bella, it's ok to be scared."

"I'm not scared."

"Ok, well... nervous... about going home. I felt the same when I left hospital."

Bella exhaled shakily. "Yeah, but you didn't try to jump off a bridge, did you?"

"No. But I thought about it."

"What?"

"I thought about it. When I left hospital and everything seemed so overwhelming... I wanted nothing more than to end it. Escape. It was weird, I dreamed about getting home all the time in Afghanistan, and once I was back, I couldn't remember anything. I felt lost and confused. All I wanted to do was close my eyes, and never open them again."

"But you didn't..."

"No. I looked at my parents, and how hard they were trying... and I had my dog... and I knew I had to keep going. For them. And then I remembered Charlie. And I knew I had a lot to live for."

"I don't want to upset my dad. Or my brother. But sometimes I feel so down... like there are black clouds all around me, suffocating me... and I can't escape. I can't think of any other way out. And if it wasn't for you..."

"For what it's worth, I don't think you'd have jumped, Bella."

She stared at him. "How do you even know that? You don't really know anything about me."

"I know a strong woman when I see one."

Blushing, she grinned. "Alright, there's no need to go all psych on me!"

"I'm not! I'm being honest. I'm proud of you. It's hard to accept help, and even harder to admit how you've been feeling. And that's exactly what you've done here, and I promise you, now people know, they'll help you. And things will get better."

"I hope so."

"I know so."

She grinned. "So, you never told me what happened with Charlie!"

"Oh. Yeah, that."

"*Yeah, that!*"

He raised one eyebrow. "I saw her in the courtyard, and we had a chat. She's going to think about it... being friends. I put my number in her phone."

"That's it?!"

"What do you mean, that's it?"

"I thought you were going to say you kissed her, or she admitted that she's still in love with you!"

Jake rolled his eyes. "Bella, it's not a film. She's *married* remember, to someone else!"

"So? She was married to you first! You can't help it when you love someone..."

"Life isn't always that straightforward."

"Well, it should be."

"Well, it's not. Anyway... she has my number now. The choice is hers. I hope she'll get in touch. I promised that we can be friends, that I don't have to be a part of her family's life if she doesn't want me to be. I mean, I hope she'll let me meet them..."

"What are you even *talking* about?! You love her! Why aren't you fighting for her?"

He frowned. "I am. I'd rather have her in my life, even as just a friend, than lose her completely. And I do want her to be happy."

"She'd be happy with you! You told me what it was like before you went to Afghanistan. You guys were so happy!"

"She might not..." his voice fading, he scratched his hand through his hair roughly. "I'm not always this person. Sometimes I wake up and the black clouds are there for me, too. Some days are a struggle. But I'm trying my best. The last thing I want to do is tear her away from the wonderful life she has now, and make her unhappy. I'm still in the army, I'm still going to be deployed occasionally. She hated it. And if something happens to me again and I ruin her life all over again... well, I couldn't forgive myself for that."

Bella blinked at him. "I get that. But what about you? What about what you want?"

Jake sighed. "When you love someone, sometimes that means taking the hardest choice on yourself, to make them happy. And this is one of those occasions."

CHAPTER ELEVEN

The carseat felt heavy and awkward in Charlie's hand. Every time it swung and hit the back of her leg her stomach lurched, worried that she might have hurt its delicate contents. She felt totally out of her depth. Here she was, presenting to the world a tiny, fragile, brand new life, who was going to rely on her for everything. Food, love, comfort... some days, it was all Charlie could do to find the energy to feed herself. How was she going to cope? What if she...

The screech of brakes and the heavy honk of a car horn stopped her in her tracks and she stood, wild eyed, her mouth gaping open. The car came to a stop inches away from them and she tightened her grip on the carseat, her legs trembling underneath her, threatening to give way.

"Have you got a death wish?!"

She opened her mouth to reply to the driver, who was now hanging out of the window, but she was shaking too much. The haunting tune of Christmas music filtered out of the car. At that moment she realised that she was never going to like Christmas again.

"Some people aren't fit to be parents!"

Shaking his head, he got back in the car, revving the engine in frustration. Eventually, Charlie came to her senses, scuttling across the road and down the path until she reached a bench, where she sat with the car seat next to her.

Her baby was fine. Fast asleep, completely unscathed, oblivious to the mammoth journey they had ahead of them.

"I can't do this..." she whispered, her bottom lip trembling and tears threatening to overspill. "I can't do this on my own."

It was Christmas Eve, a day which had always been hard for her before she moved in with Jake. People spent Christmas Eve with their families, something Charlie had never been able to do. And then she moved in with Jake, and he showed her what it was like to get excited about something - *really* excited about something. Last year, she'd had Christmas Eve off work, and they'd gone for a long woodland walk, enjoying each others' company. Then they'd come home, wrapped themselves up in bed with mugs of hot chocolate and watched a film. It had been one of the best days of her life.

"How am I going to do this?"

She looked up to the sky. She didn't really know why - it wasn't like she was expecting an answer. She needed a sign, something, *anything*, to tell her what to do. But there was nothing. Just cars whizzing past, rushing home to their families, visiting loved ones in hospital. She was on her own.

***

Charlotte bristled, the click of the front door unlocking setting her instantly on edge. Izzy's face lit up and Charlotte forced a smile, steadying her nerves.

"Daddy!"

"Don't rush..." Charlotte ordered, but Izzy completely ignored her, jumping from the sofa and running towards the hallway. "Be careful!"

"Izzyyyy! Look at your arm! You've been in the wars!"

Charlotte gulped. She could hear it in Myles's voice already - that tone. Implying that this had all happened because of her, because she was too useless not to keep an eye on her daughter properly. Accusing her.

"Hi," she forced a smile, emerging from the doorway. She put her arms around her husband, kissing him on the cheek gently. "I'm glad you're back."

"Me too," he smiled, placing his arm around her. Then he released her and crouched down, digging inside his pocket. "I have something for you, Iz."

"What is it?! What is it?!" She cried, jumping up and down.

"Izzy, be careful... stay still!" Charlotte pleaded, gritting her teeth as she watched Izzy's arm move around in its sling.

"It's a bit late for that!" Myles muttered, pulling a packet of sweets from his pocket. "Here you go!"

"Sweeties! Can I have them now?"

"It's almost bedtime..." Charlotte replied, but Myles cut in with, "of course you can!"

Izzy ignored her mum and passed the tube back to Myles so he could open them for her. Once they were open, she skipped off happily towards the kitchen.

"Would you like a drink?" Charlotte asked sheepishly, although she didn't know why.

He hung his coat on one of the pegs in the hallway. "I could murder a coffee."

Charlotte slipped away, towards the kitchen. Thick and stagnant, the atmosphere between them was almost unbearable. Bracing herself for what might come later, once Izzy had gone to bed and they had a chance to talk properly, she began to make a mug of coffee, just how he liked it.

"Daddy, can we watch a film?"

"Of course we can!" Myles sunk down next to Izzy on the sofa in the corner of the kitchen, placing his feet on top of the coffee table. Charlotte filled the mug with hot water and stirred it, Myles's gaze burning through her. She didn't look round until she heard him talking to Izzy again.

"There you go," she said brightly, placing the coffee on the table next to him.

He continued to scroll through films with Izzy, not acknowledging the coffee at all. Charlotte hovered for a moment and then sat down the other side of her daughter, leaning in to cuddle her. She felt almost like an outsider, not wanted by anyone now that Myles was back.

"Are you going to watch the film with us, Mummy?"

"Yes."

She snuggled up next to Izzy, being careful not to knock her cast. Even when she felt Myles's gaze boring into her, she focused on the film on the big screen ahead of her, pretending not to notice.

Once it was finished, she carried an almost sleeping Izzy upstairs and tucked her in, kissing her gently on the forehead. By the time she closed the curtains and switched her nightlight on, Izzy was dozing, her eyelids fluttering like butterfly wings. Charlotte hung around in the doorway for a moment, watching her daughter sleep. She was so happy. Surely that meant it was all worth it? All she had to do was stick it out, and Izzy would have the lovely, secure, enriching childhood that she had never had.

Izzy was loved. She had a beautiful home, an excellent education. A wardrobe full of immaculate clothes and all the toys she could ever need. Two parents who adored her. She would never know about her difficult start to life, about how her mum had almost let her down, falling apart because of the loss of her dad. She had a stable family now.

But Charlotte was so tired. Pretending to be someone that she wasn't was exhausting, she realised it more than ever now that she'd felt what it was like to be herself around Jake once more. And most of all, she worried about Izzy. What if she found out that her strong family unit wasn't actually one at all? What if she found out that she'd missed out on her real dad all this time? Would she grow to hate her?

"Are you going to stand there all evening?"

Charlotte jumped, turning to see Myles's silhouette behind her in the hallway. He stepped forwards and grabbed her buttock, squeezing it hard. She tried not to flinch.

"Shall we have an early night?"

She wanted nothing more than to fall into bed and close her eyes, recover from the exhausting day she'd had, but she knew better than to expect that. She knew exactly what Myles wanted, and it wasn't to sleep.

"I need to do the washing up..."

"Leave it! It will still be there in the morning."

"I don't like leaving it..."

"I said, leave it!" He raised his voice slightly, grabbing her by the wrist. Charlotte raised her eyes to his. For a minute, she felt afraid. But then his face softened.

"Come on. You've been doing all the heavy lifting while I've been away. Now it's time to relax."

He spun her around and began to massage the knots out of her shoulders, his voice suddenly full of concern. "There. That's better already, isn't it?"

"Yes. Thank you."

"Go and run a hot bath. I'll do the dishes. You deserve a break."

Curious at his sudden change of heart, her eyebrows knitted in a slight frown. A couple of hours ago he was furious that she had allowed Izzy to break her arm, now he was singing her praises? Still, she would do what he said - she couldn't deny that a hot, deep bubble bath was appealing.

Whilst he slunk off downstairs, Charlotte padded across the family bathroom, the automatic lights bathing it in a rich glow as soon as she stepped inside. She bent down and turned the tap over the bath, watching the water cascade out, splashing across the bottom of the deep tub. This tub had been one of the main things she loved about this house when they viewed it. She had never seen such a luxurious tub, let alone set foot in one. She still had to pinch herself sometimes when she entered the bathroom, knowing that it was hers.

It took a long time to fill. While waiting, she swirled some bubblebath in the water, lit some candles and then sunk down in the hot water, allowing her eyelids to droop. The door was locked, and she was alone. She let her head drop back until her ears were submerged, and all she could hear was the swoosh of water filling the tub.

An unexpected memory surfaced. Walking into the bedsit she shared with Jake after a night-shift, dead on her feet, to find the bath filled with hot, bubbly water, and candles lit. She sighed. He had always been there for her. Whenever she was wilting, he was always there to build her back up. And he still was now.

She remembered the strength of his embrace at the hospital, the look of utter love in his eyes when he stared at her through the glass. And he understood her position, he had promised to be there for her, even though she had betrayed him and married someone else. She had no reason to doubt that he'd keep to his word.

Submerging herself, she blew bubbles from her mouth forcefully. She was completely torn. She would give her last breath to make sure that Izzy had the childhood she deserved, but maybe she could have both? Maybe things could stay exactly as they were, but Charlotte could have Jake in her life too? If she was careful enough? The thought of having someone she could truly confide in, who she knew was on her side, lit her up. It had been such a long time since she had someone in her life who truly understood her and knew her inside out. She'd never had to keep a secret from him before. Until now, that was.

The squeak of the door handle brought her back to the present and she sat up, running her hands over the top of her head, pushing the soapy water down her back.

"Just a minute..."

She climbed out of the bath, wrapping herself in a soft, fluffy towel. The warmth of the towel against her skin was soothing and she sighed, closing her eyes as she patted the skin on her face.

"It's Effie on the phone."

"Ok, give me a second..."

The last person she wanted to talk to right now was Effie, after the way things had ended between them at the trampoline park. But Effie had tried to call a few times now, and Charlotte kept ignoring her calls - it was only a matter of time before she'd have to take it. Now seemed as good a time as any. She didn't want to cause tension between Myles and Connor.

Once she was dry, Charlotte wrapped the towel around her body and cocooned a second around her wet hair, then opened the door of the bathroom. Myles handed her the phone.

"Thanks. Hello, Effie."

"Finally! I've been trying to get hold of you all week!"

"Yes... sorry. I've been busy trying to keep Izzy happy, and stop her running around too much!"

"What a nightmare. Is she ok?"

"Yes, she's fine. Just a bit bored."

"Good. Listen, I'm really sorry about our disagreement. I honestly didn't mean to upset you. I know I'm not always subtle. And I don't always think before I open my mouth. I wish I had."

Charlotte smiled slightly, pulling the towel tightly around her body as she sat down on the bed. "It's alright. Apology accepted. I'm sorry I was such a moody cow."

"No, not at all. It's all my fault."

"Let's forget it ever happened?"

"Suits me! Listen... I was thinking. It's been a really long time since we had a girl's night out! We should organise one soon?"

Charlotte sighed. "I'm not really in the party mood at the moment."

"Ok, a spa day then? You can never resist a spa day!"

Charlotte paused. "Mmm... I can't deny that a spa day sounds appealing."

"Well, that's sorted then! Let's sort it out. As soon as possible. God knows, we both need a break before this baby comes. And it sounds like you need some time to get things off your chest."

"I'll speak to Myles, see when he'll next be around for the day."

"I was thinking we should go for the night! Or even two nights! Treat ourselves!"

Charlotte imagined lying on a soft lounger by a sparkling blue pool, having her feet massaged while she read a book and thought of nothing else but herself. Nobody to look after, nobody to have to think about before she thought about herself.

"Alright. I'll speak to Myles."

"Perfect! See you tomorrow then, at school?"

"Yes. See you then."

***

"Are you sure you're going to be ok?" Charlotte planted a kiss on her daughter's head.

"Of course, Mummy! Daddy and me are going to have a film night with lots of sweets! And popcorn too!"

"Hmm. Not too many sweets, ok? I don't want you to be awake all night!"

Izzy flashed a toothy grin, glancing up at Myles. Charlotte fastened her grip on the strap of her bag and leant forward, pecking him on the cheek gently, a meek smile on her face. "I'll see you tomorrow, then."

"Yep," he replied cooly, as if it was no big deal that she was going.

Despite the guilt she always felt when leaving Izzy, Charlotte's mood lifted instantly at the thought of a whole night to herself. No stepping on egg shells. Nobody to interrupt her when she wanted a long, hot bath. The crisp, cool sheets cocooning her in bed when she slept alone. She could barely even remember how long it had been since the last time she had some time to herself. And this time, she really was getting time to herself - Effie had pulled out of the spa trip that morning by text, after spending most of the night lying on the bathroom floor with a sick bug. Charlotte felt for her - she remembered how drained she'd felt when heavily pregnant with Izzy; a sick bug on top of that would have tipped her over the edge. She had been surprised when Myles said she should still go, make the most of her trip. She couldn't deny that she'd been looking forward to it. And actually, now that she was going alone, she felt a strange sense of freedom. It would be quite nice to enjoy a swim in peace.

Driving down the road past the still frosty fields, Charlotte sighed with relief, enveloped in the leather seat. She thought about the pool and the loungers, the luxurious buffet dinner she always enjoyed when she went to the spa, the cakes and coffee she could enjoy while reading a book in the lounge area.

The media screen lit up in front of her and she bit her lip, her stomach turning at the sight of the name on the screen. *Julie.* Maybe she should ignore it. Tonight was for her, a chance to get her head straight. Yet, maybe it was an opportunity for more than that...

"Hey, what's up?" She cringed a little at the sound of her own voice. She sounded like a teenager. She never spoke like that now.

"Hi. Are you ok?"

"Yes, I'm fine," she tightened her grip on the steering wheel. "I'm driving at the moment."

"Oh... sorry, I can call another time..."

"No, it's alright. Myles isn't here... I'm out on my own."

"Oh..." his voice lifted instantly. "Fair play. Where are you going?"

"I'm off for a spa break."

"Fancy!"

She grinned. "What are you doing today?"

"Nothing. Literally. I'm bored out of my brain."

"Fancy a spa break?"

There was a pause at the end of the line and Charlotte rolled her eyes at herself in the mirror. What was she even thinking? The words had come out of her mouth so quickly she'd not even thought them through.

"Sorry, it's a bit of a weird question... I was supposed to be going with a friend but she's ill, so it's only me now. I wondered if you'd like to catch up as we've not had a proper chance to. Obviously you don't have to, if the spa is not your thing..."

"I'd love to."

"Really?"

"Yeah. I mean, I've never set foot in a spa before but there's a first time for everything, I guess."

Two hours later, Charlotte was sitting in her soft towel robe on a lounger by the pool, a blend of chlorine and essential oils tickling her nose as she watched the door impatiently. Today was supposed to be about her and Effie, then it had become simply about her, and almost as though he could read her mind, he'd called her out of the blue, at the very moment she was driving to the spa. They had talked a few times over the past few weeks on the phone, when Myles was at work and Izzy was at school. She'd not mentioned the spa. Yet it was like he instinctively knew.

The door opened and she held her breath expectantly, but it was just another woman about her age in a robe. Disappointedly, she leant against the back rest, lifting her book from the coffee table next to her, being careful not to knock over her cool glass of lemonade. She opened it and looked down at the page, but although her eyes skimmed over the print, none of the words went in. Her mind was completely elsewhere.

Then, the door opened again and there he was, metres away from her, standing in his robe like an awkward little boy on his first day of school - completely out of his depth. Charlotte smiled and patted the free lounger next to her, pulling her towel off it. "I saved it for you."

Awkwardly, he sat beside her and glanced around the pool, his eyes scanning the area as though anticipating an attack.

She frowned slightly, reaching across to place her hand on his upper arm. "Are you alright?"

"Yeah," he nodded, his eyes connecting with hers. "It's really good to see you."

"You too," she leant forwards and hugged him, taking a deep breath of his scent. To her relief, it was back - that familiar smell from years ago. Same minty shampoo and musky shower gel. "I wondered if you were going to bail on me."

"I'd never do that."

His eyes were still scanning the room, taking in all the entry and exit points and the other people around them. Keen not to make a scene, Charlotte leant back against the lounger, stretching her legs out in front of her. She caught him looking, his eyes edging up her smooth skin towards the edge of her robe. Flustered, Charlotte pulled the robe down and crossed her legs, trying to ignore the butterflies dancing in her stomach.

"Would you like a drink? They have all sorts of tea, coffee and soft drinks... cake too, if you're hungry."

"I'm fine." He was still perched on the edge of the lounger, as though he wasn't stopping. He looked completely out of his depth. Charlotte could see the reflection of the water in his wide, anxious eyes.

"Fancy a swim?" She unrobed, revealing her spotty swimming costume. Jake didn't know where to look; his eyes travelled from her legs to her cleavage, then back to his lap.

"No, you go ahead."

"Come on! It's a spa, you have to swim!"

"I said, I'm fine!"

He said it more forcefully than he intended. The echo of his voice around them heightened his anxiety and he pulled his robe tighter around him. He'd almost given up when sitting in the changing room, hiding his skin under the towel robe. Nobody had seen him this exposed since he'd got back; the texture of the robe against his skin reminded him of the rags he'd worn when in captivity. The spa wasn't what he expected. He didn't realise that he'd have to take his clothes off and rely on a thin piece of fabric to hide his modesty from the rest of the world. But he'd forced himself to wear it, to come in here - because he couldn't bear to let her down. She was waiting for him, he knew that. And he'd hoped for this day for months. He couldn't waste this opportunity.

Charlotte suddenly looked nervous, and he hated that. He didn't mean to put her on edge. Tugging at his robe again, he clenched his jaw, wishing that he could feel normal, even just for one day. How could he persuade her to love him again when he didn't even like himself?

"I'm not really... big on swimming anymore."

She said nothing for a moment, then shrugged her robe back over her shoulders and stood up. "Come on."

"I don't want to ruin this for you... you should stay. I can meet you later, when you're done?"

"Nonsense. Come on. Get changed, I'll meet you outside. We'll go for a walk. You're still big on walks, right?"

He smiled. "Right."

***

Strolling through the grounds together side by side, like old times, Charlotte could almost forget how much her life had changed since the last time they walked together like this. She pulled her jacket around her, a chill creeping up and down her spine. Jake walked beside her, more relaxed now that they were on their own.

"How come you don't like swimming anymore?"

Jake pushed his hands in his pockets, his breath clouding the air in front of his face. "I don't really want to talk about it. Sorry."

"That's alright."

Circling overhead, a little bird chirped, seemingly forgotten by the rest of his flock who'd long flown their nests, ready for the winter. Jake watched it for a few moments. He knew what that felt like.

"I'm glad you came," Charlotte breathed, enjoying how it felt to have Jake next to her. She no longer felt on edge. She could breathe properly again for the first time in an incredibly long time.

"Me too," he smiled, glancing at her sideways. Charlotte caught his eye, fighting the urge to reach for his hand.

They reached a bench which overlooked the fields to the front of the building. It was almost lunchtime and there was nobody around, most of the guests either checking out at the end of the stay, or enjoying the indoor facilities as they'd just arrived.

"Shall we sit?"

"Ok," Jake perched beside her on the bench, leaning against the wooden back. It was a relief to be outside, far away from everyone else - it was much easier to keep track of his surroundings when the surrounding environment was so quiet. Out here, he'd hear the snap of a twig or the crunch of a boot long before he could see someone approaching.

"So, is this like... your favourite activity now? Coming to the spa?"

Charlotte grinned. "You make me sound posh!"

"You are."

"I'm still me, deep down. Feeling like an imposter."

Jake's brow furrowed. "Really? You don't look like one. You fit right in here."

"I feel like everyone's looking at me, all the time. Like I don't fit in at all."

Jake remembered her long, tanned legs, with their blue pearly toenails stretched out on the lounger in front of her. He gulped, forcing the image to the back of his mind. Time to change the subject.

"How's Iz?"

"Oh, she's absolutely fine! Jumping around like nothing even happened. Begging to go back to the trampoline park, not that Myles will ever let her."

"No?"

Charlotte shook her head. "Myles is very... cautious, when it comes to Izzy."

"Well, maybe you can take her when he's not around."

"He'd never forgive me if she hurt herself again. It was bad enough this time."

"It was an accident - kids have accidents all the time."

"I know. He's just very protective. Anyway, her cast's coming off next week, hopefully."

Jake's little finger brushed against hers, causing her heart to thump harder in her chest. "It's not your fault, you know. You're a great mum."

"You don't know me well enough to say that, Jake."

He recoiled, as though she'd hit him. Instantly, she felt bad. She hadn't meant it to come out the way that it had.

"I didn't mean it like that. I meant..."

"I do, actually. I can tell from the way you talk about her that you love her to bits."

"Well, love isn't the only thing that matters..."

"No, but it's a good start."

His eyes were locked on hers then, piercing and green, drawing her in like they had countless times before. Suddenly, she had an overwhelming urge to kiss him. The feelings she'd buried for the past five years were seeping through the cracks, bubbling to the surface. She wasn't sure how much longer she was going to be able to keep them inside her, but at that moment nothing else seemed to matter besides the fact that she was sat right next to him again.

But her wedding ring dug into her finger and she clenched her palm around the bench, reminding herself that she had other commitments now - and her feelings weren't the only thing that mattered. In fact, they weren't even close.

"Let's talk about you, now."

"There isn't much to say."

"How was your meeting with the brigadier?"

Jake shrugged. "It was alright."

"When do you go back?"

He puffed out his breath hard. "The psych thinks I need some more time in the unit, some more sessions before I go back. I don't know how much more I can talk about what happened. I want to get back to doing what I love, you know. It's frustrating."

She nodded patiently, waiting for him to go on.

"I feel like I'm trying to move on, but everyone around me is trying to pull me back in, you know? Asking me to go over it over and over again. And all I want to do is forget. If I keep going over it, and what they did, they win, don't they? The longer they're in my life, stopping me from moving forwards, the longer they're in control of me. And I don't want that."

He felt her hand slip around his, the warmth of her palm against his dissolving the ball of anger starting to form in the pit of his stomach. Every time he thought about what they'd done to him, fury bubbled up inside him. They had taken five years of his life, his wife and every chance of happiness he had for the future. He couldn't even sleep without waking every time a car door shut outside his bedroom window. The harder he tried to jump the psychiatrist's hurdles, the deeper he seemed to fall into a hole he might never be able to climb out of. Maybe he would never be able to go back to active duty at all. And then they'd have taken that from him too, his career, the thing he'd worked towards for his entire adult life.

"Some days, I think I'm doing ok... I'm getting there. And then some nights I go to bed wishing that it's the last time I'll ever close my eyes. Because at least then, it will stop."

"Oh, Jake." Charlotte wrapped her arms around him, drawing him into the warmth of her neck. Closing his eyes, Jake relaxed his muscles, allowing some of the tension to escape from his body. Today had been one of those days. He'd woken up at a loose end, desperate to find something that might help turn things around. So he'd called her, and here he was. Sat next to her on a bench in one of the most beautiful gardens he'd ever set foot in. The world started to make sense again, when he was with her.

"I wish I could do something to help."

"You are. Just by being here."

"I'm always here for you. Whatever you need."

He almost laughed. It was so ironic that the one thing he needed most in the world, was the one thing he could never have. Because she belonged to someone else now.

CHAPTER TWELVE

Dreary and grey, the ominous clouds reflected Charlie's mood. She pushed the pram along the pavement, creaking over every bump. She regretted buying it, now. There was no way it was going to last until Izzy grew out of it, and she wished she'd spent a little more on a better one - now she was going to have to buy two. But she was on her own, on a budget, and her options were limited. She was doing the best she could.

Raindrops began to spill from the sky, dropping onto the hood of the pram and the pavement around them. Charlie sighed. It was going to pour down. Last time it rained heavily, water had seeped through the cover of the pram and Izzy had screamed for an hour on the way home, causing Charlie to feel like the worst mum in the world because she couldn't even keep her baby girl dry.

The raindrops began to fall harder.

She stopped to pull the hood as far over the buggy as she could, then looked around for somewhere to shelter until the downpour stopped. There was a coffee shop across the road. The thought of a fresh, hot coffee made her tastebuds sting. She hadn't had anything that luxurious for months, not since before Izzy was born. She saved every penny she could now, scrimping and saving because there was nobody else her baby could rely on. She had to make sure she could afford milk and nappies for Izzy, and keep up with the bills so they had a roof over their heads.

And it was her birthday today - if she couldn't treat herself to a coffee on her birthday, when could she? It wasn't as though anyone else had remembered. She needed something to cheer her up.

That morning, the loss of Jake had hit her like a freight train. He'd been gone for months now, but she'd still expected him to burst in with a bag of fresh croissants and a bunch of flowers, as he had every other year since they'd moved in together. He had always made such a fuss of her, because he knew there had been so many years when her birthday had barely been acknowledged, and he wanted to make her feel special. So, for the past few weeks, she'd felt excitement brewing deep inside her. The anticipation that, if he was still out there - and she was sure that he was, deep in her gut - he'd make it home to her, for her birthday. Or at least get in touch. He'd find a way.

Then, she woke up and everything was the same. Exhausted from lack of sleep, having been woken three times in the night by a screaming baby, she almost cried when discovering that the milk in the fridge was sour, and all she had to eat was a bowl of dry cornflakes. Izzy didn't know it was her mum's birthday. She still needed feeding and changing around the clock, still bawled her eyes out for most of the morning because she was teething and upset, and, Charlie assumed, quite fed up of being cooped up inside every day. She waited for something, a phone call, a card in the post... the postman came and went, with only bills to deliver. Her phone never rang once.

And here she was. She'd had to come out, because the prospect of dry cornflakes for a second meal in a row wasn't at all appetising, and the thought of spending her entire birthday sitting in the tiny flat, all alone with a cranky baby, was even worse.

Struggling through the door of the coffee shop with the creaky pram, she glanced around, looking for somewhere she could sit down, have a hot drink and disappear, just for half an hour. Maybe Izzy would keep sleeping and she'd be able to enjoy some peace for a little while?

Awkwardly, she manoeuvred the pram into the corner, towards the only free table. The others were filled with couples, families, groups of people... all engrossed in conversation. Trying desperately to ignore the gnawing feeling of loneliness in her gut, she parked the pram, retrieved her purse from her bag, then headed over to the counter to order her drink. Waiting for the man in front of her to order his, she nervously glanced back at Izzy's pram in the corner. If only she'd parked it the other way; what if someone grabbed the pram and ran, before she had the chance to get back to her?

What if? What if the pram was stolen, and suddenly she only had herself to think about? She could go back to work, get her life back on track... with a decent night's sleep, she might actually have time to process the loss of Jake and move on with her life. She'd be able to eat properly, because she wouldn't have to afford nappies and milk, and clothes for someone else who never seemed to stop growing.

Almost immediately, she felt sick. Disgusted at herself for even thinking it. Voices echoing around her, the room began to spin and she felt a cold sweat prickle at the back of her neck.

"Are you alright?"

Blinking hard, she managed to focus on a pair of deep, chestnut brown eyes, peering down at her curiously. She blinked again and the room finally stopped spinning, the voices around her blending back to focus. With a gulp, she glanced at the pram, still safely tucked in the corner, the blanket in exactly the same position as it had been when she left it there. Her baby was safe.

Another voice came from behind the counter, this one sharper. "What are you having?"

She opened her mouth, but no words would come out; the words jumbled in the back of her exhausted mind.

"There are other customers waiting - what are you having?"

Charlie swallowed hard, but the words were still stuck in her throat. She looked down at her trembling hands.

"Watch your tone! Can't you see she's not well?! Cappuccino, hot and sweet," the deeper voice answered for her. "Sit down, I'll bring it over."

She nodded gratefully, fumbling in her pocket for her bank card.

"Don't worry - this one's on me."

"I..."

"It's fine. Go, take a seat. You look exhausted. I'll bring it over."

She wanted to fling her arms around him. It had been such a long time since someone had even noticed her, let alone thought about how she might feel, anxious and alone with a tiny baby. Despite her embarrassment at coming across so feebly, her knees threatened to give way and she was forced to retreat to the table, where she sank down in the seat next to Izzy's pram and pulled her coat off, running her fingertips through her damp, windswept hair.

Pulling the blanket back gently, she peered at Izzy, sleeping peacefully in her pram. Maybe she should come out more often. Izzy never slept at this time at home - it was her worst time of the day, she was always cranky and miserable, in need of a nap but desperate to fight sleep.

The tap of the coffee cup on the table brought her back to earth. She studied the man who lowered himself into the seat opposite, then pulled his gloves off and hung his coat over the back of the chair, revealing a polished suit underneath. Suddenly, to her utter embarrassment, her eyes filled with tears. Angrily, she scrubbed them away with the back of her hand, wishing that the ground would swallow her up.

"I'm sorry..." she mumbled, "and thank you. For the coffee."

"Don't mention it," he smiled, although his eyes looked full of concern. "Are you alright? Do you need me to call someone for you?"

"There isn't anyone..." she mumbled, blinking away a fresh wave of tears, which threatened to erupt. She swallowed them back hard, desperate to pull herself together before she frightened him away. It had been such a long time since she'd even spoken to another adult who didn't call her mum, as she was fourteenth on their list of appointments that day, just another mum to get through.

"Everyone has someone..." he lifted his own coffee and warmed his hands, his eyes still fixed on her. "Baby's father?"

Charlie shook her head. "He's not around. I really don't have anyone. I don't have any family, and recently I realised I don't actually have any friends, either. Nobody's been in touch since she was born."

He frowned sadly, his eyes sincere and kind. "I'm sorry. That must be tough."

"Yeah. I guess it is."

"I bet you haven't slept properly for weeks, either."

Charlie shook her head, wiping her cheeks again which were finally drying out. "No. Not since she was born. It's been tough."

They sat in silence for a couple of minutes. Charlie raised the coffee to her lips and took a sip. It was thick, creamy and sweet, and it made her taste buds prickle with delight. She'd not tasted anything so delicious in longer than she could remember.

“I’m used to not getting any sleep. I’m a nurse. Was a nurse. Before I had my baby. But now I’m just a mum.”

“You’re not just *a mum! There’s no such thing as* just *a mum. You’re a superhero, in my opinion. I couldn’t do it.”*

Charlie sipped her coffee again. Instantaneously, she felt the sugar and caffeine run into her bloodstream, providing her with a much needed boost. Maybe the rest of the day wouldn’t be so bad. “Do you have kids?”

“No.”

Warming her hands through with the coffee cup, Charlie’s cheeks flushed. She opened her mouth, ready to apologise, but the sudden warmth of his palm on the back of her hand strangled her voice.

“I’m Myles, by the way.”

Without taking her eyes off it, she let go of the coffee cup and shook his hand hesitantly. “Charlie.”

“Nice to meet you, Charlie. Tell me something about you.”

She frowned, a small smile playing on her lips. “About me? There’s nothing to tell. My life is not very interesting.”

“That’s not true. You’re a mum… you’re a nurse. That’s interesting.”

“Alright then. But it’s your turn. You know two things about me, but I know nothing about you.”

He grinned. “Ah, I was right. I knew there was some fight in there.”

She examined the creases around his eyes, the dimples that adorned his cheeks when he smiled. It felt nice to make someone else smile. She couldn't help smiling back.

"I have a pilot's licence."

"You can fly a plane?"

"Yes. And a helicopter."

"Wow. That's pretty incredible."

He raised one eyebrow. "That's two. Now, it's your turn."

Charlie pressed her lips together, her cheeks now completely dry. "Ok... it's my birthday today."

"What?! Why didn't you say before?"

"Well, I only met you ten minutes ago... I don't normally randomly stop people and tell them it's my birthday."

"And why the hell wouldn't you?!" He asked, mock-incredulously.

She grinned. "I don't know. Maybe that's where I'm going wrong."

"Maybe. So... the all important question, what are you doing to celebrate?"

She peered at him. "The best I can hope for is probably... a hot cup of tea and an hour's telly in peace once Izzy's in bed."

"Oh, come on. You can do better than that!"

She shrugged, her smile fading. "Like I said... there isn't anyone else. I'm on my own. It's just me and her."

He frowned thoughtfully, studying her. Suddenly, she felt under the spotlight. Lifting her coffee, she took another sip, enjoying the warmth inside her body.

"Alright. I've got a plan."

"A plan?"
"A plan."
She blinked at him.
"What are you doing on Saturday?"

***

His belly full of food, Jake crunched across the dingy gravel car park. The food was delicious, the nicest food he'd eaten in five years. Not that it had much competition. The further they got from the building, the more the light from inside faded, until all that was left was the glow of the moon on the tops of the cars around them.

"Thanks for inviting me," he turned to Charlotte, his eyes glimmering in the moonlight.

She smiled. "I'm glad you came. It was nice to have company. And catch up properly."

"Yeah. It was."

They stopped by his car. It was a rust bucket, picked up the week before for five hundred pounds because it was cheaper than hiring a car every time he wanted to go somewhere, and easier than answering the hundred questions his parents asked, if he wanted to borrow theirs. He was surprised it had got him all the way here. The seats were stained and the window wipers got stuck half the time, but the wheels went round and it stopped when he pushed the brake pedal, so it wasn't all bad.

"Well... bye, then."

He pulled the key out of the pocket of his

jeans, grasping it in his hand, hesitating for a moment. He didn't want to leave her, let her go back to her life. Today, for the first time since he'd returned, he felt like he was at home - with someone who truly understood him, and always had. He'd opened up more to Charlotte in one day than he had to his psychiatrist in months.

His trembling hand fumbled the key in the lock, trying to find the slot in the darkness.

"Jake..." he soaked in the energy of her body approaching, the warmth of her hand on his forearm. "Why don't you stay? I have a twin room... I feel like we haven't said all there is to say. There are still things I want to explain... things I want to know."

Clenching his jaw, he tried not to allow his hopes to leap. He fastened his hand around the key.

"Please stay? It's a quiet room... more like a little lodge, really. It's private. We can talk properly."

He never could say no to her. Within a couple of minutes, they were inside the lodge. Jake edged in behind her, watched as she casually hung her bag on the pegs by the door and slipped her shoes off, before padding barefoot across the floor towards the sitting area. Swallowing hard, he locked the door behind him, double and triple checked the handle, then slid on the door chain and followed Charlotte inside, shutting every set of curtains as he went. He examined the escape routes. There was another door off the sitting area. He checked the handle. It was locked. When he looked up, he caught Charlotte staring at him curiously.

"I er… I'm just checking…"

Silently, she nodded knowingly, then headed across the room, where there was a bottle of wine already on ice. She lifted it out of the ice bucket. "Drink?"

"Please."

After popping the cork she filled two glasses, handing him one on her way back to the sitting area. Then she settled in one of the armchairs, folding her slender legs underneath her until they disappeared under her dress. "What did you think of your first day at the spa?"

He shrugged, still hovering awkwardly by the door. It was flimsy. It wouldn't take much for someone to kick it in. He didn't like sitting with his back to it. In fact, this whole room made him uncomfortable. However he sat, he'd have his back to at least one door. His eyes fell into his glass. Maybe he shouldn't have a drink. He needed to be alert.

"Jake? What's wrong?"

"Nothing. Nothing, I'm fine."

He perched on the edge of the chair, glancing behind him self-consciously.

"It's safe here. I promise you."

He felt his cheeks flush slightly, embarrassed that someone else could see inside his mind, even just for a moment. "I know."

"It's alright… you can be honest with me. You don't need to pretend."

He gulped, cheeks still hot with embarrassment. He knew that he had to let his anxiety go, move on. But it was like a cancer, eating away at him, smothering any attempt at progress he made. And he hated it.

"We used to tell each other everything."

"We *used* to be married to each other, not other people."

He regretted the words as soon as they fell out of his mouth. But this was how he behaved when he was stressed - pushed people away when what he really needed to do, more than anything, was cling to them.

"I would never have married him if I knew you were still alive. You know that."

Jake raised his glass to his lips and took a big swig, the light catching the large stone in Charlotte's ring. Bigger and better than the one he'd given her.

"Do you still have mine?"

She frowned, confused. "What?"

"The ring."

Pressing her lips together, her eyes fell sadly to the ground. He knew the answer already.

"I still have mine. It was in my locker at the base, my parents were given it in an envelope with the rest of my belongings. They kept it safe for me. I guess you had no need for yours, once Myles came along and bought you a proper one."

"That's not how it happened."

"No?"

"Why are you *being* like this?"

"You said you had questions. Stuff you wanted to say. Well, so do I."

Narrowing her eyes, she took a sip of her drink. Then quickly downed the rest of the wine in her glass and lifted the bottle, filling it right to the top. "Alright. You want to know what happened, I'll tell you."

He was quiet then. He wasn't sure whether he really wanted to hear it. Whether he was ready to.

"I waited for you. For months. *Years.* Every day I woke up, thinking it would be the day you'd come home. And you never did. I needed you, and you never came back. Everyone said you were dead, I kept hoping. Wishing. *Praying* that you'd come home to me, turn up at the hospital, at the flat, or something. But nothing. *Nothing,* Jake. And the longer it went on, the harder it got. I knew I had to move on with my life, or I was going to die too. And I had to be strong. And it was so hard, so *bloody* hard, you have no idea."

Now her eyes were full of tears, and he felt a stab of guilt in his gut. He opened his mouth to talk, but she cut him off.

"It was suffocating, the not knowing. The waiting. And then I met Myles, and I had a chance to be happy again... to actually *live,* not just survive. So I took it."

It stung, hearing her talk about another man in that way.

"But I never, *ever* stopped loving you. And

if I'd known you were still alive, I would never have even looked at another man. I'd have waited a lifetime, if I thought there was even the slightest chance you were still alive."

"There was always a chance..."

"Everyone said you were dead. Your commanding officer, all the soldiers from your platoon who I spoke to. Even the court decided the evidence was overwhelming..."

"Only because you applied for the order," he snapped. "You gave up on me. Like they all did. Mum and Dad didn't..."

"I didn't have a choice. It was killing me. I had to move on. I didn't want to, it was the hardest thing I've ever had to do in my life."

"Didn't take you long to marry Myles afterwards, did it?"

"I had no choice, I wanted a stable home for Izzy..."

"Izzy?"

Charlotte's heart almost stopped and her stomach turned violently. Then, unexpectedly, he offered her a way out. "So, you got pregnant. You got married."

Her mouth snapped shut. She didn't correct him. She wanted to tell him the truth, but what would that achieve? Everything would unravel. He wasn't the same person he'd been when he left for Afghanistan, he was hardly a stable figure for Izzy - the little girl who knew nothing of her turbulent start to life, nothing about her real DNA. All she knew was that she had a mum and a dad, and a wonderful life, and everything she could ever want. Charlotte could grit her teeth and bear almost anything, as long as Izzy got the life she deserved - the childhood she'd never had herself.

Instead, she changed the subject. "Do you remember that boat trip?"

"What?"

"The boat trip we took on the sea. When we went camping, and we were broke, so instead of going on the proper boat trip we bought a second hand blow up one and rowed it out to sea."

Jake's face softened at the memory. "Yeah. I remember."

"I went back there. The day before I married Myles. And I rowed out to sea, all by myself, and I talked to you. I told you how I had a second chance... but I'd never forget you, or stop loving you. But I had to let you go. And I rowed out to the same spot where we stopped for that picnic... well I think it was the same spot, it was kind of hard to tell. The waves were a lot stronger that day than they were when we went. And I talked to you, for hours, until I had nothing left to say. And then I dropped the ring into the sea, and I said goodbye. It was the hardest thing I've ever done. It took all my strength to row myself back to shore, and not throw myself in after it..." her voice faltered. "If it wasn't for Izzy..."

"Charlotte..."

She blinked back tears.

"I'm sorry."

She shook her head. "What for? There was nothing you could have done. It's not like you chose to be captured."

He said nothing. No, he hadn't chosen to be captured, but it was his own decision to disobey orders that had led to it. If he'd listened to his commanding officer, stayed on the vehicle and waited for orders, then he wouldn't have played into the ambush. He hadn't been thinking straight, his judgment clouded by loss. How could he blame Charlotte for how she had reacted to losing him, when his own reaction to losing someone he loved had been so unpredictable?

"I should have stayed on the truck..." he breathed. "But he was all I could see."

He could see Cam right in front of him, clear as day, desperately firing at the surrounding insurgents. He had been all on his own, with his comrades only yards away, following instructions. If only Jake had followed his gut that day, disobeyed orders, charged forwards with the others - well, they could have reached Cam when he was still alive. By the time they took out the insurgents and reached his best friend, he was lying on the ground in a pool of blood, his lifeless eyes wide open. Not even the medic could bring him back. It was too late. Sometimes when Jake gave in to sleep, Cam's lifeless face was all he could see.

He saw him that day too, when he was waiting in the truck, that familiar sound of bullets ricocheting off the ground and vehicles around them. He had to help the others. He could not let it happen again. His platoon were like his family. He got that gut feeling. Get up, run. Help them. So he did.

"You were not responsible for what happened to Cam."

He looked up. "I know. But I didn't help him, either. I could have done. But I made a bad decision. Like I did when I got out of the truck."

His mistake had almost cost him his life. And the ramifications on his family and others around him had been huge, as they had been for Cam's family and friends when he died. In a way, Jake thought that what he'd put his family through was actually worse. They had no certainty, no closure. Charlotte may have moved on with her life, but his parents hadn't. They'd gone through hell for five years, not prepared to give up on their son when the rest of the world had.

"We're only human. Humans make mistakes. We all do what we think is best."

"I did."

"I know."

Solemnly, she topped his glass up. Jake looked down at it. He'd not even realised it was empty. "I don't..."

"Drink it. You don't need to go anywhere tonight. It's safe here, I promise. Myles wouldn't let me come if it wasn't."

Jake nodded, although he didn't feel at all reassured. Anyone could have a key to this room, absolutely anyone. Not that they needed one. He knew he wouldn't be getting much sleep tonight. But he couldn't leave now, how things were. He needed to make amends, persuade Charlotte that they were still a good team.

"Did you tell the psychiatrist about Cam?"

He stared at her, then dropped his eyes to the floor. He couldn't lie to her.

"Why not?"

"It's not come up."

"Don't you think it would help?"

"No."

"Why?"

He shook his head, setting his glass on the coffee table next to the chair. Suddenly his stomach was churning, he couldn't drink anymore. "It was a long time ago. And he's dead, talking about it won't change what happened."

Charlotte set her glass down too and padded across the rug towards him. Slowly, she lowered herself onto the arm of his chair. He tilted his head and looked up at her, her tousled hair framing her face. Wavy from the warmth and damp of the spa, it only intensified her beauty.

"You weren't the same person when you came back from that tour. I think Cam's death has affected you far more than you realise. And I think if you really want to get better, you need to go right back to that time. Talk about what it was like."

Jake's heart was thumping in his chest. "I don't want to think about it. I need to go."

Scrambling out of the chair, he reached for his keys.

"You can't drive, Jake, you've had too much to drink..."

"I need to go."

He tried to push past her but she stood firm in his way, blocking his escape. There was no way she was going to let him run away from this again. She should have been more forceful last time. Made sure he spoke to someone about how he felt. He had run away then, back to Afghanistan, and then she had lost him. She wouldn't make the same mistake twice.

"Jake, stop!"

Grabbing him by the arms, she held him steady. For a moment, he stopped trying to push past and stood still, his chest heaving with exertion, his eyes wild. She hated seeing him like this.

"We don't have to talk anymore. We can go to bed. Please, don't drive home in this state. It's not safe. You can leave first thing if you want to..."

"Charlotte, get out of my way. Please."

"No! I'm not going to sit back and watch you drive away in the state you're in. You need to sleep on it. You're safe here, I promise you."

"Stop saying that. You don't know that..."

"I do, Jake. It's safe here..."

"You have no idea what you're talking about! You're a civilian, you walk around every day without a care in the world, with absolutely no *idea* about all the things we have to fight to keep you safe. Even here. At home. They're *everywhere,* Charlotte. There could be someone on the other side of this door, *right now,* and you'd have no idea."

Trying her best to remain calm, she pressed her lips together, but she could feel herself becoming exasperated. "There's nobody on the other side of the door."

"How do you *know* that?!" He shouted then, taken aback by the tone of his own voice.

She stood in front of him for a few seconds, then sighed. "Let's see, shall we?"

"Charlotte, *no*... I said... *stop*!"

He tried to grab her but she was too quick, dodging around him, making her way to the door. He flung himself at her as she reached for the key, pushed her away so hard she fell against the wall in a crumpled heap. He heard her head smash against it like a coconut and recoiled in horror, his hands on the back of his head, eyes filling with tears at what he had done.

"Charlotte..."

He scrambled down to the floor where she was rubbing her head, slightly dazed. When she looked up at him, her disappointed eyes were filled with tears. The knot in his gut tightened and the wine he'd drunk curdled with the remnants of the food in his stomach.

"I'm so sorry..."

"I'm fine..."

He tried to pick her up but she pushed him away, pulling her knees to her chest defensively.

"I'll call for help..."

"Jake, there's no need. I'm ok..."

"No, you hit your head..."

"I'm fine. I've had far worse. I'll be ok."

Distraught, he didn't dwell on what she'd said for more than a second. He sat beside her, his back to the cold wall, finally feeling a little safer with his body facing the door. Which was, thankfully, still locked.

"I don't know what's happened to me..." he whispered, anxiously running his shaking hands through his hair. "I was never like this before."

"It's not your fault. After everything you've been through..."

Turning to her, his eyes fell on the angry purple bruise coming up under her hairline. His hands trembling violently, he reached across and inched the hair away from it carefully, his fingertips sorrowfully dancing over the bruise. "Charlotte, I'm so sorry..."

"I know."

He couldn't hold it in anymore. His pent up anxiety and frustration came pouring out and he sobbed, resting his head on his knees as his back heaved up and down. He hated the man he had become. He hated that, even now he had escaped them, they *still* controlled him. What was he going to do if this was how things were going to be, for the rest of his life?

"Come here."

He felt the soft hairs on her arm brush against

his neck as she pulled him into her, her body warm and comforting against his. He cried and cried until he had no tears left. Charlotte rested her chin on the top of his head, shushing him until he'd calmed down and stopped sobbing.

"I hate you seeing me like this," he sniffed, wiping his dewey cheeks on the back of his hand. "I was always strong for you... what must you think of me now..."

She shook her head. "I think you've been through something awful. And everything you ever knew has been turned on its head. You're still hurting. And you don't need to be strong for me, I'm fine."

He didn't know what to say. He leant back, resting the back of his head on the wall, his mind and body exhausted.

"Shall we go to bed?"

He hesitated, then nodded. He wasn't sure how much sleep he'd get, but perhaps lying in the dark would help.

CHAPTER THIRTEEN

Relaxing on the patio, Charlie enjoyed the fresh spring breeze as it came up over the rolling hills beyond the garden. She could happily sit here all day, enjoying the sound of the birds singing in the trees, the relaxing hiss of the wind teasing the leaves. It was a far cry from the sound of passing traffic in her own cramped flat.

"Looks like someone's exhausted!"

She turned towards the approaching voice, just in time to accept a glass.

"Yeah. I've not heard a thing from her since we got back. The beach tired her out! We should go more often." She smiled curiously at the bubbles rising in the glass. "Are we celebrating?"

"I don't need a celebration as an excuse to treat you! You deserve the best!"

Her cheeks flushing slightly, she took a sip. She still couldn't get used to the fact that Myles wanted to spend time with her. Who would have thought it, a single mum with a young baby, hanging out with a wealthy businessman? Especially one as kind as him.

"Although... there was something I wanted to ask you."

"Oh?" She took another sip, butterflies dancing in her stomach.

It was strange; she'd not known Myles that long, but already she felt like he had her back. Sometimes she couldn't believe that it had only been a couple of months since they'd met, by chance, in the coffee shop on her birthday. Thankfully, she was in a vastly different place now; it embarrassed her to think about what life had been like back then. She still missed Jake terribly, and her heart still broke every morning when she turned over in bed and found his space empty. But now that Myles was around and she had someone to talk to and spend time with, she felt like there was hope. Perhaps, one day, she could be happy again.

"I know we've not known each other that long Charlotte, but... sometimes people come into your life, and it feels like they've always been there. And that's how I feel about you... I feel like I've known you for years. And we have a lovely time together, the three of us."

She smiled, touched by his words. "We do!"

"I wondered... and if it's too soon, do say, I won't be offended... but I thought, perhaps you'd like to move in with me, the two of you? Then I can look after you properly?"

She blinked at him, gobsmacked. It wasn't at all

what she had expected. She opened her mouth to speak, but the words were stuck in her throat like barbs, the guilt of betrayal sitting heavy in her stomach. But then she glanced at the new pram next to her, bought by Myles to replace her existing one two weeks before, when it had suddenly given up on her. Jake was gone, and everyone else seemed to have resigned themselves to the fact that he was never coming back. And Izzy deserved a good life, full of delicious food, nice clothes, new toys - not a life of rations and hardship. She wanted her to have a comfortable home, a happy family life - all the things that Charlotte herself had never had. Myles was offering her that.

"Think about it..." Myles said, taking a sip of his own drink. "You don't have to decide now. Like I said, it might be too soon. But I can't deny how I feel, Charlotte. These last couple of months... since you came into my life... well, I've been happier than I've ever been. And I would love nothing more than to look after you. Give Izzy the life she deserves. Right, I'll get some food. Chinese or Indian?"

"Whatever you fancy," she managed.

"Ok."

He was almost inside the kitchen when she opened her mouth. "Myles, wait."

He turned around, his eyebrows raised expectantly.

"Yes."

"Yes?"

"We'd love to move in with you. Thank you."

***

Jake shot upright, approaching gunfire ringing in his ears. He licked his dry, cracked lips and leant against the dusty wall as his head began to spin. It had been months since he'd had a proper meal. His clothes hung off him like rags and his bones now protruded from his skin so much that it hurt to stay in one position for too long. It was barely light, but the ominous glow of the newly rising sun on the horizon announced the start of another dangerous day.

Within a couple of hours, the heat would be stifling again, and he'd be forced to beg for water. Sometimes he felt like begging for mercy instead. If they would put a gun to his head and put an end to his misery, rather than stringing it out for as long as possible, then perhaps it would be easier for everyone. It certainly felt like it would be best for him.

At the sound of distant footsteps crunching across the sandy floor, he narrowed his eyes, trying to focus on the figures coming towards him in the dim light. As they got closer he could make out the image of one of the fighters, holding another hostage like him by the scruff of the neck. Jake watched, trying to keep his head down, wondering if he could simply disappear. He wasn't sure whether he had the strength to endure another beating, or another torture session, or any of the other things they put him through on a daily basis.

The figures stopped in the central area, where the beatings always took place. Yet this time, the captor was holding a long gun, which he used to force the hostage down to the ground. The hairs on the back of Jake's neck stood on end as he heard the captor shout. The hostage said something back, and suddenly Jake's stomach turned. That voice was familiar. The fighter ripped the cover off the hostage's head and Jake forced himself upright, holding onto the bars of the cell, screaming as loud as his lungs would let him. It was Charlie.

Suddenly, he shot up in bed, his whole body soaked in sweat, the sheets wrapped around him like tourniquets where he'd been thrashing around. She was safe, lying in her bed a couple of metres away, her hair splayed across the pillow, her chest rising and falling peacefully. He consciously breathed in, and out, slower and slower until his heart was beating at a normal pace and he had the strength to get out of bed. He pulled his sodden clothes off and dropped them to the floor, before throwing the sheet back over the mattress in embarrassment and slipping into the bathroom before he woke her.

Standing under the raindrop shower head he tilted his head back, allowing steaming hot water to cascade over his head and over his chest and back, washing the sweat away. He felt tears leaking from his eyes as he sobbed, the sight of Charlie being held by a captor with a gun to her head refusing to budge from his mind. It was relentless. Most nights he relived the awful things he'd experienced and seen, but sometimes his mind played cruel tricks on him and instead of seeing himself, he saw people he cared about in his place. Those were the worst nights. Sometimes the images stayed with him for weeks.

Once his skin was red hot, he stepped out of the shower, wrapping himself in a towel which was barely large enough. He found it really strange that a beautiful spa hotel like this wouldn't have proper sized towels. Suddenly, he remembered that he'd not brought any spare clothes with him - only his swimming shorts. He'd have to spread his t-shirt out on the radiator and hope it didn't smell too bad by morning.

Carefully, he opened the bathroom door and crept back over to the bed. He knew that he wouldn't be sleeping again tonight. Turning the bathroom light off, he plunged the room into darkness, and found his way across the room. He smoothed the sheet and perched on the edge of the bed, the towel tied around his middle. Then he saw something move in front of him.

"Jake? What's wrong?"

She flicked the switch for the bedside lamp, bathing the room in a dim glow.

"I couldn't sleep..." he whispered. "It's ok. Go back to sleep, it's still the middle of the night."

He caught her eyes travelling from his face to his torso and downwards, examining the scars that covered his skin. Wishing that he had a larger towel, he swallowed hard.

"This is why you didn't want to swim..."

He hesitated, then nodded silently. She pushed her sheets back and stood up, crossing the space between them in her immaculate silk pyjamas, lowering herself carefully down beside him on the bed. Her eyes full of concern, she ran her fingertips across one of the largest scars, which ran across his shoulder. It was still red and angry, caused by one of the deepest cuts he'd sustained, which had become infected not long before he was recovered. He was probably only hours from death when Special Forces stormed the compound, hallucinating as the infection ravaged his body. When her fingers reached the end she looked up, her sad eyes connecting with his.

"How did you get this?"

"I don't really... think it's a good idea..."

"Please. I want you to tell me. I can take it."

He opened his mouth and closed it, then opened it again. "Are you sure?"

"Please tell me, Jake."

She ran her fingers across it again, wishing that she could erase not only the scar, but the pain and suffering deeper inside.

"One day, not long before I was rescued, I almost escaped. I'd planned it for weeks, down to the tiniest detail. I waited until they were all in prayer and then I took my chance. But they caught me, and they lashed me over and over again until I lost consciousness. The cut was so deep and they left it open. It wasn't long before it got infected."

Catching sight of the tears gathering in her eyes, he shook his head. "I shouldn't have..."

"No, I want to know. I need to know..." she ran her fingers across his skin delicately, until they were resting on another deep red scar on his upper arm, this one round rather than long.

"Bullet wound. They used to put a cover on my head, tell me to run while they shot at me. Sometimes I wished they'd aim at my head, get the job done, put me out of my misery. But they never did. Or maybe they did and they were just a crap shot."

Silently, her fingers edged down to the rippled skin which covered his ribs.

"Burns," he explained softly. "I had to work in the sun all day, it was boiling. Sometimes I collapsed because of dehydration. And they'd leave me there, the sun beating down, until I woke up again in the night."

"I'm so sorry..." her bottom lip wobbled, fingers skimming over the rest of his skin, over every single bump and ridge and scar. Once she was done, she cupped the side of his cheek, her thumb skimming his nose which was bumpy and crooked from being broken so many times during beatings.

"Some days I begged them to do it properly, finish me off. I didn't think I had the strength to survive another day in that place."

Now, tears were running down both their cheeks. She pulled his forehead to hers, closing her eyes, enjoying the closeness she'd missed for so many years. Jake closed his eyes, his heart full, remembering what it was like to be close to her. Then he felt her head tilt, her soft lips brushing against his, which were still a little rough round the edges. She didn't mind. She pressed her lips to his and kissed him, gently to start with but then with a little more urgency, her tongue finding its way inside and dancing with his. She raised her palm to his and laced their fingers together, squeezing his hand as she kissed him. Jake's stomach turned over. Even after all these years, even though she lived a completely different life now, she kissed exactly the same. If he closed his eyes and tried to forget what the last five years had been like, he could almost imagine that he was returning from deployment, and they were picking up where they left off.

Eventually, she broke away, her forehead returning to his. He gently wiped the tears out of her eyes with his thumbs, as though she was fragile enough to break. Charlotte felt butterflies in her stomach; she longed to get closer to him. But her wedding ring felt heavy on her finger; even though nothing had ever felt more natural than their kiss had, she couldn't shake the thought of her daughter out of her mind.

"I wish things were different," she whispered, pulling away so that she could study his face. His eyes gazed at her longingly and adoringly.

"Why can't we go back to how we were before... try again..."

She shook her head sadly. "I wish it was that easy. I have to think about what's best for Izzy..."

"She can still see her dad... we'll find a way to make it work..."

Charlotte squeezed his hands. "He'd take her from me, Jake. I know he would."

"He couldn't..."

"He could! He has all the money he could ever need, I rely on him for everything. I couldn't survive, if he took her. She needs me..."

"You won't lose her." His arms enveloped around her, squeezing her tightly as she cried against his chest. "I promise."

"You don't know that, Jake. He could throw as much money as he needs at it, I could never compete with that. And I don't want her to have a life like I did... she'd have to leave her school, her home, everything she knows. I could never give her the sort of life he can."

Jake didn't know what to say. At that moment, all he wanted to do was stop time, spend the rest of his life with Charlotte. It had always been them, and it always would be. She had a little piece of his heart, which he knew he'd never get back. His whole body ached for her.

"I don't want to lose you again, Jake. If things were different then of course I'd come back with you, but... I have to think about Izzy now. And I have to do what's best for her."

Jake held her, running his fingers through the soft strands of her hair. There had to be a solution. A way they could be together, but her family wouldn't be destroyed. "Maybe you don't have to choose... we could still see each other... work out what we're going to do. You could get legal advice, I'll work through my issues... I understand that you won't want me anywhere near Izzy at the moment, not until I've got my head sorted. When the time is right, we can make the next step. I promise I won't push you. The ball's in your court. I need you in my life, I can't lose you again. Having you sometimes is better than not having you in my life at all."

"I don't want to hurt you. You deserve better than that..."

"Honestly, I don't care. All I want is you."

He cupped his palms around her cheeks and again kissed her firmly, showing her just how much she meant to him. "I've always been there for you, haven't I? And that's not changed. I'd give anything to have you in my life. And I understand that your daughter comes first, of course I do. Let's try? See how it goes?"

She knew that it was wrong, that she ought to put her marriage first, stick to the vows she'd given when she married Myles. But she'd vowed to stand by Jake too, hadn't she? And although their marriage had ended, surely she still had a moral duty to stand by Jake? She couldn't deny that she still loved him, more than she'd ever loved anyone else in her life, with the exception of Izzy.

She nodded.

This time, she was going with her heart, not

her head.

Whilst ignoring the nagging doubt in her stomach that she still wasn't being entirely truthful with him.

***

"Where've you been?!"

Alana stumbled out of the living room the minute Jake opened the door. He sighed, closing the door behind him, and placed his keys on the sideboard. "I stayed out at a friend's."

"Well, you could have let us know! We were worried about you!"

Jake nodded. "Sorry. But you don't need to worry. I'm twenty-seven, Mum."

"I know. But... after everything you've been through..."

"I need to move on with my life. I don't need you wrapping me up in cotton wool. I'm a grown man."

He couldn't stand the disappointment in her face, so before she said anything else, he took her by surprise, pulling her in for a hug. She stood awkwardly in his arms for a couple of seconds, not sure how to react to his sudden embrace, but eventually relaxed. He pulled away from her. "I'm going to be ok, you know? Everything's going to be alright."

Peering at him, she held him at arms length, examining every inch of his face. He looked different. She was sure she could see a flicker of something new in his eyes. Hope, maybe?

"Has something happened?" She asked, hesitantly.

"What do you mean?"

"You seem a little… different."

"Nothing's happened," he patted her on the shoulder gently. "I'm fine. But I am hungry. I need to make a snack."

Edging past her, he headed for the kitchen. Alana watched him retrieve some ingredients. She watched him crack some eggs into a pan, whisk them up briskly with a fork. He was standing taller, and much to her surprise, as he whisked he began to whistle. Alana raised her eyebrows. Something had happened, for sure. She'd not seen him this happy since he'd come home.

"Jake?"

"Mmm," he mumbled in reply, not looking up from his eggs.

"Was it Charlie? Who you stayed with?"

He froze for a second. Then, unable to keep a smile from creeping onto his face, he turned to her. "Yeah."

"And?"

"And, what?"

Alana rolled her eyes, exasperated. "What did she say?"

Jake shrugged. "It's complicated. We'll see." He lifted the pan and poured the eggs onto a plate.

"What does that mean?!"

"It means we'll see."

Taking his plate, he walked past her into the living room, leaving Alana standing in the kitchen, just as in the dark as she had been before.

***

The house was quiet when Charlotte arrived home. Myles's car was not on the drive and she instantly relaxed. Her mind was swimming with the night before and she needed some time to get her head straight before she had to pretend to Myles that everything was normal. It was something she was going to have to get used to, if she was going to make sure nothing changed for Izzy, but she could still have Jake in her life.

She hated lying to everyone, but she couldn't see any other solution. Now that she'd allowed Jake back into her heart, there was no way she could shut him out again. Her feelings for him had flooded back, stronger than ever before, and the thought of never seeing him again was unbearable. Having barely survived the last time he was torn from her, she was certain that she couldn't survive saying goodbye to him again. Yet the strength of her feelings about Izzy's future hadn't faded. She couldn't do anything to compromise that.

So this was the only way. Once Izzy was older, old enough to make her own decisions and understand the truth, and Jake was in a better place mentally, she would tell them. But for now, this was the only way. She prayed that they would both understand why she'd done what she had, when the time came.

Once in the utility room, Charlotte loaded her swimwear and clothes into the washing machine and closed the door. She couldn't risk Myles getting the slightest hint that she'd spent time with another man. She turned the wash up to 60 and filled the drawer with detergent, then watched the clothes turn round and round for a few minutes, allowing the sloshing sound to cleanse her mind. Everything had to be normal. She had to get used to this, living a double life, if this was to work. She desperately needed it to. Last night, when kissing Jake, she'd been the happiest she had been for as long as she could remember.

Absent-mindedly, she raised a hand to her lips, brushing her fingertips across them gently. She closed her eyes and remembered the roughness of Jake's lips on hers, the way their lips fitted together. How she wished things could have been different. If only she'd never met Myles, and Jake had been rescued sooner, they could have given Izzy a life together. Jake and Charlie would have been the only parents she'd ever known.

The sound of the front door opening broke her from her thoughts and she stood up, smoothing her hair back from her face and painting on a fake smile. Normal. She just had to act normal.

CHAPTER FOURTEEN

Gently brushing a loose curl of hair off Izzy's face, Charlotte watched her daughter sleep. She was the picture of beauty, lying on the deep plum velvet pouffe in her white dress, her hair splayed across the pillow and a sparkly wand clenched in her left hand.

Charlotte's eyes travelled to the beautiful, hand tied bouquet of roses, nestled in tissue paper on the dressing table in the corner. It was her wedding day, and she was in the most beautiful place she'd ever set foot in, but she had never felt so alone. She thought that saying goodbye to Jake yesterday would give her some closure, but it hadn't. She felt more torn than ever.

Protectively, she moved a pillow next to Izzy, in case she rolled over in her sleep. Then she stood carefully, smoothing her dress and lifting the front so that she wouldn't tread on it. Approaching the dressing table, she caught sight of herself in the mirror. She barely recognised herself. The wedding was going to be a new start for her and Izzy - a new family, a new name, and in the next few months, a new home in a new town too - they were relocating, as Myles merged the family business with one owned by an old friend named Connor, who he'd not seen for several years. It was going to be an intimate ceremony - only Myles's closest family members and a handful of his friends were coming to watch them get married. Charlotte had no family or friends to invite.

She wasn't sure whether a new start was what she needed or not. She was going to have to reinvent herself, get used to living the life of a millionaire's wife and pretend that it was no big deal. This morning she'd had her hair, nails and make up done ready for the big day, but when she looked at herself in the mirror, all she wanted was to scrub it all off, get changed and leave - maybe she wasn't ready to leave her old life behind.

But, as always, her focus returned to Izzy, still sleeping peacefully, and she remembered why she didn't have a choice. Her little girl was going to grow up in a beautiful home, with a private education and an enriching childhood. She would never go hungry, or wear clothes stained and stretched by someone else, or sit in a classroom for a week working out of a textbook because most of her year had gone on a ski trip, but nobody could afford to send her.

And so, Charlotte had to do this. She had no choice. She closed her eyes, allowing herself to think about Jake one last time. Then she took a deep breath, closed the box in her mind, and locked it. A new start.

***

Expectantly, Jake sat in the window seat, scanning the busy street outside. He wanted her here. Waiting made him anxious, especially when he was tired. He'd had a two hour session with the psychiatrist that morning, and his mind was exhausted. But the thought of seeing Charlotte had been enough to drag him out of his hole, and he had practically run to the coffee shop.

Then he saw her. She crossed the road, her hair blowing in the wind as she headed for the coffee shop. She saw him as soon as she walked in the door and waved awkwardly, quickly scanning the shop before she sat down to make sure she didn't recognise anyone.

"Hey. How are you?"

He reached across the table and took her gloved hand, squeezing it tightly. She pressed her lips together, and he imagined the taste of her mouth on his.

"I'm alright," she smiled nervously.

Reassuringly, he squeezed her hand again. "Nobody will recognise you here. Why would they?"

She shrugged, taking her hand and unravelling her scarf from around her neck. "I don't know. There's always the potential."

"We can get coffee to go? Go for a walk somewhere quieter?"

She bit her lip, her face relaxing slightly. "Yes. I'd like that."

Five minutes later, they found themselves heading down a woodland path, bordered on both sides by thick trees. They weren't far from the village, but buildings quickly faded away and before long they were alone, hidden from the outside world by thick, barbed bushes.

"How are things?"

Jake breathed in sharply. "Ok, I guess."

"Just ok?"

He shrugged. "They still won't let me back with my platoon. I'm beginning to wonder whether they ever will."

They were walking so close that their arms brushed together a few times. Charlotte tried to adjust her position to give him more room, but it was fruitless - within seconds, their bodies had closed the gap again, as though drawn together by an invisible force. She took a sip of her coffee. "Of course they will. You're a good soldier."

"Was a good soldier..."

Jake's voice trailed off and Charlotte took another sip of her coffee, then took Jake's free hand in her own. "You're going to be ok. But it's not going to happen overnight. Give it time."

"And what about you?"

"I'm alright. I've been busy, getting everything ready for Christmas."

A smile played on Jake's lips. "You do Christmas now?"

"I do it for Izzy. That's not to say that I find it easy, or remotely enjoy it."

He squeezed her hand, turning to study her features. She looked even more beautiful than normal, the bold plum colour of her scarf highlighting her delicate skin and the sparkle of her eyes.

She caught him looking. "What?"

He stopped in his tracks. Unable to fight the urge anymore he grabbed her, pushing her up against the fence which ran alongside the path, pressing his lips to hers. Charlotte relaxed in his arms, her own around his neck, enjoying the warmth of his body. Their lips danced together until Jake had to pull away, the desire to go further rising within him. He knew she wasn't ready for that. Not yet and not here. He couldn't spoil what they had right now.

"I'm not sure I want you to let go..." she mumbled against his lips, pulling him against her again. Their lips collided together more roughly this time and she pressed her body to his, pulling him closer to her. Jake groaned and pulled away. "Don't... I won't be able to...."

She leant her forehead against his, feeling the pant of his hot breath on her face. She looked up, right into his eyes, and she could see it right there - his desperation for her. Yet he had never once pushed her to do anything.

"I don't know how I'll go a whole two weeks without seeing or speaking to you," she admitted, pulling out of his arms. "It's going to be hard."

"I know. But you'll be busy, with Christmas... and then we can see each other again."

After checking behind them to make sure they were still alone, they continued to walk down the path, their boots crunching through the odd patch of frost which was shaded, and hadn't been melted by the late morning sun.

"He's starting to get suspicious. He asked about entries on our bank statement the other day. Why I'd gone all the way there, last time... that's why I paid cash today."

Jake mulled the thought over in his mind. "We need to be more careful. I don't want to jeopardise things for you. I can't risk losing you."

"You'll never lose me. I think we're incapable of losing each other!"

For a few minutes they walked in silence, their hands finding their way together again. Jake enjoyed the warmth of Charlotte's soft glove against his skin.

"James is arriving tomorrow, from New Zealand," he said eventually.

"Oh, you never said he was coming! That's great."

"Yeah. It's going to be a bit strange though... seeing him again after all this time. And Kelly. They're married now, I told you that, didn't I?"

"Yes. You did."

"I do want to see him. But I don't really know what we're going to say..."

"You're brothers. It will be like he never left,

you'll see," Charlotte smiled confidently.

"Hmm... it's not him that's the problem though, is it? I'm not the same person I was when we last saw each other."

"It will be alright. You'll see. I think you'll have a great Christmas. And hopefully, the New Year will be a new start. For both of us."

"Oh?"

Charlotte held her breath for a few seconds, then puffed it out slowly. "I er... I've been thinking."

"Sounds ominous?"

Jake flashed her a grin and her own lips formed a mischievous smile. "Why do you have to do that? I'm trying to have a serious conversation with you."

"Sorry," he grinned, although they both knew that he wasn't.

"I want to go back to work."

"As a nurse?"

"Mmm," she nodded. "I miss it, a lot. And I've been so lucky to be able to spend this time with Izzy, but she's getting older now... and I know I don't need to work, but I feel like I need to do something for me. Get part of myself back. Does that sound mad?"

"Not at all. Makes perfect sense. You were born to be a nurse."

They continued to walk deeper into the trees. The further they got from the village, the more Charlotte felt her body relax. "I need to speak to Myles about it. Hopefully he'll come around to the idea."

"Come around to the idea?"

"We spoke about it... a long time ago. To say he wasn't keen on the idea of me going back to work is an understatement."

Jake frowned. "So you need his permission?"

She sighed. "Yes... no... well, sort of. He works away a lot. He wants me at home."

"And what about what you want? Why does he get to decide what you do?"

"Well... he's looked after us all this time. I'm lucky to have him. I wouldn't have coped without him."

"I think you'd cope better than you give yourself credit for."

She shook her head. "No. You weren't there, Jake. You don't know what it was like, being on my own... if it wasn't for Myles, I'm not sure Izzy and I would even be here now."

Jake's brow furrowed in confusion. "Well no... obviously not, as he's her dad..."

Charlotte opened her mouth, her stomach lurching violently as though she'd been dropped from a plane. She felt her pulse pounding in her forehead and her chest felt tight, her mouth suddenly dry.

"Charlotte..."

She could see it in his eyes, he could see it in hers. He wasn't going to give her a way out this time. Her face was telling the story all on its own. She couldn't breathe.

"He is her dad, isn't he?"

She stared at him, speechless.

"Charlotte... how old is Izzy..."

It had been staring him in the face all along. Charlotte's reluctance to show him any pictures of Izzy, the petrified look on her face when he suggested that he could become part of her family's lives. There had always been a nugget of doubt at the back of his mind, when Charlotte had explained she couldn't do anything to jeopardise the life Izzy had now. He knew that she wanted the best for her daughter, of course she did - didn't all parents? But there had been something else. Something that didn't quite sit right with him. Charlie had never been materialistic, all she had yearned for as a child was love, a parent who loved her, and really wanted her. Izzy would always have that, no matter what happened. But he trusted her, and so he hadn't probed.

"I need you to tell me the truth..." he whispered, his voice hoarse.

Charlotte opened her mouth to speak, but no words would come out. She blinked at him, watching as devastation and betrayal clouded his eyes and he staggered away from her as though she'd shot him.

"Is she mine?"

Her eyes prickled with tears and she pressed her lips together, bracing herself for his reaction. He lifted his arms and she held her breath, her body stiff, waiting for impact. But it never came. Instead, he fell against the fence behind him, bent over, his hands on his thighs.

"Jesus, Charlotte."

Eventually, she found her voice. "I need to go and collect her..."

"No, you don't..." he grabbed her by the arm, the force of his grip twisting her towards his body. "You can't just leave, not like this."

He saw her staring at his fingers on her arm, the alarmed expression on her face telling him that he was hurting her. Quickly, he released her. "I'm sorry... I didn't mean to..."

They stood in silence, their bodies still parallel. But Charlotte couldn't raise her eyes to his. She kept her eyes on the floor, petrified and stuck. What was she going to do?

"I know I'm not the sort of person you want in Izzy's life right now. But didn't you think I have a right to know?"

Charlotte lifted her gaze to his. "I wanted to tell you. But I didn't know how. I was scared."

"Of what? You could have told me at any point over the past few months. But you chose to lie to me instead! Why would you do that? Surely this makes things easier?"

"How can I possibly make the right decision? Whatever I do, someone loses out. I had to be sure that person wouldn't be Izzy."

"And you never thought she might lose out from being lied to her whole life? From not knowing her dad?"

"She *has* a dad, Jake. Myles is her dad. And there's no reason she would ever doubt that..."

"But he's *not* her dad! And one day, she'll question it - why she doesn't look like him. What if she finds a news report about me, and puts two and two together? Didn't you ever think about that? And what about me? You've been meeting up with me for weeks, what did you think you could just carry on like this forever, and never tell me the truth? Don't you feel even the slightest bit guilty about that?!"

"Of course I do!" Charlotte cried. "But right now, she's happy, she has a mum and a dad who love her, and all the things she needs. I thought you were dead, Jake, I thought the chances of you returning were zero. One day, if she starts to question things I'll tell her the truth. But if I tell her now, it's going to rip her apart. She's four years old! She never asked for any of this!"

"Neither did I."

"And neither did I, remember."

Jake stared at her, unable to unpick the feelings he had towards her at that moment - whether it was contempt or love, he couldn't tell.

"Don't you see? Whatever I do, someone gets hurt. And that's why I was so reluctant to see you at first, and I tried so hard to fight my feelings, but... I *love* you, Jake. I always have, and I always will. And I want nothing more than to come back to you, and continue where we left off five years ago, but I *can't.* It's not just me I have to think about, do you understand? It will destroy her if I tell her Myles isn't her dad, that her whole life is a lie. Don't you see that?!"

Tears began to leak from her eyes and run down her cheeks. His hand was drawn towards her skin, brushing them away with his thumbs. She looked up at him through clumped, teary eyelashes, her eyes wide and sincere.

"I love you, too..." he found himself saying, unable to fight the furious love he felt for her deep inside. But inside his gut, betrayal and anger was bubbling up, threatening to erupt - he let go of her face and turned, punching the fence with a loud crack. Charlotte watched, devastated, as he let out a howl like a dying animal and then leant his back against the fence, panting heavily.

Instinctively she stepped forwards, gently taking his hand in hers, using a tissue from her pocket to press hard on his bleeding knuckles. "I'm so sorry I kept this from you..." she mumbled through tears, dabbing at them with the tissue once the bleeding slowed. "I wanted to tell you. I just didn't know what to do. What would happen if I did. And selfishly, I needed you in my life. You walked straight back in, and at that moment I knew I could never lose you again."

"I understand..." he found himself saying. "I'm a mess. Of course you don't want me anywhere near her."

Charlotte returned her gaze to his. "No! That's not why at all, please don't ever think that. I just... I can't risk losing her. She's my daughter, I'd give my life for her. If Myles took her... if he got custody... I couldn't live with that."

"But she's my daughter too, isn't she? So how do you think I feel, being kept away from her? Being lied to, by you of all people? Surely you know that I would *never* do anything to compromise her best interests. I would never tear your family apart, Charlotte. Not if you were happy. But I don't think you are. You wouldn't be here with me now if you were."

She pulled her hand away from his. "Myles saved me, Jake. I've loved you longer than I've ever loved anyone, but when I lost you... Myles saved me. I owe him my life, and Izzy's. How can I take her away from him, when I owe him so much?"

Jake frowned. "Feeling indebted to someone isn't the same as loving them, and wanting to be with them. If you took everything and everyone else out of the equation, what do *you* want? What would make you happy?"

Charlotte closed her eyes for a few moments, allowing herself to imagine what her life could be like if Jake had never left for Afghanistan, if she'd never sunk lower than she ever thought she could, if Myles had never found her. She opened her eyes again and she knew the answer to his question. But getting there seemed so impossibly hard.

"Life doesn't work like that though, does it? I can't only make the decision based on what I want."

"So you do want me..."

She swallowed a lump which had grown in

her throat. She couldn't speak. She wanted him so much it hurt. But Izzy. She had to think of Izzy. "I want what's best for Izzy."

***

Arriving at school with seconds to spare, Charlotte had to jog to get to the entrance doors in time to greet Izzy. She was dressed up in her Christmas jumper and designer jeans, a crooked tinsel crown balanced on her head. As soon as she saw Charlotte, her eyes lit up and she said goodbye to her teacher, before running down the steps.

"Mummy!"

Charlotte opened her arms and lifted her daughter, squeezing her tighter than she ever had before. She took a deep breath and managed a smile, feigning excitement even though she desperately wanted to cry. "It's the Christmas holidays! Do you have everything?"

"Yep! PE kit, hat, all my pictures I've been making... all in my bag."

"Great! Say goodbye to everyone, then."

Izzy waved goodbye and they crossed the playground to the car, before climbing in. Charlotte took Izzy's bags and lay them on the back seats.

"Mummy, you've got a leaf in your hair!" Izzy laughed, reaching up to pluck a stray brown leaf from Charlotte's parting.

Charlotte's stomach turned with guilt, the weight of her lies firmly resting on her shoulders.

But she managed to force a smile, pretending that everything was normal. "Oh, look at that! It must have blown there earlier when I was tidying up in the garden. Clearing a path for Santa to land his sleigh!"

Izzy squealed. "How many days, Mummy? How many?"

"Only seven now!"

"And even less until my birthday!"

Izzy squealed again, turning the dial to raise the volume of the radio, as a Christmas song filled the car. Charlotte clenched her jaw, trying to force herself to feel happy about her daughter's favourite time of the year.

"Do you think Santa got my letter?" Izzy asked, her little head bobbing along in time with the music.

"I'm certain he did!" Charlotte replied, her eyes on the road. "I'm sure he has your presents loaded in his sleigh already, ready for the big day."

"Claudia says she's asked Santa for a pony. A pony! As *if* he's going to fit that on his sleigh!"

"That does sound quite unrealistic! Hopefully she won't be too disappointed."

"Oh, she won't be disappointed. Her mum and dad will buy one for her, she gets *everything* she wants. And she's still *never* happy."

Charlotte quickly glanced at her daughter before returning her eyes to the road, indicating as they approached the roundabout. "Are you happy, Izzy?"

Izzy peered at her strangely. “Of course I am! It’s almost my birthday and Christmas!”

Charlotte smiled weakly. “Of course.”

“Are you alright, Mummy?” Izzy asked.

“Yes, I’m fine. Absolutely fine. Now, how about hot chocolate and a Christmas film tonight?”

“Yayyy!” Izzy’s excited squeals filled the car, clouding Charlotte’s mind, for now pushing out the monumental decision she needed to make.

CHAPTER FIFTEEN

As Myles walked through the front door, a bunch of flowers in one hand and his keys in the other, the smell of freshly baked bread filtered through his nostrils, making his mouth water. He placed his keys on the sideboard and dropped his bag on the floor, flicking his shoes off before heading down the hallway towards the kitchen.

"Something smells nice," he smiled, his eyes on his wife who was dancing around the kitchen with the sound of the radio in the background.

"Hello," Charlotte grinned, reaching out for the flowers. "Ah, they're beautiful! Thank you!"

"Not as beautiful as you," he grinned, kissing her.

"Dada!"

Feeling a little tug on the knee of his trousers, he looked down to see Izzy standing next to him, a beaming smile on her face.

"Hello, beautiful!"

Quickly, he lifted her, spinning her around in the

air, making her laugh right from the depths of her gut. Charlotte watched them happily, then reached inside the oven for two freshly based pizzas. Myles's mouth watered again.

"Are you ready to eat?" Charlotte placed the pizza stones on the smooth, shiny hob.

"Yes, I'm ravenous," he replied, planting Izzy back on the floor before loosening his tie. "What a busy day."

He took Izzy's hand and walked her to the dining table, where he fastened her into her high chair. Izzy spun the wheel attached to the high chair tray, which made the sound of raindrops.

"Here we are," Charlotte announced, placing the pizzas on hot plates in the centre of the table, which was already laid with plates and cutlery. "Dig in!"

Myles reached for the pizza cutter and sliced a piece for Izzy, then for himself. He began to eat, enjoying the hot, satisfying pizza inside his stomach.

"Mmm, these are delicious! That new kitchen was worth every penny, with all these treats you keep cooking up!"

Charlotte beamed, taking a seat opposite. "Well, it's the least I can do. That kitchen is the stuff of dreams! I still can't believe it's mine."

"What did you two do today?" Myles asked, before taking another bite.

"We went to the park, didn't we, Izzy?"

"Yes! Park! We fed ducks!"

"You fed the ducks?" Myles repeated. "That sounds fun!"

"Daddy not there," Izzy said sadly.

"No. Daddy wasn't there. But hopefully I can come next time!"

Izzy's smile returned and she continued to eat, a string of mozzarella hanging down her chin.

"And then Izzy had a nap. So I had some time to myself. And I've got some exciting news, actually!"

"Oh?" Myles asked, his mouth still full of pizza.

"I applied for a job!"

Myles almost choked, coughing heavily before managing to swallow his mouthful, much to Charlotte's relief. "A job?"

"Yes. Only a few hours a week initially, but it's a start."

Myles stared at her, the smile gone from his face. "Why would you do that?"

"I know it won't really make any difference to our finances, but at least I'll be able to contribute something..."

"There's no need," Myles interrupted, taking a large sip of the wine Charlotte had already poured for him.

"I know, but I want to. It's not fair that all the responsibility is on you, I want to do my bit."

Myles wiped his mouth and crushed his napkin in his fist, before dropping it onto his plate. "We'll talk about this later."

Then he left the table, leaving Charlotte confused, wondering what on earth she had said to warrant such a reaction. She didn't understand why he wouldn't be pleased - she was getting her life back on track, slowly peeling away from the reliance she had upon him. Alright, it was a small step, but it was a step nonetheless.

Once she'd settled Izzy to sleep, Charlotte entered the living room, where Myles was now sitting watching television, a large whisky in his hand. The atmosphere was thick and uncomfortable. Charlotte hovered in the doorway for a few seconds, before taking a seat in the arm chair nearest to the door.

"It's a few hours a week at a school... covering lunchtimes, to start with. That's all. I might not even get it..."

"And what are you going to do with Izzy?"

"There are plenty of childminders who could have her... lots of one and two year olds go to childminders or nurseries, Myles. It would be good for her."

"What's good *for her is being at home, with her family. People who love her."*

"Or, I was thinking I could come to an arrangement with Effie, maybe she could have Izzy for a couple of hours and I could have Callum in return..."

"Have you spoken to Effie about this?!"

"No, not yet... I might not even get the job..."

Myles said nothing. Lifting his glass to his mouth, he took a large gulp. Charlotte could tell that he was angry - in fact, he was absolutely fuming. She just couldn't understand why.

"Myles, I'm not sure why you're getting yourself so worked up about this... I know you're busy with work, I'm not expecting you to drop your commitments to take care of Izzy. I'll make arrangements..."

"Worked up?!" He interrupted, his voice now

raised. "Worked up? I'll tell you why I'm worked up! You're so ungrateful, do you know that? You don't know how lucky you are!"

Charlotte stared at him, stunned.

"I was there for you, when you had nothing. Nothing! Not a single pound to your name, living in a cramped, damp little flat with Izzy, she didn't even have a decent pram when I met you, remember? Do you remember that? Have you forgotten all that I've done for you, all that I've sacrificed for you?!"

Charlotte bit her lip, her stomach churning. She had been so excited to tell Myles about the application, so hopeful that she'd get the job. And now she felt sick.

"I know you have... and I am grateful, Myles, so grateful! I want to give something back... work hard, like you do..."

"I give you everything you need! You want for nothing! There's no need for you to work, how would it make me look, you working in a minimum wage job? I give you everything! Is that not enough?"

Charlotte's chest felt tight, she could hardly breathe. She swallowed hard, then dropped her eyes to the carpet, feeling incredibly guilty. She had made Myles angry. He had given her so much, and she had upset him.

"I'm sorry, Myles..." she mumbled. "I had no idea you'd react like this. I thought you'd be pleased."

He tutted. "Pleased!"

They sat in silence for a few minutes, then Charlotte stood and left the room. She padded across the tiled floor in her slippers towards the kitchen, where she opened her laptop and stared at the screen for a few seconds, the glow of the screen reflecting in her eyes. Sadly, with a sigh, she clicked the button on the webpage, cancelling her application.

Picking at a roast potato with his fork, Jake chewed the piece of beef in his mouth over and over until it was tasteless. Across the table, his sister-in-law Kelly told his mum all about the beach near to their home in New Zealand, how great the local schools were, and how their home had the most beautiful veranda overlooking woodland. He swallowed hard, allowing his mind to wander, like it always did, back to Charlotte.

Suddenly, there was a gasp and a clatter. Gravy splattered across the table as Alana dropped her fork, reaching quickly for Kelly's hands.

"Oh, that's the most wonderful news! Truly wonderful!"

Jake looked up to see his mum pull Kelly into her arms, and his dad clap his brother, James, on the back. "Good job, son!"

James grinned. "We're having a little girl! She's due in June!"

"Oh, wow, that's even better!"

James's gaze travelled to his brother, and Jake swallowed his next mouthful, forcing himself to smile. "Congratulations, that's great."

"Thanks, mate," James said, although Jake saw his smile fade slightly.

Jake wished that the ground would swallow him up. He wanted to be pleased for his brother; he really did. But hearing how happy James was with his wife, and that they were expecting a baby, only cemented in Jake's mind the disappointment and devastation that he'd lost the love of his life - and that another man was bringing up his child. He took a big glug of his wine, which now tasted acidic, then set his glass back on the table abruptly. Wine sloshed up the side of the glass, threatening to over-spill. Feeling his dad's gaze on him, he cleared his throat. "I er... I'll be back in a moment."

Leaving the table abruptly, he felt four pairs of eyes on him. Nobody said anything as he left the room. Jake couldn't look back. He marched down the hallway and up the stairs, until he was alone in his room. He shut the door behind him and sat on the edge of the bed, his head in his hands. Playing happy families was the last thing he needed right now.

He pulled his phone out of his pocket, turning it over and over in his hands. He knew that he couldn't call her, and that she wouldn't be able to call him, not until the New Year when Myles went back to work. If she ever did again. But that didn't stop him wishing that she would. Unpicking his feelings was a monumental task. One minute he hated her, furious at her for keeping this from him, for not telling him the truth as soon as she knew he was alive. But the next, he felt his heart swell and he loved her, and he thought he could probably forgive her for what she'd done. He had no choice - he had to forgive her, because he simply couldn't live without her.

There was a knock at the door and Jake sat up straight, taking a deep breath. "Come in."

After a moment the door opened slowly, and James stood in the doorway. "Are you alright, mate? Sorry, it was insensitive of us to make the announcement today. We should have waited."

"No, you shouldn't. *I'm* sorry, for being like this. I am happy for you, honestly."

James crossed the room and sat next to Jake on the bed, as he had fifteen or twenty years ago when they were kids and then teenagers, confiding in each other about the girls they'd fancied. There had only ever been one for Jake. James used to laugh at him for it.

"I'm sorry to hear about Charlie... it's shit. I don't really know what to say."

"It is what it is."

"I can't believe she married someone else... after how long you guys were together. It was always you two, wasn't it? Ever since you were kids."

Jake shrugged. "I can't blame her. She thought I was dead. She moved on. I'm happy for her."

"Are you? I'm not sure I could be, if it was the other way round. If someone else had their hands all over Kelly." He cringed, watching Jake crack his knuckles in his lap. "I'm sorry. That was insensitive too. I need to shut my mouth."

Jake shook his head. "It's fine. You always did

have a big gob."

He grinned then, and his brother visibly relaxed.

"Listen, I didn't want to ask you about it because I wasn't sure if you'd want to talk about it... but I'm always here for you. Whatever you want to talk about. Charlie... Afghan... whatever. When I'm here, or on the phone, when I'm back in New Zealand... I'm always here for you. I feel awful that I've not come back before now, but I had to sort out work and everything... and the plane tickets aren't cheap... with a baby to save up for..."

Jake shook his head. "Not at all. I completely understand. You have your own lives."

"I'll always have time for my brother, though."

Jake nodded, then turned to his brother. "Do you know she's married to a millionaire?"

"What?"

"Charlie... she's married to a millionaire."

"Oh. Yeah. Mum said."

"Did she tell you she has a kid, too?"

James nodded regretfully. "Yeah. She did."

"Mmm. Izzy. She's mine, by the way."

Jake watched as his brother's eyes widened. "Yours? Like... you mean..."

"Yep."

"Shit! Does Mum know?"

"Nope."

"When did you find out?"

"Yesterday. And before you ask, she knows

nothing about me. She thinks Myles is her dad. Myles the millionaire. How disappointed she'd be if she found out her real dad was a useless, penniless lump like me."

"What are you even *talking* about?! You're a war hero!"

Jake snorted. "Hero. Yeah, right."

Slowly, James shook his head. "There aren't many men who could go through what you have, and bounce back so quickly. Put the uniform back on and ask to go back. You're really brave, mate!"

Jake said nothing, dropping his gaze back to his lap.

"What are you going to do? Is she going to leave her husband?"

"I don't think so. Would you? They have the perfect lives - what can I offer them that he can't? Nowhere to live and a man who jumps at his own shadow. There's not really any comparison, is there?"

"I wish you'd stop putting yourself down like that. You were held by terrorists for *five years,* Jake. Nobody expects you to walk back into your old life as if nothing happened."

"Yeah well, I wish I could."

"Focus on how far you've come since you got back. Mum said you were in a state... I was expecting you to be much worse than you are now. You look alright to me. A few grey hairs and all that, but..." he nudged him.

"Well, you can't see inside my head."

"So, let me in. Tell me."

Jake opened his mouth, but hesitated. "You don't want to hear it. Trust me. You'll have nightmares."

"I do. I want to know. All of it."

"Are you sure?"

"Yes."

Jake sighed. Then he opened his mouth, and began to speak.

***

Surrounded by plastic penguins and musty white fake snow, Charlotte pressed her lips together to form a smile, watching Izzy run in excited circles, her eyes wide with anticipation. The garden centre was heaving, and there were a hundred places Charlotte would rather have been at that moment. But at least it provided a welcome distraction from the constant internal dilemma she played over and over in her head.

"Come on, Mummy!" Izzy cried, her voice squeaking with excitement. "Come *on*!"

"I'm right here," Charlotte lifted her watch. "We have about... half an hour before we can see Santa. Why don't we walk around the Christmas trees outside, while we wait for Effie and Callum to arrive?"

"Ohhhh!" Izzy whined. "But I want to see Santa *now!*"

"Well you can't, it's not your turn."

"Why?! I want it to be my turn! I want to see him *now*! Daddy would let me see him now, if he was here!" Izzy stomped her foot petulantly.

Charlotte took a deep breath, her cheeks burning as she noticed people around her staring. Maybe it was mostly her imagination - but she was sure she heard someone tut in their direction.

Quickly, she crouched, her smile faded. "Isobel, you listen to me. You're lucky to be able to see Santa, do you hear me? There are lots of little boys and girls who won't be able to come and see Santa this year. You're being very ungrateful. If I hear one more tantrum or whine from you, we'll be going home, do you understand?"

Izzy said nothing but she nodded slowly, her eyes falling to the floor.

"Right. That's settled then. Let's go outside and get some fresh air before Callum arrives."

Silently, they walked in the direction of the automatic doors. As the crisp air hit their skin, Charlotte felt Izzy's hand creep its way into her grip, and she squeezed it tightly. She looked down at Izzy and they exchanged a smile.

"Wow! Look at all these *trees!*"

Izzy let go and began to run towards a big stack of huge fir trees. As much as she hated Christmas, Charlotte couldn't deny that the smell was enjoyable; crisp and fresh, like the smell of new beginnings. She was surprised to see so many trees so close to Christmas - it was just days away, what would happen to all the trees that were left? Would they be disposed of? What a waste.

"Mummy! Where am I?"

Charlotte couldn't help but grin as Izzy darted behind one of the trees, then crouched underneath its heavy lower branches. She put her hands on her hips theatrically. "Oh, no! Where's Izzy gone? I can't have lost her! What will I do?"

She peered behind some of the nearest trees, enjoying the sound of Izzy giggling from behind her chosen tree. "Hmm... not behind here... and not under here! Oh, no! I think I really have lost her! I'll have to go and see Santa by myself..."

"I'm right here, Mummy!"

Izzy jumped out, roaring with laughter.

"Oh, thank goodness! I thought I'd lost you."

The automatic doors clunked open behind them, and another excited shriek filled the air. Effie and Callum appeared, dressed for the occasion in matching Christmas jumpers.

"Well, you certainly came dressed for the occasion!" Charlotte laughed, hugging Effie as best she could with her bump between them.

"Where's yours?!" Effie protested. "It's almost *Christmas,* Charlotte! Even I found one to fit, I don't know what your excuse is. You're such a scrooge!"

"Yeah, well. You know it's not my favourite time of the year."

"Like I said, Scrooge! How can it not be your favourite time of the year? Look how happy they are!"

Their gazes returned to their children, who

were now playing tag around the trees. They watched them for a few minutes, then Charlotte looked at her watch again, keen to change the subject. Effie knew nothing of her life before Myles.

"How about we go and see Santa?"

"Yay!" Two voices cried immediately.

"Come on, then. Let's see if we can get in a little early."

It felt like they queued forever. The dimly lit, enclosed tunnel in which they had to wait was hot and stuffy, and that, together with the echo of excited children screeching at the little characters which periodically popped out from under the fake snow, was stifling. Unzipping her coat, Charlotte exhaled deeply, wondering whether to take it off completely. Today was the very epitome of why she hated Christmas, but when she looked at Izzy, it all seemed worth it.

Finally, they reached the front of the queue, and were confronted by a spotty teenager dressed in an elf costume who clearly shared Charlotte's enthusiasm for the grotto.

"Welcome to Father Christmas's cottage. You've waited really nicely, Father Christmas can't wait to see you. Only a few more minutes, then it'll be your turn."

"Yayyy!" Izzy cried, jumping up and down in time with Callum, oblivious to the elf's lack of enthusiasm.

The watch on Charlotte's wrist buzzed, sending an unexpected current through her arm. She jumped, raising her wrist. *Julie.* She gulped. He had *promised* not to call over Christmas, to give her time to get her head straight. Why was he calling now?

She stuffed her hand in her pocket dismissively, just as the big wooden door behind the elf opened a crack, and the elf broke out in a forced smile.

"The big man's ready for you now!"

Izzy looked up at her hopefully.

"Go on, then!" Charlotte forced a smile too.

On the other side of the door was another musty tunnel, covered in glitter and fake snow. Izzy and Callum pressed forward, tailed by Charlotte and Effie. They reached another big wooden door, with yet another elf, this one female.

"Are you guys ready?" She smiled, a lot more enthusiastically than the first. The children nodded and she opened the door. "Merry Christmas!"

They filed inside the room, which was thankfully a lot brighter than the tunnel they'd walked through, but had a similar musty odour. In the corner sat Santa, dressed in a luminous red suit, his snow white beard shining under the strip lights. Charlotte had to admit that he looked quite authentic. The children were transfixed, entirely convinced that they were standing before the real thing. And so it was all worth it, she thought.

"Ho, ho, ho! Merry Christmas!"

Charlotte and Effie exchanged an amused glance as the children stood and stared.

"Come and take a seat!" Santa patted a large

empty space on the bench next to him.

"Go on!" Effie pushed Callum forwards gently.

Slowly, the children edged forwards and sat on the bench, pressed together anxiously, in silence. Santa peered at them over the top of his round glasses, his face kind. "Who do we have here then?"

Callum stared, completely silent. Izzy glanced at Charlotte who nodded reassuringly, then she turned back to Santa. "I'm Izzy. And this is Callum. He's my best friend."

"Well, it's lovely to meet you both. Are you looking forward to Christmas?"

Callum found his voice; they replied in chorus, "yes!"

"Me too! My elves have been really busy making lots of toys for all of you boys and girls. And I've been giving my reindeer lots of food, so they have lots of energy for their long flight!"

The children grinned.

"So, what do you both want this year?"

"I want... a big car transporter, with cars, red, yellow, blue and green ones!" Callum grinned.

"Wow, that sounds lots of fun," Santa replied. "And what about you?"

Suddenly, Izzy seemed to have forgotten her voice. She looked over at Charlotte nervously.

"Izzy? What do you want for Christmas?" Santa repeated. "You can tell me anything you like!"

Izzy glanced at Charlotte again, and then she smiled. "I'd like a new doll, with clothes."

"Oh, that sounds fun!" Santa nodded. "Would

you like a photo before you go?"

They both nodded. Charlotte and Effie produced their phones and snapped some photos, then another elf appeared, and Santa smiled kindly. "It was lovely to meet you both! I hope you have a lovely Christmas."

Callum happily skipped back to Effie. Before Izzy reached her mum, she turned back to Santa and stopped for a moment. "I forgot... there is something else I want."

"Quickly then, Izzy! It's someone else's turn..." Charlotte held her hand out, but Izzy was still facing the opposite direction. She jogged back to Santa and then said very quietly, but loudly enough for both Charlotte and Effie to hear, "Please can you bring my mummy a present this year? Sometimes Daddy makes her sad, and I really, *really* want her to have a nice Christmas."

CHAPTER SIXTEEN

"Happy Anniversary!"

Groggy from sleep, Charlotte opened her eyes to find a huge bunch of flowers in her face, her husband holding them out to her with a big smile on his face. She rubbed her eyes and sat up, reaching for the flowers. "Wow! They're lovely. Thank you so much."

"Anything for my wonderful wife," Myles grinned, kissing her gently on the top of the head. "Now, you rest. I've got Izzy up, she's had breakfast, she's dressed. I've asked Effie if she wants to come over this evening, keep you company."

"This evening? Why? I thought we were going to have dinner together?"

"I'm sorry, something urgent has come up. I've got to fly out to Boston at lunchtime. I got the call ten minutes ago."

"But... it's our first anniversary." Charlotte

struggled to hide the disappointment in her voice.

"I know. But like I said, it's urgent. I'll make it up to you when I'm back, I promise."

Charlotte nodded, but she said nothing.

"I made you breakfast," Myles continued, looking at the tray on the bedside table.

Charlotte followed his gaze. She hadn't even noticed the tray, set with a plate of toast, jam and butter, a cup of tea, and a small flower in a jar. "Thank you."

Myles kissed the top of her head again. "I'll leave you to it. I'll be downstairs with Izzy."

Then he left the room. Charlotte grabbed a piece of toast. She took a bite, but it sat heavy in her mouth, churning round and round like cardboard, almost impossible to swallow. She had been married twice, yet neither time had she celebrated her first wedding anniversary with her husband. The first time, Jake was missing, presumed dead... and this time, Myles didn't even care for her enough to spend the whole day with her.

She swallowed hard, forcing the toast down. The rest was too unpalatable for her to continue.

***

Jake's boots squelched through the soggy mud, Bee trotting happily by his side. The long hair on her belly was practically dragging in the mud, and Jake knew that he was going to have to bathe her as soon as they got home - otherwise his mum would go mad. She'd spent the past few days scrubbing the house spotless ready for Christmas Day. He didn't really understand why. The house had looked fine before; James and Kelly had been there since the start of the week. It was only going to be the five of them on Christmas Day, so there was nobody else to impress.

Jake was relieved to get out and clear his head, now that there was a break in the rain. The weather was unseasonably mild and wet - so much for the crisp, frosty mornings he remembered from past Christmases, before he was last deployed.

Not being able to contact Charlotte was doing his head in. He'd broken his promise and called her a couple of days ago, but she hadn't answered. Now he was kicking himself. What if he'd unintentionally pushed her away? What if he'd forced her to admit everything to Myles? What if Myles spent Christmas talking her around, and she decided she never wanted to see him again?

He shook his head, as though trying to shake the anxiety from his mind. He needed to focus on something else. In another week, they'd be able to meet again and have a proper conversation about what they were going to do.

Bee scampered through the bushes, chasing after a little bird. Jake called her back and then pulled out his phone. There was someone else he'd been meaning to call all week.

"Hi, Jake! Merry Christmas!"

Answering quickly, Bella sounded happy. It brought him a great sense of relief.

"You too. How are you?"

"I'm good, actually. Surprisingly. I've not felt this positive about Christmas for a while."

"Well, that's great. I'm really happy for you. Do you have much planned?"

"I persuaded Dad to invite my aunts and all our cousins over, from Mum's side. We haven't seen them so much lately, but I feel like it's time to move on... I thought it might help my recovery, facing up to it... and actually, I really can't wait to see them now."

"Well done, Bella. I'm proud of you."

"Thanks."

He could hear the chatter of voices in the background, the faint hum of Christmas music. He glanced over at Bee again, who was happily sniffing the leaves. "Are you busy? Sorry, it's probably not a good time to call."

"Oh, no, it's fine! We're just peeling the veg, but I can take a break. It's good to hear from you."

He heard the clatter of a knife being dropped on a worktop, then the background noise diminished. "How are you?"

"I'm ok. My brother's over from New Zealand, I've been talking to him a lot this week. It feels good to open up to him."

"That's great. Were you close? Before you went to Afghanistan?"

"Yeah... we were quite close. But I was worried that things might not feel the same... like he might not understand me anymore. His life has moved on a lot since I left. He's married now, living in a different country... he's busy with work. But turns out I didn't need to worry. It's been really nice to have him around, actually. I'll miss him when he goes back."

"How long is he over for?"

"Until New Year's Eve. Flights are cheaper then, apparently."

"Well, you still have a week together. Make the most of it. And maybe you can go visit him over there sometime?"

"Yeah... maybe."

There was silence then, as Jake continued to squelch through the woods, following Bee who knew the route well. She always seemed to sniff the same trees, treading in yesterday's paw prints.

"Did you hear from Charlie?"

Jake clenched his jaw. He'd not spoken to Bella for a few weeks, not since he'd discovered that Izzy was his. How was he going to put it into words?

"I've been meeting up with her for a while. Every week or so, when I have a rest day. But not at the moment obviously, because it's Christmas."

"That's great, Jake! Has she fallen in love with you again yet?"

A large drip of water fell from a nearby tree and landed on Jake's forehead, splattering down his face. He wiped it off with his spare hand. "It's complicated."

"I *knew* it!"

"The last time we saw each other, things didn't exactly go to plan..."

"What do you mean? Did you have a fight?"

"Not really..."

"What does that mean?"

"I er... you know I said that she has a child? A girl?"

"Yes."

"She's mine."

"What?!"

"She's mine. She's my kid."

"Oh, Jake!"

Bella was stunned to silence. Momentarily, Bee went out of sight, but then came trotting back as soon as Jake whistled for her, faithfully by his side as always.

"Well that makes it even more straightforward, surely? What's she still doing with her husband? She was married to you first, you have a kid together, she still loves you!"

"Well, she loves him too. And he has a hell of a lot more going for him than I do. And Izzy... she thinks Myles is her dad. If Charlotte tells her, she'll turn her life upside down."

"But... but, she has to!" Bella replied, indignant. "She can't continue to lie to her! She'll have to tell her one day - she'll find out! She'll question things!"

"Mmm. Maybe."

"What do you mean, maybe? Jake, we've been through this - you need to fight! She's your daughter! You have rights!"

"But I love Charlotte, and I don't want to

ruin things for Izzy... one minute all I want is to take them away, keep them for myself. Tell Izzy the truth. And then the next, I think maybe it's for the best... she has a mum and a dad who love her, she goes to private school, lives in an amazing house - I can't provide her with that. If she loses Myles, she loses everything she's ever known."

"But you're her *dad!*"

"Yeah. I know."

"Does anyone else know?"

"I told my brother. He thinks I should go in, all guns blazing. But Charlotte had an awful childhood, she had nothing. Her worst fear is Izzy going without. If I do that, she could lose everything. She might hate me. She has to decide for herself."

"And what if she says you can't see Izzy? Ever? How will you feel about that?"

The rain was starting again. Quickly, Jake pulled his hood up, glancing up at the ominous looking clouds through the breaks in the trees. "I hate it. It makes me feel sick. I can't stop thinking about them... sat around the Christmas tree together, having a lovely Christmas. It's doing my head in."

"Oh, Jake."

He could hear sympathy in her voice and he hated that - it was the last thing he wanted.

"He's at home this week, so obviously we can't see or talk to each other. He goes away again in the New Year, so I'm hoping we'll see each other then. And she'll let me know what her decision is."

"I'm sure she's going to choose you, Jake! I know he has money and stuff, but you can't buy love. And I know you say she loves him too, but you were the first one she loved, she'd never have even met him if it wasn't for you going missing. I'm sure she will choose you. She'll make the right decision. And if she doesn't, she doesn't deserve you."

Jake nodded, although he didn't know why, as Bella couldn't see him. He would give anything for her to be right.

***

Izzy had asked how many hours until Santa came at least a hundred times by lunchtime, and Myles's patience was wearing thin. He had snapped at her at least four times and was about to make it a fifth when, spotting a break in the rain, Charlotte bundled her into her rain suit and wellies and took her to the park. Although she wasn't keen on getting wet and they didn't often visit the local park, preferring to play in the garden where Izzy had her own playground large enough for thirty children, getting away from the stifling atmosphere in the house was a relief.

They had reached the park and Izzy had run off to play on the slide when the metal gate swung open, and Effie and Connor appeared with Callum in similar clothing.

Effie smiled. "Fancy seeing you here!"

"We needed to get out," Charlotte explained.

"And Izzy needed to burn off some energy. She's been driving us mad all morning."

"Oh, I know that feeling!" Connor laughed. "This one's a bit over excited too!"

He glanced down at Callum, who was holding his hand. "Can we go on the swings, Daddy?"

"Sure!" Connor said. "Come on, Izzy's over there. Let's go say hi."

They squelched across the play area, which was deserted other than a couple of other young children who were braving the weather, presumably too hyper to sit through a Christmas film. Once they were out of earshot, Effie turned to Charlotte.

"Myles didn't fancy coming then?"

Charlotte shook her head. "No, not his scene."

Effie pressed her lips together. For once she didn't say anything, but Charlotte could feel her hard stare. She busied herself with watching Izzy, who was waving at her from the top of the slide in the distance.

"What did Izzy mean? At the grotto? And why were you so reluctant to talk about it afterwards?"

Charlotte swallowed hard. "Because I don't know why she said it."

"Don't you?"

Silently, Charlotte waved to Izzy again, who had now slid down the slide and almost shot off the end, morphed by her plastic rain suit into a human torpedo.

"She seemed quite certain."

Charlotte pressed her lips together. "We've been arguing a bit recently, that's all."

"About what?"

"The usual things. To be honest, Effie, it's not really any of your business..."

"There's no reason to be defensive! I'm your friend, remember, Charlotte. And our husbands might be business partners and best friends, but I won't say anything to Connor. You can talk to me."

Charlotte watched as both Izzy and Callum climbed onto Connor's back. He stomped around the park, pretending to be a huge monster, while they screamed with excitement. She opened her mouth. The thought of opening up, removing the bottle top, was so tempting. But what if Effie said something to Connor? What if she broke her promise? Things would become even more complicated.

"Has Myles changed his mind about having a baby?"

If only, Charlotte thought. "No... it's not that."

"Then what is it? You've been weird for months... and don't deny it, Charlotte. It's like you changed overnight! Has Myles done something to hurt you?"

Her heart thumping in her chest, Charlotte turned to Effie, her eyes watering; whether it was because of the cold, or because of her emotions, she didn't know. Just as she was about to speak, there was a thud and then a scream, as Izzy fell from one of the swings in a crumbled heap.

"I'm coming, Izzy!" Charlotte cried, and left Effie standing alone at the edge of the playground.

CHAPTER SEVENTEEN

"Have you seen my lilac shirt?" Myles asked, banging from one wardrobe door to the next.

Charlotte opened her eyes, her sight fuzzy from lack of sleep. She managed to focus on the blue digits of her alarm clock - it was only 4am!

"No..." she replied, her eyes closing again as she drifted back to sleep.

"Well, did you take it to the dry cleaners like I asked you to? Charlotte?"

She didn't open her eyes. "I don't know... can't you wear another one..."

Myles exhaled deeply. "I don't believe this! I asked *you to take it to the dry cleaners with the others." He stomped around the bedroom and rooted through the laundry basket. After a few seconds he found the shirt, and threw it in a ball in a crumpled heap. "Do I have to do everything around here?!"*

Charlotte sighed, sitting up in bed. "I'm sorry... I must have forgotten to take it with me. Please, wear another one, I'll take it to the cleaners today..."

"What else do you have to do all day? How could you forget? I work hard so you can have a nice life, the least you can do is make sure you do the odd thing I ask you to..."

"I do lots of things for you! I look after Izzy, look after the house, cook meals..."

"I wish that's all I had to do!"

"Well, I never said I wanted to stay at home. In fact, I wanted to go back to work, to contribute... but you weren't happy for me to do so..."

"Why'd you have to be so ungrateful?! Have you forgotten what your life was like when you met me?! There are so many people who would do anything to be in your position - take a look around you, Charlotte! Look at this house! A bit of gratitude wouldn't go amiss."

"Myles... I am grateful, you know I am..."

"Well, show it then!"

He was almost shouting now. Charlotte was stunned, she didn't know what to say. Myles had woken Izzy, she was stirring in the next room. Now, she would be up for the day.

"I'll see you on Friday."

Then he left, leaving Charlotte alone at 4am with a tired, grizzly toddler who hadn't had enough sleep.

***

Jake tried his best to enjoy Christmas. He knew that his parents were trying, especially his mum, who wanted everything to be perfect for the first Christmas that Jake had celebrated in five years. On Christmas Eve they had an Indian takeaway; it had been their tradition, before he moved in with Charlie. They spent the evening watching Christmas films, and on Christmas day he woke up to the smell of freshly cooked bacon. At lunchtime there was enough roast turkey and beef to feed twenty people, with all his favourites, and in the evening she had gone all out on party food. Underneath the Christmas tree was a huge mound of presents, almost as many as there had been when Jake and James were little boys.

"I wanted to treat you," Alana mumbled emotionally, handing him the first present she took from under the tree. "To make up for all the Christmases you've missed."

For a moment, they sat in silence. Jake stared at the present in his hands, feeling out of place because everyone else in the room felt like something they'd been missing for the past five Christmases had returned - but he didn't. In fact, the last piece of his own Christmas jigsaw was missing, and perhaps it always would be. Then John filled the glass in Alana's hand with bubbly and Jake forced a smile, ripping the present open like a little boy. "Thanks, Mum!"

By nine in the evening, John was snoring

loudly in the armchair while everyone else lounged across the sofas, watching Christmas soaps. Jake looked around him. Every so often he caught Alana staring at him, a look of adoration and relief on her face. He knew that his presence had made her Christmas. On the other sofa, Kelly lay with her head resting on James's leg, his hand casually resting on her lower belly. Jake's mouth suddenly felt dry. He'd missed all of this with Charlie. He'd never felt the soft curve of their child growing under her skin. The first light kicks of their baby as she made her presence known. The excitement and anticipation of meeting her when she made her entrance. He'd missed all of it. The whole pregnancy, the birth, and the first four years of their child's life.

Standing up, he cleared the knot from his throat. "I'm going to take Bee out."

"Don't worry about her, Jake, she's had more than enough excitement for one day, she can wait until tomorrow..."

"No, I want to. She's been a good dog. I always did take her for a Christmas walk. Can't break the tradition now."

As though summonsed, Bee stretched then stood in front of him, her tail wagging with excitement. She had got used to her daily walks with Jake, and had no doubt been waiting all day when he'd not taken her out that morning.

"Come on, then," Jake patted her on the head. "Let's go. I'm going to take you somewhere a bit different today, seeing as it's Christmas. What d'you think about that, hey? A Christmas treat for you."

"Where are you going?" Alana asked.

"I'm going to take her to that big field we used to take her to, when we first got her. I've not taken her there in years."

"Oh, we could come?" Alana gave John a nudge and he snorted in his sleep, opening his eyes briefly.

"No, don't wake him! Let him rest. You stay here and watch the soaps, I know you've been waiting for them and you'll miss them all - it'll take me an hour to get there. I don't mind being on my own. Honestly."

Alana glanced back at John, who was snoring again. "Well... if you're sure..."

"Of course! I'll be back late. Don't wait up. Today's been great, thank you."

He planted a kiss on Alana's head, nodded to James and Kelly, then went to retrieve Bee's lead. Within a few minutes they were heading down the dark road, Bee sitting to attention in the passenger seat beside him, her long tongue hanging from her mouth. Once they were out of sight, Jake pulled over in a lay-by and withdrew his phone from his pocket. He scrolled through the first few photos until he got to the one he needed. Then he memorised the address and typed it into the sat nav app on his phone. It would take him just over an hour to get there.

He had taken a photo of Charlotte's driving licence a few weeks before. He hadn't intended to get her address, but she had left her purse on the table in a coffee shop when she went to the toilet. Curiosity had got the better of him, and he found himself pulling her driving licence out of her purse, quickly taking a photo of it and putting it back. He had never intended to turn up out of the blue. He wouldn't put her at risk. But after searching the internet for information on where she lived, he found out that the house backed onto a large woodland area, laced with public footpaths. He'd not been there before, but today the distance between them felt almost unbearable, and the knowledge that he could be close to her - maybe he would even catch a glimpse of her through a window - gave him comfort. Maybe he would catch sight of Izzy, too.

First, he drove past the house. He could barely see it, hidden behind a large set of gates and thick bushes, with a long driveway. He continued to drive up the road for a few minutes until he reached a small car park, then got out of the car and let Bee jump down from the passenger seat.

"Come on, then. Walkies!"

He pulled a torch from the glovebox and flicked it on, then they began to follow a path through the trees. The darkness and quiet was soothing. Jake could tell that there was nobody around - they were all at home, probably lying on the sofa like his parents had been, almost comatose from eating two or three days' worth of food in one sitting. Playing charades and dominos. Watching films together. Was that what Charlotte would be doing, with Myles and Izzy?

They headed deeper into the woods. Eventually, the path began to snake behind the large gardens, and he could see from the map on his phone that they were heading in the direction of Charlotte's house. Bee was excited, animatedly sniffing at the leaves and mud as they pressed forwards. She would be covered in mud by the time they got home.

After ten minutes or so, Jake could see that they were about to pass the end of Charlotte's garden, although there was a thick section of forest between the path and the row of houses; he could no longer see them. Twigs snapped under his boots as he headed off the path and into the dense trees, Bee at his heels. Low lying branches scraped at his shins as he pressed forwards and at one point, he thought the trees were going to be too thick to penetrate - but just as he was about to give up and turn back, they began to thin and he could see the faint glow of lights in the distance. Lowering his torch to the ground so that they wouldn't be spotted, he whistled softly, keeping Bee in his sight.

Within a minute, the trees cleared and he could see down the muddy bank, expansive, luxury gardens beyond the fence at the bottom. They were well manicured and lit with beautiful, soft white lights. Jake switched off his torch, staying close to the trees where his dark clothing would blend in. All the houses had lots of glass on the back, luxurious bifold doors. The curtains on the first house were closed and he was relieved to see from his phone that Charlotte's house was a few more along. When he got to the house he stopped, looking up to make sure he had the right one. He could see right inside the back of the house, a huge, twinkling Christmas tree to one side of the room, surrounded by brightly coloured toys which were scattered across the carpet.

He couldn't see anyone inside, but he had a feeling. She was here, he could feel it deep inside him. This was her house. Edging closer to the trees, he pushed back until satisfied that nobody would be able to see him, his body concealed by the branches. Then he stood, placing his hand on Bee's head to settle her down by his side, and waited.

Eyes skimming across the clean, shiny glass doors, he took in everything he could see on the other side. Expensive furniture, a beautiful gloss tiled floor. What looked like a real Christmas tree, covered in decadent decorations. Two bin bags full of wrapping paper in the corner of the room, next to a pile of stacked up boxes. Brand new toys scattered across the floor, a shiny new scooter with clean, white wheels abandoned on the patio.

And then he saw movement.

At first, he couldn't make out who it was, but his stomach did somersaults when he caught sight of her in checked pyjama bottoms and a black hoodie, her hair thrown up in a messy bun. He watched her cross the kitchen and pull open the dishwasher, then start to load dirty plates and cutlery inside. There was no sign of Izzy, nor Myles. Jake glanced at his watch. It was late, past nine o'clock - Myles was probably putting Izzy to bed. Peering at the upstairs windows, Jake longed to catch a first glimpse of his daughter, but all of the upstairs windows were dark - either the lights were off, or they were covered with curtains.

Jake watched Charlotte instead. He analysed her body language, the way her body moved when she bent down to place each item in the dishwasher and reach for the next. He watched her shoulders sag as though the weight of the world was bearing down on them. She looks kind of sad, he thought, wondering if that meant she'd made her decision.

There was another flurry of movement in the corner of the room. Suddenly Myles appeared, dressed in dark jeans and a brightly coloured shirt, the silvery flecks in his dark hair catching the light. Jake gulped as he crossed the kitchen and stood close to Charlotte, reaching for a wine glass which was half-full on the side. Charlotte barely acknowledged him as he leant against the worktop, drinking a long sip of wine while watching his wife clear the kitchen. He looked like a predator, sizing up its prey.

Swallowing a wave of nausea which bubbled up from his stomach, Jake wondered whether he should leave; perhaps this was a stupid idea. He couldn't bear the thought of Charlotte touching her husband, it made him sick to his stomach. Reading his body language, Bee whimpered beside him. She could sense that he was on edge.

"Shall we go home?" Jake whispered, glancing down at her. Having adjusted to the darkness, his eyes could see the shine of hers against the blackness around them.

But he couldn't leave. She was like an addiction, pulling him in, even though he knew that he ought to go. He barely blinked, desperate not to miss a thing as Myles, watching his wife close the door of the dishwasher, placed the glass on the side. Then, he made his move. Clenching his fist around Bee's lead, Jake watched Myles approach Charlotte, clumsily dropping his arm around her waist. Still bent over the sink, rinsing it down, she didn't look up, but Jake saw her body unmistakably tense.

Myles tried again, this time more forcefully. Jake closed his eyes for a moment, nausea and rage bubbling inside, threatening to spill over. All the food he'd eaten sat heavy in his stomach. He watched Myles's fingers run up Charlotte's back, caressing her shoulders; his lips brush her neck. Jake couldn't bear it. After reaching for Bee's collar, he snapped her lead on, ready to go back to the car. But as he turned to leave, his eyes locked onto Charlotte again and he was surprised by what he saw.

Charlotte turned in her husband's arms, but she looked far from comfortable. She wasn't smiling; in fact, she looked upset. She raised her hands and, when he continued as though completely oblivious, she pushed him gently back until he got the message. Curiously, Jake watched them exchange words. He couldn't hear a thing from so far away, on the other side of the glass, but he studied their expressions. Charlotte looked upset, stressed, exhausted. Myles looked disappointed and angry. He tried to push himself on her again but Charlotte stood firm, this time shoving him back harder when he forced himself on her.

It was difficult for Jake to control himself. Every fibre of his body pleaded with him to ignore his brain and jump the fence, run to her, save her from the husband who she clearly didn't want. But eventually, Myles got the message, taking a few steps back. Jake could tell from their gestures and the way their lips moved that their words were becoming more heated; Charlotte's body became more and more tense with every minute that passed. He watched them argue for a good five minutes, before Myles stormed from the room, leaving Charlotte standing alone in the middle of the kitchen.

After a few moments, she leant over the worktop, strands of hair spilling over her face. Jake knew her well enough to know that she was crying. He could tell from the way she stood, the way her shoulders edged up and down slightly. From the way she reached up to her face every so often. Jake clenched his jaw, his heart swelling with love for this woman. How could Myles bear to hurt her like this? Even the thought of making her sad caused Jake discomfort.

Eventually, she straightened up and visibly

sighed, wiping her cheeks with her palms. Then she turned and crossed the room to the doors, staring out into the garden and the darkness beyond. For a split second, Jake thought she was staring straight at him - but she was simply staring into space, not looking at anything in particular. Opening her arms, she pulled the curtains shut, killing most of the light to the garden. All that was left was the soft glow of the garden lights.

Jake clicked on his torch and headed back through the trees, Bee trotting down by his side. In silence, they began the walk back to the car.

***

Focusing on the gentle fizz of the bubbles in her glass popping on the surface, Charlotte stared at the contents, running her fingertips around the base of the glass. Effie roared with laughter opposite her but she barely noticed; her eyes narrowed as she concentrated on the bubbles rising from the bottom of the glass.

Suddenly, everyone went quiet. When she looked up, they were all staring at her intently.

"Charlotte? What do you think?" Connor took a sip from his own glass.

Charlotte felt her cheeks flush. "Sorry... what was the question? I was miles away!"

Her eyes travelled to Myles, who was sat quietly next to her, his eyes narrowed in disapproval. She'd shown him up. Taking a large sip from her glass, she closed her eyes, savouring the burn of the alcohol as it slid down her throat. Once upon a time... even a few months ago, she'd have been mortified to have done such a thing, and tried desperately to play along for the rest of the evening. But this Christmas, she seemed to have lost all motivation to please him.

Spending time with Jake had opened her eyes to what Myles was really like. She hadn't realised how much control he exerted over her until now. When she thought about it - *really* thought about it - she couldn't remember the last time she had bought something because she liked it - there was always an underlying reason. Because Myles wanted one, or because he'd bought her similar clothes before and she knew he liked them. They always went on holiday where he wanted. Her life revolved around him. It was obvious to her now - ever since the first day they met, she had tried desperately to please him. And she had tried so hard that she'd completely lost herself, even dropping her shortened name not long after they got together, as he started calling her Charlotte one day and she didn't correct him. Now, nobody knew her as Charlie. Nobody, except for Jake.

And Izzy was right - he did make her sad. And that wasn't all - she made herself sad too, because she no longer existed as a person, except as Izzy's mum and Myles's wife.

"We were taking bets on when and where this one's going to make an appearance," Connor slurred, his pupils swimming. "On the bathroom floor, or in the taxi on the way to the hospital! Callum popped out the minute we got to the labour ward, and they say second ones come out faster..."

"Maybe you could have a home birth," Charlotte quietly suggested. "Then there wouldn't be any rush..."

Myles pulled a face. "Eurgh, no, imagine the mess! There'd be blood and guts everywhere! That's the last thing Connor would want in his house."

"Well, it's not only Connor's house, is it? Effie gets just as much a say, if not more of a say, seeing as she's the one that has to go through it."

Myles said nothing, but he looked furious. Out of the corner of her eye, Charlotte could see him peering at her, wondering what on earth had come over her. Normally, she agreed with everything he said.

"Yeah, too right!" Effie laughed, giving Connor a playful shove. "But actually... yeah, there's nothing I'd like less than Callum hearing me in labour. Poor kid would have nightmares for years!"

After draining her glass, Charlotte stood quickly. "Top up? I'll get another bottle."

She slinked away from the table, Myles's hard stare burning through her back like a dagger. Walking cooly away, she wondered how long it would be before he followed. But he didn't. She made it to the cellar door and opened it, the automatic lights bathing the cellar in a soft glow. After making her way down the stairs with the empty bottle in her hand, she dropped it inside the black recycling box at the bottom, then retrieved another from the fridge. The ice coolness of the bottle against her skin gave her goosebumps but she gripped it tightly, closing the fridge door gently.

He took her by surprise. She almost dropped the bottle. Grabbing her by the arm, he shoved her against the wall, his eyebrows knitted in a furious frown. "What are you playing at?"

"I'm getting another bottle…".

"It's not like you to drink so much. You're showing yourself up. You've barely spoken for an hour, and when you do, it's like someone else is speaking for you…"

"I can say whatever I like," Charlotte retorted bravely, a glimmer of her old self shining through. "I don't know what your problem is."

Myles tightened his grip, turning her skin under his fingers white. "My *problem* is that you're showing yourself up in front of our friends. You'll regret it."

"Why would I regret it? I'm letting my hair down. That's what you said I should do…"

"I didn't mean you should get blind drunk!"

"I'm not. You're hurting me."

Eyes travelling to his hand, his grip loosened, just enough for Charlotte to pull her arm away. "Let's not keep our guests waiting."

On the outside she was as cool as a cucumber, but on the inside her heart fluttered in her chest like butterfly wings. She never stood up to

Myles like this - she was always the one to back down, not wanting to upset the delicate balance in their house. But Izzy was asleep, she had been for hours, and Charlotte knew that there was no way she would overhear their conversation down here. Standing up to Myles felt good.

Dodging past him, she made her way back up the stairs, through the kitchen to the dining area. She held the bottle up. "Here we are! Top up, Connor?"

"And I got another bottle of elderflower for you, Effie," Myles said from behind, putting his arm around Charlotte's waist possessively. "Didn't want you to feel left out."

"Ahh, that's kind of you. Thanks, Myles."

He unscrewed the lid and poured Effie a glass, while Charlotte filled hers and Connor's glasses up to the top. Nobody noticed the angry red marks on her forearm. The whack of the bottle on the table as Charlotte placed it down harder than she intended made everyone jump.

"Sorry!" She giggled, then retired to her chair to continue with her glass.

Effie and Connor exchanged a look, so briefly that Charlotte barely noticed. They had never seen Charlotte get noticeably drunk - certainly not like this.

"So... New Year, and all that. What have you got planned this year?" Connor took another sip.

Myles fastened his hand around the stem of his wine glass. "I think it's going to be a busy one, with everything we have lined up. Hopefully we'll get time for a holiday. Somewhere hot. I'm thinking maybe Bali..."

"Ooh, a hot beach! What could be better?!" Effie crowed. "I'll be so jealous if you guys to go Bali. I don't think we'll have a chance of a decent holiday for a good couple of years now."

"Well... that's why I want to make this year one to remember. I'm sure it will happen for us too, sooner or later."

Raising her eyebrows, Charlotte took another long sip of her drink. The bubbles seemed to bring an unexpected surge of bravery to the surface. Bravery or stupidity, she wasn't really sure. She opened her mouth and the words tumbled out. "I'm thinking about going back to work, actually."

"Oh! Where?" Effie asked.

"I was a nurse, before I met Myles. Now that Izzy's getting older, I'd like to go back to it."

"Were you really?! How did I not know this?"

Myles almost choked on his drink. "Well, yes, but we discussed this before, didn't we? And if we're going to have another baby, then you'll have your hands full..."

"Well, it's not happened yet, has it? Maybe it's not the right time."

"It will happen. I told you, we'll get booked in with that specialist, they'll be able to help..."

"Everything happens for a reason, Myles. Maybe it's a sign that we shouldn't be trying at all."

There was silence around the table as Myles

glared at Charlotte incredulously, as though she'd confessed to murder. She stared back at him for a few moments, oblivious to their guests who were cringing, fidgeting in their seats on the opposite side of the table. Eventually, Myles backed down. Standing abruptly, he scraped the chair legs back on the tiled floor. "I'm going to check on Izzy," he announced, then glared at Charlotte again before leaving the room.

Shortly afterwards, Connor rose too. "Just popping to the loo."

Once they were alone, Effie watched her friend chug back her glass again. "Charlotte… are you alright?"

Charlotte swallowed her mouthful. "Of course! Why wouldn't I be?"

"I dunno… you seem a bit… well, you're not yourself. Are you sure everything's ok?"

"Oh, it's never been better!" Charlotte replied, blinking hard as the room in front of her began to spin. Her vision felt strange - almost like she was in a goldfish bowl, with Effie watching her from the other side of the glass. "Like I said the other day, we've been arguing a bit lately. That's all."

"Maybe it's time we called it a night…" Effie rubbed her bump thoughtfully. "I'm exhausted, and I think you'd better call it a night too before you pass out!"

"Oh, don't be dramatic! The party's only just started."

Connor padded across the floor in his socks, taking his seat next to Effie. She smiled weakly, squeezing his leg. Charlotte watched the way he smiled at her lovingly. She realised that she couldn't remember the last time Myles had looked at her like that.

"Are you alright? Are you ready to go?"

"Yeah," Effie nodded, leaning her head on his shoulder. "I'm struggling to keep my eyes open! And I expect this one will keep me up for most of the night, kicking."

"Mmm," Connor smiled, rubbing her bump gently.

Charlotte realised that she was staring. She gulped, standing to collect the glasses from the table. "I didn't mean to make you feel uncomfortable. Sorry. We should have saved that conversation for later!"

"Oh, not at all! It's late anyway, we need to get back for the babysitter," Connor glanced at his watch, then held an arm out to Effie. "Come on. Let's get you home!"

Once they had left, Charlotte busied herself clearing the glasses and plates. Tense under the burn of Myles's stare, she didn't feel quite so brave now that they were alone. Izzy was fast asleep and there was nobody to witness how he behaved. Her head was spinning; all she wanted was to close her eyes and find herself in bed.

Myles's barbed voice shattered the thick silence. "What were you playing at?"

Charlotte pressed her lips together, closing the dishwasher door with a clunk. It whirred into life and she stood back, reaching for a tea towel to dry her damp hands.

"Oh, so you drop a bomb like that, and now you're giving me the silent treatment? Really mature, Charlotte."

She sighed, dropping the tea towel on the shiny worktop. "I'm tired. Let's talk about it tomorrow?"

He narrowed his eyes. "But you brought it up this evening - and made it so awkward, our friends left!"

"No, they left because Effie was tired, and it's late."

"They would have stayed much later if you hadn't opened your mouth, and you know it."

"Alright. Whatever. I don't think it's a good idea to have this conversation now, we've both had too much to drink."

The scrape of the chair legs echoed in Charlotte's head and she gripped the worktop behind her tightly. He padded across the tiles towards her until he was a couple of feet away. She clenched her jaw, raising her eyes to his.

"Why did you say that? That you want to go back to work?"

"Because I do."

"But we discussed this before, didn't we... and we decided..."

"No, Myles - *you* decided. And I went along

with it, because I wanted to make you happy. But over the past few weeks I've realised that it's important for me to be happy too."

Myles stared at her for a few seconds, and then to her surprise, his face softened for a second. Then it contorted into a laugh. "Happy? You're not happy, now? After everything I've given you?"

"Not always, no."

"And how does Izzy fit into this?"

"Izzy will be fine, Myles. She adores nursery, and it won't be long before she starts school. And lots of children have two working parents. In fact, she's one of the only ones that doesn't..."

"And the baby? What about him or her? Have you forgotten what life was like, with a small baby?"

"No. I haven't. Alright, I'm going to be completely honest with you. I don't want that at the moment."

Raising an eyebrow, he shook his head, his eyes wide. "Ok... so you've changed your mind. Why, Charlotte? A few weeks ago we were trying... you were excited about having another baby, you *wanted* another baby."

Charlotte bit her lip. "Actually, Myles, it was *you* who wanted a baby. I never said that I did. You assumed."

He inhaled sharply. "Assumed? Ok... alright... if that's the case, why the hell didn't you say something? No, I'm not buying this. Not at all. What's changed? Why are you suddenly desperate to stick Izzy with a nanny and go back to work? Abandon our plans to expand our family? What is your problem?"

"I've not suddenly done anything, Myles. I told you months ago that I wanted to go back to work. You dismissed it. I tried to tell you I wasn't ready to have another child... but you wouldn't listen. You kept going on and on about it. I feel like I don't even have a choice."

He was silent then, his chest heaving up and down as adrenaline coursed through his veins. Charlotte heard his teeth grind, he clenched them so hard. He was furious. But now she had started, she couldn't stop. The words kept tumbling out, forced out by the bubbles of the champagne she'd consumed. "I don't feel like I've had a choice for a long time."

He laughed again. "You've had nothing but choices since I brought you here. You had *nothing* when we met, you could barely even afford a decent coffee. I saved you, you and Izzy. I've given you everything you could possibly want. A beautiful home, luxury holidays, a credit card to buy whatever you want. Your life is unrecognisable from what it was before. Why are you being so ungrateful?!"

"I'm not ungrateful, I've said a million times that I'm grateful for everything you've given me and Izzy. But that doesn't mean I don't deserve to make my own choices too. I want to go back to work, I want to get myself back now she's getting older. I don't feel ready to start over again with a newborn."

"If you're worried about managing after what happened last time then I get that... we can get a nanny to help..."

"No, Myles! You're *still* not listening to me! I'm not worried about coping, I don't want to have to." She yawned. "I'm tired. I'm going to go to bed. We can talk about this again tomorrow, once we've both slept on it."

She turned to leave, but he quickly grabbed her, pushing her against the worktop with the weight of his body. The bottom of her spine smashed against the hard edge of the work surface and she cried out, wriggling in his grip - but the harder she fought, the harder he pushed.

"It's not just *you* who gets to make the decision, is it? I've done everything for you these past few years! I could have walked away that day at the coffee shop... let you get on with your life, deal with the fall out of your decisions. But I didn't! I was there for you! I helped you look after your daughter when you couldn't do it on your own... nobody else was there for you."

"Myles, please... let go, you're hurting me..."

"You wouldn't be here now if it wasn't for me!" His face was inches from hers, she could feel his angry breath on her face. "Neither of you! Izzy is only alive because of me! What sort of a life would she have now, if it wasn't for me?!"

Charlotte tried to wriggle free, begging for him to let her go, but it was as though a curtain of fury had fallen over him and he couldn't see past it. He was pushing her back so hard she could hardly breathe; the pressure of her ribs on her lungs was making her light headed, and his face began to disappear behind a wall of white spots.

"You need to learn to be more grateful, you waste of space," he hissed.

Finally, after what seemed like forever, he released her. She fell to the floor like a sack of potatoes, crumpled and bruised. Gasping for breath, she leant back against the kitchen units, cradling one wrist in her hand. Eventually her vision returned and there was the familiar sight of him sitting on one of the dining chairs, his head in his hands. She took a deep breath and managed to stand up shakily, smoothing down the bottom of her dress with one hand. He looked up.

"I didn't mean to hurt you... if you didn't say what you said, I wouldn't have done..."

She stared at him for a few moments, steadying herself on the worktop. He was waiting for her to apologise as she always did, to insist that this was all her fault, and promise not to provoke him again. But at that moment, something inside her snapped. She realised that she didn't love or respect him at all. How could she respect someone who held so little respect for her?

Silently, she pressed her lips together, and left the kitchen.

CHAPTER EIGHTEEN

Lying on the sun lounger with her wireless headphones in her ears and a book balanced on her thighs, Charlotte could barely hear the commotion going on in the kitchen. She turned the page, enjoying the warmth of the sun on her skin. Suddenly, her bubble was broken. Movement in the corner of her eye caught her attention and she looked up to see Myles standing on the patio, a bright orange stain down his light blue shirt. She tried to stifle a grin.

"Hilarious, isn't it?! I'm going to have to change again before my meeting now, as if I wasn't already in a rush."

With her back to him, she rolled her eyes, pulling her headphones out and setting them down on the lounger with her book. She knew it was too good to be true. Just an hour to herself, before Myles went off on yet another overnight stay.

"Don't worry. I'll take over. You go and get changed."

He stalked in front, through the kitchen and out to the hallway. Charlotte's eyes widened at the sight that greeted her inside - her two year old was covered almost from head to toe in spaghetti hoops. She rolled her eyes again. It was hardly rocket science, getting a meal into her.

"Did Daddy let you hold the bowl again?" She murmured, reaching for a cloth and wiping down Izzy as best she could. "You're going to need a bath!"

"Bath time!" Izzy grinned, smacking her spoon on the tray.

"You are a cheeky girl! How did this happen, hey? You know how to eat nicely! You always eat nicely for me."

"Izzy dirty," Izzy held up her hands and stared at them. "Food... messy."

"Yes! Very messy!"

Charlotte pulled her from the highchair and peeled off her clothes, holding her at arms length until they reached the bathroom. She plonked her in the tub and turned the taps, swirling bubbles through the water as it filled. Izzy lay down and sloshed around in the water like a fish, the food dissolving and leaving only bubbles behind.

Myles peered around the door, fastening his cufflinks. Charlotte smiled at him, but his face was blank. "Oh, come on! It was an accident!"

"Yeah. Hilarious. Now I've had to faff around getting changed..."

"Well, you still have plenty of time, so there's no harm done! Lighten up a bit, she's only two!"

"I'd like to see you get covered in kids food and find it funny..."

"Oh, come on, Myles! I get covered in food most days. It's hardly the end of the world."

Rolling his eyes, he left the room. Satisfied that Izzy would be alright for a moment, happily splashing away in the water, Charlotte peered around the door into the hallway. Bent over, Myles was tying up his shiny shoes. She glanced back at Izzy, then quickly stepped out of the room.

"Are you going already?"

"Yes. Might as well. It's not like you appreciate me being here."

"Oh, don't be so silly! Of course we do."

She tried to snake her arms around his neck but he shrugged her away, lifting his briefcase from the carpet next to him.

She sighed. "See you on Thursday then?"

"Yes."

Before she could attempt to kiss him goodbye, he pushed past her and descended the stairs, leaving her alone in the hallway with a sinking feeling deep in her stomach.

***

"Don't forget your new bag!" Charlotte reached behind the front seats to retrieve Izzy's shiny new rucksack, one of her Christmas gifts.

To her surprise, Izzy didn't move. She looked down at her lap, her hands folded together and her hair half covering her face.

"Izzy?" Charlotte frowned. "What's the matter?"

"I don't want to go to school," Izzy muttered. "Can we go home? I want to stay with you."

Charlotte wrapped her arms around her. "Oh, Iz! Come on. This isn't like you. You've had three weeks off, normally you're desperate to go back!"

"I feel sick..."

Charlotte raised her eyebrows. "Oh, come on! You gobbled your breakfast up half an hour ago, you had seconds. Do you really expect me to believe that?"

"I do! Can we go home? Please?!"

Charlotte held her at arms length. Something was up. Izzy never behaved like this - she loved nursery. Normally, she went running in without a backwards glance.

"I know it's always disappointing when Christmas is over, but your friends will be pleased to see you! And your teachers. You'll have a great time."

Izzy said nothing.

"Has someone upset you at school? I can come and speak to your teacher, if they have?"

Izzy shook her head.

"Are you sure? You don't look happy, Izzy. Tell me the truth, please. Who's upset you?"

Izzy gulped, lifting her gaze to her mum's, her

hands still folded in her lap. Charlotte could see little creases in her forehead; she looked as though she had the weight of the world on her tiny shoulders.

"You can tell me anything, you know? Whatever it is, I won't be cross. And if you don't want me to say anything, I won't. It can be our secret."

"Are you sure? Do you promise?"

"Of course!" Charlotte reached for her daughter's hand and squeezed it. "Come on then - spit it out! What's up?"

Izzy bit her lip. "I'm scared, Mummy."

"Scared? Of what?"

"I don't want you to go."

"Izzy, it's the same school it was before the Christmas break. You'll have a wonderful time..."

"I'm not scared of school."

"Then what?!"

Izzy's eyes were swimming with tears. "I'm scared that Daddy's going to hurt you."

Her stomach turning upside down, every hair on Charlotte's body stood on end. Suddenly, her whole body felt freezing, as though she'd been dropped into an ice bath.

"What?" She whispered.

"Like he did last week."

Charlotte stared at her, speechless.

"I heard him shouting, and I heard you crying. In the bathroom."

Charlotte swallowed the huge lump in her throat. "I wasn't crying. I'm absolutely fine. We had a bit of an argument, but it's fine now - don't worry.

You mustn't worry. Daddy wouldn't hurt me..."

"But he does. I saw him before. He pushed you, and you got a bruise on your arm. You told me that I must tell someone if anyone pushes or hurts me at school, because it's bullying and it's wrong. So why does Daddy do it to you?"

Anxious and lost for words, Charlotte fiddled with the sleeves of her jumper.

"Daddy's not going to hurt me," she said eventually, forcing a smile. "I'm absolutely fine, Izzy. Daddy didn't give me a bruise, I fell and banged my arm on the radiator. And he didn't push me on purpose, it was an accident..."

"Are you sure?"

"Yes. You don't need to worry. It's a misunderstanding, that's all. What you think you saw... well, you didn't. Please don't think about it again."

After that, Izzy climbed out of the car and went into class, like she always did. Charlotte waved, a huge smile plastered across her face, and she managed to hold it together long enough to get back in the car and drive off. It wasn't until she reached the main road that the tears began to fall, and they wouldn't stop.

When she eventually parked the car, Charlotte realised that she'd been so consumed by her thoughts that she couldn't remember the journey at all. Gripping the steering wheel, she stared out of the passenger window at the house across the street. The driveway was empty and for a moment, she wondered whether the long drive had been wasted - perhaps he'd already left. But something kept her pressed to her seat, the engine off. A feeling. And after a couple of minutes, the front door opened.

Jake had been on the phone to his commanding officer when he heard the purr of the car engine outside. He knew that it was her without even checking. The hairs on the back of his neck stood on end. The call was important, but every bone of his body ached for her. He forced himself to concentrate on the call, stay professional, because he knew that if Charlotte did want him in her life, he needed to get himself sorted - get his own life back on track. His efforts were finally being rewarded. He would go to the barracks for a meeting on Thursday. Hopefully after that, he would be able to reintegrate with his platoon.

Once the call was finished, he opened the front door. He could tell that she was upset from the way her back arched in the seat, from the shadow of the make up smudged around her eyes - even though she was thirty or forty feet away. He stood tall in the doorway, then when she made no move to exit the vehicle he put the door on the latch and marched outside, down the driveway, across the road to her car. For the first time in a long time, he barely took in his surroundings, the only thing that mattered in that moment was her. She stared at him solemnly from inside, and he felt a pang of sadness in his chest when he saw how broken she looked.

He tried the door handle. It was locked. He

tried it again. Charlotte didn't move.

"Open the door?" He asked softly, tapping on the window. The tapping seemed to break her from her trance and she flinched, reaching for the door handle.

"Hey," he said simply, resisting the urge to reach for her now that the physical barrier between them was gone.

"Hello," she gulped, her bottom lip quivering slightly.

"Do you want to come in? Everyone's out. James and Kelly have gone back home, and Mum and Dad have gone away for a couple of nights. I bought them a hotel stay for Christmas. A spa break. You inspired that one!"

A weak, relieved smile spread across her face. "Yes. That would be nice."

Following Jake across the road and into the house, Charlotte locked the car behind her. She stuffed her trembling hands in the pockets of her navy coat and felt a wave of nausea rise up from her stomach, remembering the exact day Myles had bought her it. She had wanted the coat in brown, but Myles had insisted that the navy looked nicer. And as always, she had let his opinion override hers.

The door clunked heavily behind her and she folded her arms across her stomach, as though defending herself. The house was warm and homely, but her whole body was still trembling.

"I'll get us a coffee," Jake muttered, slipping his boots off on the door mat. "A strong one."

"Thank you," she copied, but she placed her boots perfectly parallel, on one shelf of the shoe rack. Then, she unbuttoned her coat and slowly withdrew one arm, wincing slightly as the bruised muscles in her back flexed.

"Are you ok?" Jake reached for her coat, which he hung on one of the free pegs.

She nodded, although her eyes betrayed her, filling with tears. Slowly, his hand crept towards hers, closing the distance between them. Their little fingers brushed together and she allowed his whole hand to engulf hers, closing around it. The first tear escaped and ran down her cheek, coming to rest on her jumper.

"What's happened?"

"I can't do this anymore..." she whispered.

"Can't do what?" Jake asked, suddenly nervous. He had been desperate to see her for weeks, but now she was here, he was petrified that this might be the last time. That she had made her decision. Was that why she was so upset?

"Lie. I need to tell the truth. All of it."

Pressing his lips together, he nodded slightly. "Ok. We could sit in the kitchen..."

Anxiously, Charlotte glanced behind her at the glass panes in the front door. "Can we go up to your room? I don't mean... I just think I'd feel safer up there."

"Of course. Do you want to go up and I'll bring the coffee?"

She nodded. "Thank you."

After squeezing her hand, he released it. "I'll be quick."

Charlotte padded up the stairs, towards his room. It had been years, but she didn't even need to think about where she was going - her legs took her all by themselves. She crossed the hallway and opened his bedroom door, the handle making the familiar squeak it had all those years ago. When she opened the door, her eyes travelled around the same furniture, the same bed, even the same curtains she remembered. The posters were gone from the walls and his possessions were more grown up - the room was certainly tidier than it had been when they'd last hung out in it, before they moved in together all those years ago. But the familiarity comforted her and she smoothed the duvet down, before perching on the edge.

Jake appeared in the doorway a couple of minutes later, a mug in each hand. He set them down on top of the chest of drawers then took a seat next to her, following her gaze around the room.

"It feels strange being back here," she smiled weakly. "It even smells the same."

"Mum still uses the same laundry powder."

"I can tell."

They sat in silence for another minute, before Jake caught her gaze. Slowly, his arm crept behind her and his hand came to rest on her hip. She flinched, causing him to jump back.

"I'm sorry, I didn't mean to overstep... you look like you need a hug, that's all..."

Charlotte shook her head. "No, I'm sorry. I didn't..."

"You don't have to apologise for the fact you don't want me to touch you. Not ever."

"It's not that I don't want you to touch me. In fact, that's all I want right now."

Surprised, Jake cupped her cheek with his palm, his thumb wiping the tears from her wet eyelashes. She closed her eyes and breathed him in, a feeling of safety and relief washing over her. She was on the edge, and she needed to jump. But she knew that once she did, there would be no going back. And she was terrified.

"So, Christmas wasn't great, then?"

"No. Christmas wasn't great."

Blinking back tears, she raised her gaze to Jake's, wishing that he would just kiss her. But he didn't. He wiped her tears again, then withdrew his hand, placing it in his lap. "Do you want to talk about it?"

She truly didn't know where to begin. Her daughter's words that morning had really brought it home to her, the fact that she had been lying to everyone all this time, including herself. She couldn't bury her head in the sand and do nothing anymore. In trying to do the right thing for her daughter, she had failed her.

"I don't know where to start."

Sitting back on the bed, Jake leant against the wall, bringing his knees up to his chest. "Take your time. There's no rush."

"It might be easier if I show you."

He frowned curiously. "Show me?"

She nodded. Slowly, she fastened her grip around one sleeve of her ochre jumper and pushed it up, slowly revealing a string of angry purple bruises. Jake's heart began to pound in his chest as soon as he saw them. He clenched his fists. "Did he do this…"

"Yes."

"Son of a…"

His voice trailed off as she replaced the sleeve and then reached for the bottom of the jumper, pulling it up over her head and then off her arms until she was sitting on his bed in only her jeans and bra, her long hair trailing down her chest and over her breasts. Jake gulped. In silence, she turned away from him until she heard him sharply suck in his breath, and she knew that he could see. She didn't have to explain.

Jake delicately traced his fingers over the huge, angry, multi-coloured bruise at the bottom of her back, his hand trembling. It was linear and he could see that she'd been forced against something hard. "Has this happened before?"

"A couple of times. But never like this."

She pulled her hair into a loose bunch. Tucking it over one shoulder, she revealed an older bruise at the base of her neck.

Jake felt sick. "How could he do this to you? You're his wife, he's supposed to look after you."

"It's not all his fault. I provoke him…"

"Can you hear yourself? You provoke him?

That's no excuse for him to lay a hand on you. Ever."

"I know. I'm tired of making excuses. I want this to end."

Jake nodded, tracing his fingers up her spine to the base of her neck. Charlotte felt the tingle of his skin against hers and she couldn't ignore it. She turned around, her hair still spilling over one shoulder, until their faces were merely inches apart.

He kissed her gently and sensually, as though trying to heal her. She reached her arms around his neck and pulled him close to her until the fabric of his t-shirt scuffed against her bare skin. Then she reached for the bottom seam and lifted it over his stomach, then his chest, then his head, until his torso was bare too and his scars were exposed.

"I wish we could rewind," she whispered. "Back to how it was then... when neither of us had these scars."

"Me too. That's all I want."

She moved her lips to his, wrapping her arms around his body, pulling him close. The warmth of his body against hers was soothing and she closed her eyes, taking a deep breath of him, trying to erase all the hurt and damage they'd both endured. Maybe for one day - even for one hour - it could be just like it was before. She could forget about everything and everyone else and just be with him, with Jake, the man she was supposed to be with all along.

They slipped out of the rest of their clothes and under the duvet, their bodies moving together sadly, their lips never once breaking contact. Jake could feel her, she was still the same girl he'd fallen in love with all those years ago, the one who had kept him going during his captivity.

"I love you," he mumbled against her skin, gently kissing an old bruise at the base of her collarbone. He didn't expect her to respond, but she did, and when she said that she loved him too, he felt like his heart was about to burst.

He held her afterwards for over an hour, neither of them wanting to move from the warmth of the other's body. Jake ran his fingertips through her hair, his other hand entwined with hers on his chest. "I'm not scared, you know. Of him. I'll do whatever it takes to keep you and Izzy safe."

Charlotte sighed. "You should be. I am. He has a lot of money, Jake. More than you or I could ever gather. If he wants something, he gets it. What if he takes her away from me?"

"He can't. She's not even his daughter."

"He'll find a way. And how will I manage without him? I know he's done some bad things. I know what he does to me isn't right. But Izzy has the most wonderful life, because of him. I know I have to do this... it's the right thing to do. I can't go through this anymore. But she's going to lose everything. What if she blames me? She's going to lose her home, her school, her friends... everything changes for her. And it's my fault."

"No, it's his fault. He broke your trust, the day he laid hands on you."

"What if this ruins her life?"

"She's four years old, Charlotte. She doesn't need a fancy school, or pony lessons, or whatever else your rich friends tell you she needs. Do you know, I've never been happier than right before I was deployed. We had nothing, did we, the two of us, besides each other? But we were happy, *so* happy."

"I don't want her to grow up with nothing. Like I did."

"She's *not* going to grow up with nothing. Because she has a family who love her, and she'll have a roof over her head and food in her belly, and I can provide for her, and for you, I promise you. And even if you decide you don't want me, because I do understand that I'm not the best bet for you two right now, you'll be a million times better off without him controlling you, and hurting you. It will only get worse. And she knows, she *knows* that how he treats you is wrong. At four years old. If you stay, all you're teaching her is that it's fine to put up with it, because of his money. Is that what you want her to learn?"

Charlotte shook her head. "No, of course it's not."

"Then you have to do this. You have to be brave. For her, and for you. You deserve to be happy."

Charlotte said nothing for a few moments, then she sighed. "You're right. I have to do this. But I don't know how... what do I do? I can't just up and leave out of nowhere..."

"Speak to a lawyer. I know a good one. Let me give her a call?"

CHAPTER NINETEEN

"Izzy's out of trousers," Myles declared, appearing in the doorway of the snug. "Did you do any washing this week, or…"

"Of course I did!" Charlotte frowned. "Are you sure? There were loads in there a few days ago…"

"Are you saying I'm making it up?"

"No… of course not… I can't believe she's got through them so quickly, that's all."

Myles huffed. "Well, if you can't find the time to keep on top of the washing, buy some more. I don't understand why you always make things so difficult for yourself. Forward thinking… that's all it takes. A bit of organisation."

Charlotte opened her mouth to reply, but quickly closed it. There was no getting through to Myles when he was like this. Anything she said in response would only make things worse. She had been walking on eggshells for weeks now, she could never seem to say the right thing no matter how hard she tried.

"Also, I thought you were going to go to the supermarket yesterday."

"I was... but Izzy was playing up, so I didn't get the chance..."

"Didn't get the chance?" Myles raised one eyebrow. "Really? But you're at home all day. I honestly don't know what you do all day, it's not like you have to keep on top of the cleaning. We have people in to do it!"

Charlotte clenched her jaw, bubbles of frustration rising inside her. "You don't know what it's like Myles, to look after her all day, drop her off... pick her up... take her to classes... it's relentless! Sometimes it's a task just to wash my hair..."

He said nothing then, staring at her for a while, but then his face softened. "Yes. You're right. I'm sorry. Forgive me."

Approaching from behind, he squeezed her shoulders firmly. "I know you find it hard. And I'm here to help, that's what I signed up for when we got married, wasn't it?"

Charlotte relaxed in his grip, relieved that the situation had been diffused. "No, I'm sorry. I will try harder, I promise."

"I know you will. Now, text me a list, and I'll pop to the shop now."

"Are you sure? I can go tomorrow..."

"No, you put your feet up. I'll go." He kissed her on the forehead. "I promised to take care of you, and I will."

***

"Are you sure you want to do this? We can reschedule for another time, when I can go with you..."

Charlotte smoothed the lapel of Jake's uniform, her stomach turning at the distant memory it evoked. She smiled weakly. "No. I need to do this. You go to your meeting, it's important."

He paused for a moment, his eyes searching hers for any sign that she needed him. But he could see it in her eyes - she was ready. "Walk through that alleyway, then turn right. You'll see it ahead, on the other side of the road."

"Thank you."

He pulled her into his arms, his breath tickling the hairs at the nape of her neck. Charlotte closed her eyes and took a deep breath, then withdrew from his grip.

"And you'll be alright... getting home?"

"Yes. I'll take the train back to where you picked me up."

"Don't forget to use cash to buy your ticket."

"I know. I will. Good luck for your meeting. Stay calm, whatever he says. Even if it doesn't go your way today... well, we both need to wait out, don't we? Play the long game. It'll be alright in the end."

Jake smiled briefly. "Yeah. You're right."

"Myles will be back this evening, so I won't be

able to call. But I'll give you a ring tomorrow, once he's gone to work."

"Ok. Good luck."

"You too."

Glancing back at Jake one last time, she climbed out of the car and closed the door behind her. Smoothing her coat, she crossed the carpark towards the alleyway, her heart pounding in her chest. Was she doing the right thing? She had thought of nothing but this meeting for the past few days, since she agreed with Jake that she would do it. But now it was finally here, fear was taking over her body again, and it took all her strength to put one heeled foot in front of the other and make it to the office.

Exactly where Jake had said, it wasn't hard to find. Charlotte climbed the stairs, the steady tap of her heels echoing around the empty corridor in time with the thud of her heart. She swung open the double doors at the top of the stairs and approached the reception desk.

"Hello," she forced a nervous smile. "Charlotte Bond. I'm here to see Ruhi."

The receptionist looked up with a warm, reassuring smile. "Hi, Charlotte. If you'd like to take a seat, I'll let Ruhi know you're here."

"Thank you."

Charlotte settled in one of the seats which overlooked a window. Hugging her coat around her, she watched the people passing by below, once again immersed in their busy lives after the Christmas break. She wondered how many of them were considering such a major life change for the new year.

"Mrs Bond?"

She looked up.

"Nice to meet you. I'm Ruhi."

Charlotte stood, her legs trembling underneath her body. She extended her hand. "Charlotte. Please call me Charlotte."

"Charlotte," Ruhi gestured down the corridor. "Follow me."

Once inside the meeting room, Ruhi closed the door. Charlotte took a seat at the desk, examining the sparse room around her. It was clean, almost sterile. Devoid of emotion.

"Would you like a tea or coffee?" Ruhi reached for the handle of a glass jug on the table. "Water?"

"No, thank you."

"Let's start at the beginning then. How can I help you?"

Charlotte stared at the wilting pot plant in the corner of the room. It looked desperate, trapped in this sparse room with no natural sunlight.

"Charlotte?"

She jumped slightly, realising that she'd been in a world of her own for a minute or two. "Sorry. I think… I'm thinking about leaving my husband."

Ruhi nodded gently, encouraging her to go on.

"You know who he is?"

"Yes. I do."

"You must think I'm crazy for even thinking about leaving a man like him."

"I don't think that at all."

Charlotte stared, then bowed her head, returning her gaze to her lap. "I know I should be grateful, for everything he's done for me. But I just... I don't think I love him anymore. I don't think I've loved him for a while. In fact..." she pressed her lips together, swallowing the lump that had formed in her throat. "I'm not sure I ever loved him at all. Not really. I didn't have a choice."

"About your marriage?"

"Yes... no... when I met him, I was in a terrible place. I had a small baby, my husband was missing in Afghanistan, everyone thought he was dead. I could barely manage, financially... physically... I was on the edge. Sometimes I walked down the street with the pram, and I watched the cars driving past, and I thought... no, I wished... I wished that one of them would lose control, swerve at us, take us out in one second..."

She reached across the desk for a tissue, ripping it from the box and dabbing at her eyes. "I'm ashamed to say that out loud. I've never told anyone that before."

"Don't be. It sounds like you went through an awful time."

"I am ashamed. My daughter... she's amazing. I look at her now and I can't imagine ever thinking like that."

"Having a baby is hard. Especially in circumstances like you've described."

Charlotte sighed. "It was. Impossibly hard."

"And so your husband... he offered you a way out?"

"Yes. But at the time, I believed that I loved him, I wouldn't have married him if I didn't. But now, looking back... I realise that I've only ever truly loved one man. And it's not Myles. I think... well, he actually saw me... treated me nicely, talked to me like an adult for the first time in weeks. And I fell in love with that. He was there, right when I needed someone. And he's been there ever since."

Ruhi nodded. "But now things have changed?"

Charlotte wriggled uncomfortably on the stiff chair. "I think I'm starting to see him for who he really is. He's not the man I thought he was."

"In what way?"

Charlotte lifted the jug, pouring herself a glass of water. "When Jake came back into my life and I started to spend time with him again, I remembered what life was like, before I met Myles... before I lost Jake... and I realised that I've lost myself along the way. And I think that Myles has been a large part of that.

"When we got together, everything was lovely... he was lovely. I was vulnerable, in a really bad place, and he offered me a way out. A safe, warm, home, all the things I wanted for Izzy that I couldn't afford on my own. I didn't have to go back to work, because he was happy to provide for us. I couldn't believe my luck. Then we moved to a completely different town, he reassured me that I could stay at home with Izzy, I didn't need to work. He introduced me to people who have become my only friends. He gave me a credit card, he said I could buy whatever I wanted. He got us a cleaner, signed me up for a gym membership, booked me hair and nail appointments... encouraged me to take care of myself. It was all great, for a while."

Ruhi was silent, patiently waiting for her to continue.

"And I know I sound ungrateful. I should be grateful to him for giving me all the things that he has, and I am... but I feel like I don't have my own life anymore. Everything I have is down to him. He says I can buy whatever I want, but I can't really... I only ever buy things if I think he'll approve. I even have my hair cut like this because he likes it, I have my nails done in the colours I know he likes. I have nothing of my own. He won't even let me work, because he says it would embarrass him, people thinking that he can't provide for me. But I'm lonely. He works away all the time. All the friends I have are his, I can't really confide in them. I don't have any family. And until Jake came back, I had nobody else..."

Inhaling deeply, she tried desperately to steady her nerves. "And I suppose... being with Jake has made me realise that some of the things Myles does aren't normal. And they're not right. And I thought I was protecting Izzy, making sure she has the childhood she deserves... but I think I've made a massive mistake. I'm teaching her all the wrong things. And now I'm petrified that I might lose her completely."

"Why would you lose her completely?"

"Because when Myles finds out..." Charlotte felt panic rise in her stomach, bubbling through the cracks in the strong exterior she had learnt to put on in public. "I need to know that I won't lose her. If there's any possibility that I'll lose her, I can't go through with this, do you understand?"

"What do you think Myles will do?"

"He's a millionaire. He'll get the best lawyer money can buy. And he'll try to take her from me, I know he will."

"Does Myles have parental responsibility for Izzy?"

"No. But you mustn't underestimate what he might do when he finds out I'm planning to leave him. He won't let this go. He's not used to not getting his own way. I'm absolutely terrified he'll try to get custody of her. He knows things about me that nobody else does. Horrible things."

"It would be very unusual for the court to award custody to a step parent. He can apply for a child arrangement order and the court may decide that it's in Izzy's best interests to spend some time with Myles, but it's unlikely he'd get full custody."

"I'm not opposed to him seeing her. I would never stop him from seeing her, he does love her and she loves him. But she's my daughter. Not his."

Ruhi nodded. "I understand. Please try not to worry, Charlotte. We can get the best counsel for you, someone who'll represent you in court and get the best result for Izzy. And remember that the court will be deciding what's in Izzy's best interests, not what Myles wants."

Charlotte took another sip of water. "When I met Myles, I was in a bad place. What if he uses that against me? To show that I'm an unfit parent? Would the court award custody to him then?"

"Only if they feel that Izzy is safer living with Myles now. Do you ever feel like that now?"

Charlotte shook her head. "No, never. I've been fine for a few years. I saw a psychiatrist when Myles and I first got together... Myles arranged it. They diagnosed postnatal depression. I had regular sessions for several months, and eventually, I started to feel better."

"Ok. That's really positive."

"But what if he gets that doctor to say things which aren't true? I'm always forgetting things, winding Myles up. Doing things wrong. Maybe the court would decide that she's better off with him after all... what if..."

Tears were streaming down her cheeks now and she stood abruptly, splashing the glass of water all over the table. "I'm sorry! See? I always mess things up. I shouldn't have come here, it was a mistake... I'm sorry to waste your time..."

"Charlotte, wait!"

Ruhi's voice echoed around the little room.

Her hand on the door handle, Charlotte pressed her eyes shut, wishing that it was possible to simply disappear, taking Izzy with her. Maybe that was what she would have to do - disappear, take Izzy a long way away, somewhere where Myles couldn't find them.

"You're not wasting my time. I'm here to listen and advise you. Please give yourself a chance to do this, to speak to me about all of this properly. Then at the end, if you decide you need more time, or you're not sure, or you don't want to do this after all, then that's completely fine. But give yourself a chance to make a decision. We can take this as slowly as you want. Even if you want to see me three or four times, and we simply go over things each time, and you still can't make a decision, that's completely ok."

Slowly, Charlotte loosened her grip on the door handle. She wiped her eyes with the back of her hand before turning back to Ruhi, who was now standing the other side of the desk.

"I've been doing this job long enough to know that appearances can be deceptive. You see a couple from afar and they look happy, comfortable with each other, in love even. But once you see them up close, you start to see the cracks. And you realise that everything's not as it seems."

Charlotte gulped, hovering by the door, her hand now by her side.

"And I wonder whether you're telling me the whole story... because you paint this picture of a husband who's saved you, who's given you everything... and you make it sound like it's all your fault, that you're the one who doesn't love him anymore, that you're the one that was a mess after Izzy was born, and the one who messes things up. But I wonder... is that because it's true, or is it because someone else is telling you that it is?"

For a few seconds, Charlotte's mind wandered to a time when Myles swiped their dinner plates clean off the dining table because she'd forgotten to pick his new watch up from the jewellers, then apologised, saying that he'd had a bad day; he hadn't meant to take it out on her, but the thought of his new watch had kept him going all day. Blinking hard, she remembered the resounding clatter the plates had made as they smashed all over the tiled floor. She'd felt terribly guilty, made him a fresh dinner and then the next day, made sure she was at the jewellers as soon as it opened.

"Are you afraid of him?"

Charlotte pressed her lips together, then opened her mouth to speak, but immediately the wind was knocked out of her as she remembered the time he'd shoved her against the bathroom sink one night when she'd become tearful, and couldn't explain why. *What have you got to be upset about? You live a life of luxury, women would kill to be in your position. You don't know how lucky you are.*

She pressed her eyelids together, ashamed of the tears that were gathering in her eyes. *Sort yourself out, for goodness sake. What's the matter with you?*

Turn off the crocodile tears. She fought the image of him out of her mind and opened her eyes to see Ruhi sitting in her chair again. "I think I am."

"It's going to be ok, Charlotte. I can help you. But I need you to be 100% honest with me. I need to know everything. Every tiny detail. If you're not up to that today, that's absolutely fine, but I need to understand what we're dealing with. And if you're in immediate danger, we can look at getting you a place in a refuge, move you and Izzy away from him..."

"No, that won't be necessary," Charlotte shook her head firmly, lowering herself back into her seat. "I can't take Izzy somewhere like that."

"You'd be safe. It would only be temporary. It's better to go to a refuge than be unsafe..."

"As long as he doesn't know what's going on, we'll be fine. He would never hurt Izzy. He loves her, like his own daughter. That's what makes this so difficult. I know I have to do this, because otherwise Izzy will grow up thinking that the way we are... the way he treats me... that it's normal. And I can't have that. But they adore each other, and this is going to blow her world apart."

Ruhi lifted her pen, and Charlotte took a deep breath. "From the beginning?"

"Please."

"Alright."

Charlotte opened her mouth, and then to her surprise, the words started to tumble out. And they didn't stop coming for almost an hour.

***

Jake stood to attention at the end of the room. Upon command, he marched forwards, his forehead up and his chest puffed out as he addressed his superior.

"Welcome back, Corporal Parsons. At ease."

Relaxing, Jake glanced at his section around him. He knew that the vast majority of his original section had moved on; in fact, besides Captain Williams, the only person he vaguely recognised out of the six young soldiers was a man called Taffy, who'd been a wet behind the ears private when Jake went missing, but had since been promoted to Lance Corporal. But being here, with his section, who were no longer people he recognised, was hard. He knew they'd have moved on, of course; five years was a long time in the army. People came and went. Progressed, moved to other companies, left the army altogether. Got blown to bits in Afghanistan. But it surprised him how unsettled he felt; almost like he was a young private again, meeting his first section for the first time, with Cam at his side.

"Thank you, Sir." He clenched his jaw, keeping his emotions in check.

"It's good to have you back. You lot are going to learn a great deal from Corporal Parsons. He'll have you up to speed in no time."

"Sir," came a resounding chorus in reply. Jake glanced around at the soldiers again. The vast majority of them were young, enthusiastic, probably only several months out of phase one training. His eyes locked with the private on his left's, who puffed up his chest, mumbling a respectful, "Corporal," at Jake.

It was nice to be respected. Jake breathed it in, allowing the private's nerves to boost his confidence, reassure him that he was back; a proper soldier, a corporal; someone the privates would look up to.

"Right, I'll leave you in the capable hands of Corporal Parsons. Parsons, report back to me at the end of the day, alright?"

"Yes, Sir."

Williams nodded and turned, his boots thudding across the room and down the corridor once he'd left.

"Get your kit. We're going on a run. Move."

The bark of Jake's voice got them moving. They obeyed like children, following his command perfectly. Within seconds they had their bergens on their backs, waiting for his next command. He stood in front of them, inspecting their uniforms, the shine of their newly polished shoes.

"Good," he nodded. "Do exactly as you're ordered, and we'll get along fine. Courtyard. Let's move!"

He followed them as they marched down the corridor, out into the courtyard and then assembled in a perfect line again. So they were fresh, but they were well disciplined. Could do with of a bit of tightening up here and there, but they were well rehearsed on the basics. Jake stood in front of the soldiers, with Taffy to his side.

"Taffy will set the pace. We're going on a ten miler. I don't want to see any of you flagging, do you understand? I'll be at the back, so don't think I won't notice."

"Yes, Corporal."

"Good. Move!"

They crossed the garrison at a good pace, then jogged through the gates and into the countryside. The pound of their boots in unison, together with the pressure in his chest felt strangely calming, and for the first time since he'd been recovered, Jake felt like he was where he belonged again. With his section - alright, not the same section he'd grown to love like brothers when they were in the Afghan desert, but *his* section all the same. This was day one, within a few weeks they'd all know each other well, and he'd have them working with him like a well oiled machine, ready to take on any task Captain Williams threw their way.

Once they were back at the garrison, Jake instructed the soldiers to take a shower. They fell out of line, marching off towards the shower block, leaving Taffy and Jake alone.

"It's good to have you back, Parsons," Taffy muttered.

Jake took a deep breath of air. "It's bloody good to be back."

"I wasn't sure if we'd see you again. After

what you went through, in Afghan."

Jake raised one eyebrow. "You should give me more credit, Taffy. I'm made of tougher stuff than that. I almost took a bullet for you once, remember."

"I know... I didn't mean... five years is a long time, that's all. It must have been one hell of a long five years, being stuck in that place, with them..."

"It was." Jake couldn't think of much else to say. "Now go and get a bloody shower, Taffy. You stink."

"Corporal." Taffy nodded, then jogged off in the direction of the shower block.

Shaking his head, Jake rubbed his hand through his hair wearily, clearing his throat at the stale smell radiating from him. He stank too. Marching across the tarmac, a satisfied feeling in the pit of his stomach, Jake sighed. It had been a good day. He went to his locker, retrieving his belongings, including his mobile. He stared at the screen momentarily, feeling slightly deflated at the lack of calls or texts. He knew that Charlotte wouldn't call him this afternoon - Myles was due home, and as soon as she got back she'd have to pick up Izzy - she couldn't risk being overheard. But he'd kind of expected a text. Only one - as she came out of the meeting, to let him know how it had gone.

CHAPTER TWENTY

Charlotte fell asleep as soon as her head hit the pillow. She was exhausted, the demands of a pre-schooler and a pushy husband taking their toll. But to-night, she was alone. She'd got Izzy to bed early, and Myles was working late, out at a dinnertime meet-ing. Charlotte had toyed with the idea of watching TV by herself for a few hours, choosing exactly what she wanted to watch while eating ice cream from the tub with a spoon, because there was nobody here to tell her to use a bowl and stop eating like a slob. But the thought of her cloud-like pillows and feather down duvet had been too much, and she allowed her mind to wander.

She had been asleep for a few hours when she woke with a jolt. The bed swayed as she felt a heavy weight fall onto it, startling her. Groggy with sleep she opened her eyes, but she could smell him from a mile off, his heavy aftershave mixed with the strong smell of alcohol.

"I'm home!" He announced, seemingly oblivious to the fact that she had been sleeping. Or maybe he didn't care. "Aren't you pleased to see me?"

He nudged her. Charlotte mumbled, her mind trying to persuade her back to sleep. She was still exhausted.

"I'm pleased to see you."

She felt his hands roam under the duvet, down her body, all the way from her chest down to her legs. She groaned. "Myles, don't."

"Myles, don't," he imitated, then chuckled. "What's the matter with you? Don't you love *me?"*

"You know I do," Charlotte mumbled. "But it's the middle of the night, I was asleep..."

"Oh, nonsense!" He flicked on the light. "It's only... only..."

He squinted at the alarm clock on the bedside table for a few seconds, his body swaying as his head spun. "Oh. It's half one. I didn't realise it was so late..."

"That's ok," Charlotte closed her eyes again, wrapping the duvet around her like a cocoon. "Get your clothes off, and come to bed. You have to be up early tomorrow."

"At last! There's *an offer I can't resist!"*

He stood up, his body leaning over, his balance shot to bits by the alcohol running through his body. Charlotte sighed, waiting for him to hurry up and turn the light off. Eventually, he did. He groaned, wriggling around in the bed, his head still spinning.

"Shit, I knew I should have gone easy on the

whisky."

She said nothing, hoping that if she didn't respond, he'd go to sleep. Unfortunately it didn't work.

"I was thinking," he turned to face her in the dark. She couldn't see him, because her eyes were shut, but she could feel his hot breath on her face and it made her stomach turn. "We should have another baby."

She was fully awake, then. "What?"

"A baby. A brother or sister for Izzy."

When Charlotte didn't respond, he sat up and snapped the light on again. Charlotte threw her arm over her eyes, shielding them from the burning brightness of the spotlights above the bed.

"Myles, please can you turn the light off?"

"We're having a conversation*."*

"We can talk with the light off. And can we talk about this tomorrow, please? You have another meeting in the morning and Izzy will have me up early. I'm exhausted."

"You're *exhausted?" He laughed exaggeratedly. "Yeah, alright then."*

"What's that supposed to mean?"

"Nothing, nothing," he muttered, then shoved his hand under the sheets until it was roaming unwelcome across her belly. "I think we should go for it. Why wouldn't we?"

"It's not a decision we should make, just like that. We need to talk about this properly, Myles. And now isn't the time, you've been drinking..."

"I'm perfectly in control of my mind, thank you very much. I don't need you going on at me because I've

had a few drinks."

"I'm not. But I don't want to have this conversation at two in the morning when you've been drinking heavily. We can talk about this tomorrow evening, when you're back from work."

"Well, what is there to talk about? I love you, you love me... Izzy would benefit a lot from having a sibling. We don't want her to grow up spoilt, do we?"

"She's not spoilt," Charlotte retorted. "She's fine as she is."

"Is she? How would you know?"

"Because she's my daughter."

"Oh... yes... there we have it again. She's your *daughter."*

Charlotte sighed. "Myles, that's not what I meant, and you know it."

"Of course it is. You're forever rubbing it in my face. You love to hold it over me, that she's yours*. As in,* not mine*. But you couldn't do that, could you, if we had another?"*

"You're being ridiculous. I've never held it over you at all. Izzy adores you, you're her dad. Regardless of her genes. And she's ours, she has been since you came into our lives. Where has all this come from, all of a sudden?"

Myles sighed. "Nowhere. I just want a baby with my wife. Why is that so hard for you to understand? What possible reason could you have for not wanting another? It makes perfect sense, while you're at home with Izzy anyway."

"Well... actually, there are plenty of reasons. But

like I said, we'll discuss this tomorrow."

"No, I want to discuss it now," Myles replied firmly. "What reasons?"

Charlotte hesitated. "Well... like I said before, as Izzy's getting older, I feel like it's almost time for me to get some of my life back. Maybe go back to work... she'll be doing more hours at nursery soon, I'll have more time..."

"I've told *you. You don't need to go back to work. I earn plenty for the both of us."*

"No, but..."

"Any other reasons?"

"I don't know if I feel ready... not after last time."

Myles sighed again. "Oh, Charlotte. It won't be like last time. You have me now, you'll have the best private medical care. You're not in the same place you were back then. And there are two of us , aren't there? I'm not going to disappear and leave you high and dry like that complete waste of space..."

Charlotte bristled, anger bubbling up in her stomach as she heard Myles talk about Jake like that. Not that it was entirely Myles's fault. She'd never told him the whole truth about Jake. As far as he was concerned, Izzy's father had disappeared during the pregnancy, because he couldn't face being a dad, leaving Charlotte pregnant and alone. She'd never found the right words to tell him the truth.

"Any other reasons, or is that all you've got?"

"Myles, it's not a point scoring exercise. It's not a decision to be taken lightly."

"I'm not a complete idiot, Charlotte. Don't patronise me."

"I'm not, but you're making it sound like having another child is the default decision unless we can think of a reason otherwise... actually, it should be the other way round. We should only even consider it if we're both absolutely sure."

"And I am, absolutely sure. And I can't think of a possible reason why you wouldn't be. It's not like you've got anything else to do. Now come on. Let's practice."

"Myles..." Charlotte squirmed away from his roaming hands, from his hot, stewing breath. "Not now! Get off me!"

"Come on, Charlotte. Don't be like that. You'll hurt my feelings."

"I said no, Myles. Because it's 2am and I want to go to sleep, and you've been drinking..."

His hands were round her wrists now and he was clambering on top of her clumsily, hurting her arms with the pressure of his fingers.

"Myles! What are you doing?! Get off me!"

"Shhh," he said, releasing one of her arms once his weight was on top of her, clamping his hand over her mouth. "I know you want this, Charlotte, as much as I do. Another baby, something for you to focus on. You're at home, it's the perfect time. Imagine it, the four of us. It would be perfect. Stop thinking of reasons why not, and start being more positive. After all I've done for you. It's not much to ask."

"Myles, I don't want..." she tried to talk through his hand, but it was pointless. She couldn't even hear

what she was saying, let alone expect him to understand her. "Please!" She wriggled in his grip, but it was pointless. He was a lot stronger than her, and the harder she struggled, the tighter he pressed down.

Eventually she lay silent and still on the bed, a single tear silently running down her face as he took what he wanted and then rolled off, groaning. She waited until his breathing had levelled and he was still, and then she turned onto her side, pulling her pyjamas up haphazardly as she rolled onto her side. Once he was snoring loudly she stopped holding her breath and let her desperate sobs escape, her stomach churning with the shock of what had happened. And the horrible realisation that their relationship had changed forever, diving in a direction from which it would never return.

***

Charlotte felt a lot lighter during the train journey home. Finally opening up to someone about how Myles had treated her was a huge relief, especially as it was someone independent, someone she could trust to give her an honest opinion. Opening up to Jake had been invaluable, but she knew that he would always side with her. Now that Ruhi was on her side too, she knew that she wasn't going mad. The way Myles treated her was wrong.

And there was a way out. It was not going to be easy, she knew that. She had a mountain to climb, one which was monumental and steep, rugged and dangerous, but once she got to the top there was fresh air, sunlight; she would be free. She could escape. There was a way for Izzy to have the life she deserved, and they would be safe. Charlotte could get herself back. She didn't have to grind her teeth and put up with being treated the way Myles treated her for the rest of her life. She'd have another chance at love with Jake. Eventually. Once she put Izzy first, once Izzy was settled and it was time for them to move on.

She hummed along to the radio all the way to school, listening to a station that she never listened to, full of the latest upbeat music. She didn't know the words. But she didn't care. She had another person in her corner. She was going to be ok.

All the way home, Charlotte listened to Izzy's animated chatter; what she'd done that day, what she'd eaten for lunch, the treasures she'd found when the class went out for a walk in the woods after lunch. Charlotte nodded along, making encouraging noises in all the right places, but suddenly, all she could think about was how Izzy was going to react to being torn away from the life she knew. The situation should be far better than she'd originally envisaged - they'd be ok, they'd have a decent home, Izzy may even still be able to attend the same school. But Izzy loved Myles, and as far as she knew, he was her dad. How was Charlotte going to break the news that he wasn't?

"Mummy? Are you ok?"

Charlotte turned to her daughter, whose face was full of concern. She realised that her eyes were watering. "Yes! Of course I am, my eyes are a little itchy today. I think it's the new make up I bought. It doesn't agree with my eyes."

"Good. I thought you were sad!"

"Of course not. I'm happy. Happy to see you! Now, what would you like for tea this evening?"

"Can we have... spaghetti bolognese?"

Charlotte nodded. "Of course. Garlic bread, too?"

"Yes, please!"

Grinding to a stop on the driveway, Charlotte's stomach lurched. Right in front of the house was Myles's car. He wasn't due back until later that evening, after Izzy's bedtime.

"Daddy's home!" Izzy squealed excitedly. "I thought he wasn't coming home until tonight!"

"He wasn't..." Charlotte found herself frowning, but she forced a smile. "He must have caught an earlier flight and surprised us!"

"Yay!" Suddenly, Izzy's face fell. "We'll have to have something else for dinner. Daddy hates spag bol."

"I'm sure he can live with it, for one night."

"Do you think?"

"Yes. He'll be pleased to see you, I'm sure he won't care what's for dinner."

They climbed out of the car and Charlotte locked it, before swiping her fob on the front door lock to open it.

"Daddy!" Izzy skipped down the hallway, peering into each room excitedly. "Daddy? I'm home!"

"Izzy!" Charlotte heard him greet her from inside the kitchen. She hung up her coat and slipped off her boots, glancing at her phone before she slipped it inside the pocket of her jeans. Nothing from Jake. She wondered how his day had gone. She couldn't wait to fill him in on the meeting with Ruhi.

Taking a deep breath, Charlotte smoothed her hair then forced a smile, padding down the hallway and into the kitchen.

"You're home!" She beamed. "I wasn't expecting you until ten."

He stared at her cooly for a couple of seconds, making her stomach lurch. But then, to her relief, his face relaxed into a smile. "I got an earlier flight. I missed you both, and my meeting this afternoon was cancelled. So I thought, why not? I thought I'd surprise you both!"

"Lovely," Charlotte smiled through gritted teeth, watching Myles lift Izzy and fly her through the air like a plane. "Izzy's asked for spaghetti bolognese tonight. I know you don't like it... perhaps I could cook you something different?"

"Oh, no, that's fine," Myles replied, planting Izzy back on the floor. "I'm not that hungry anyway, I had a big lunch. I only want a small portion."

"Right," Charlotte nodded, slightly uneasy at his sudden personality transplant. He was never this easy going, at least not unless he'd hurt her or done something else he needed to make up for. "I'll start cooking, then."

"Izzy, why don't you go upstairs and get changed?" Myles suggested. "I left some presents in your room. Some things to try on. Perhaps you could try them all on?"

"Presents?!" Izzy shrieked with excitement. "Thank you, Daddy! Thank you, thank you, thank you!" She thew herself into his arms.

He chuckled. "You're welcome. Now go upstairs, be a good girl."

Charlotte pulled open the larder cabinet and retrieved a couple of onions, then withdrew some tomatoes and herbs from the fridge. She began to chop, trying her best to breathe steadily even though her heart was pounding in her chest. She had become used to living a double life over the past few months, but this - this was completely different. In a matter of weeks, a letter would arrive that told Myles the truth. That Charlotte was escaping his clutches, that she wanted a new life. And she and Izzy would be far away, at least to start with, while he digested the news. Before then, Charlotte had a lot to do. She needed to squirrel away what she could, start moving some of their essential possessions somewhere safe. She still needed to talk to Jake about that. Hopefully, his parents would allow her to keep some of their things in their loft for a while.

"So, what have you been doing this week? Anything interesting?" Myles asked, opening the cabinet behind her with a clunk, retrieving some glasses. Their firm tap on the worktop echoed through her ears as he set them down, then the cork popped and the wine splashed into the glasses.

"Oh, not much. You know. The usual."

Her shoulders tense, she roughly chopped the onion and wiped it off the chopping board with the knife, into the frying pan. "Same old."

"Mmm."

Izzy was quiet upstairs. It was silent in the kitchen too, except for the steady chop of the knife against the chopping board. Charlotte could just about hear her own heart, drumming in her chest.

"Did you go anywhere interesting today? Anywhere out of the ordinary?"

Her stomach lurched but she retained composure, not faltering whilst chopping the tomatoes. "Nope. Just got my nails done. I went for the lilac, I know you like that."

"Mmm. Where did you go?"

"Sinead's. Same as always."

Behind her, she heard him exhale deeply. The hairs on the back of her neck stood on end as his breath tickled her skin. Body tense, she held her breath, but let it out a few seconds later when she heard the clink of the glass being placed on the worktop beside her.

"Thank you," she forced a smile.

"You're welcome."

She wiped the chopped tomatoes off the board, into the pan, then returned to the fridge for some minced beef. After opening the packet, she turned the hob on. The pan was sizzling within seconds.

"So you didn't go anywhere else today?"

Charlotte gulped, but shook her head breezily. "No. Just to school, then got my nails done... grabbed a coffee and sat with a magazine for a while, across the road from the nail bar. Then I had lunch and went back to school."

"Are you sure?"

Her heart was now pounding so hard in her chest she thought it might split open. But she frowned as she faced him, trying her best to look completely unruffled. "What's with all the questions, Myles? I feel a little like I'm being interrogated..."

"I do apologise. I'm interested, that's all."

Charlotte nodded, smiling with relief. "That's alright. Sorry, I didn't mean to sound huffy..."

"Not at all."

Gently, he set his glass down on the worktop, its rich contents glowing under the hanging lights which lit up the kitchen island.

"I do have one more question though, if I may."

Charlotte stirred the contents of the pan. "What's that?"

"If you went straight from school to have your nails done and then you went for a coffee, and you went nowhere else before you picked Izzy up... what were you doing in Castleton, in the other direction?"

Charlotte continued to stir, pushing so hard with the wooden spoon she thought it might splinter and snap. How did he know? "I don't know what you mean..."

Feeling her cheeks flush, she fixed her eyes on the pan. She could absolutely not give anything away to him.

"I was nowhere near Castleton..."

"Oh, don't give me that *shit,* Charlotte."

Without warning, his grip fastened around her wrist and he spun her, causing her to drop the spoon with a clatter. "You better start talking, and fast."

"Myles, please..." Charlotte tried to talk steadily, but she was suddenly so petrified, she thought she might faint. She was out of her depth.

"I *said,* what were you doing in Castleton? And I want the truth. I want in now. Because whatever you say can't be any worse than what's playing out in my head right now."

Charlotte stared at him, her hand tingling, deprived of oxygen. She tried to wriggle from his grip and return to the pan - she could smell that the meat was starting to brown. "It's going to burn..."

The pressure of his grip only intensified. "I said, *start talking.*"

Charlotte heard the pad of footsteps across the landing above their heads and she swallowed hard, trying to compose herself. "Can we discuss this later? Izzy is upstairs..."

"No, we cannot. We discuss this right here, right now."

The strong smell of burning meat made Charlotte's stomach turn. "Myles... the dinner..."

"I don't give a *shit* about the dinner!" He roared, shoving her out of the way.

He grabbed the pan and hurled it at the opposite wall, splattering the contents up its pale greyness. With an ear splitting crash, it hit the floor, then clanged on the tiles below.

"Myles, for God's sake! Calm down! Think about Izzy..."

"Think about Izzy?" He roared. "Think about Izzy?! Well I've heard it all now. You're the one who's lying, who's putting Izzy at risk. *You!* Not me."

"I would *never* put Izzy at risk," Charlotte stood up to him, although as soon as the words left her mouth she knew it was a lie. She had put Izzy at risk. The day she'd moved in with Myles, given up her independence and allowed herself to rely on a man who would end up controlling every part of their lives.

"Alright, I'll make this easier for you," he grabbed her by the hair, ignoring her yelp as he steered her around the kitchen island and slammed her against the fridge, still grasping a handful of her hair. "I know exactly where you've been, and I suspect I know exactly why you went there. What you were hoping to achieve from your meeting with Castleton's finest solicitor's firm?" He let out a strangled laugh. "Jesus, Charlotte. If you want to clear me out, you'll have to do better than that!"

"I don't want to clear you out," Charlotte yelped again as he tugged her hair.

"Liar!"

"I don't."

"Then, is there someone else? You want out from this, because you want in somewhere else?"

"Myles, please... let's talk about this, like rational adults."

"DON'T PATRONISE ME!"

He showered her with saliva, his booming voice echoing through her chest like waves. Closing her eyes, she tried to find the energy to stand up for herself, the energy she used to have before she let him take over her. She was not always this weak.

"Alright! You want the truth? Then you let go of me. And I'll tell you, I'll tell you all of it."

He contemplated it for a moment. Then, finally, he released her. Charlotte toppled against the fridge, scrambling to stand up tall, smoothing her hair back into place. "But I want Izzy out of here. I'll call Effie, she can stay there this evening..."

"What, and let you off the hook? I'm not an idiot, Charlotte. I'm not letting you run away from this. From us."

"I'm not running anywhere," she said, more confidently than she felt. "But I don't want Izzy to be frightened or upset."

Suddenly, the sound of little sobs in the hallway seemed to break Myles from his rage for a few seconds. He scowled at Charlotte before striding across the kitchen. Charlotte took her chance. She reached into her back pocket for her mobile, and quickly typed a message. She had seconds before he came back. She had barely pressed the send button when she heard Izzy's footsteps back up the stairs, and hastily slid the phone into silent mode before slamming it back on the worktop. Seconds later, Myles reappeared in the kitchen, firmly closing the door behind them.

"She's gone upstairs. I told her to put the TV on in our room, and shut the door. She won't hear a thing."

"I don't want her to hear this, Myles. Please..."

"Don't you tell me what to do!" He spat, pointing his finger straight at her chest, as though it was a loaded gun. "You lost the right to have any say in this the moment you walked across the threshold of that law firm, and told them you want to leave me." He laughed again. "I still can't believe this, you know. After everything I've done for you. All the money I've spent, putting a roof over your head, over her head. All the school fees I've paid, so your little brat can have an education that's worth something."

"Don't talk about her like that!" Charlotte retorted fiercely. "None of this is her fault! None of it! And she loves you!"

"Yeah, she does. And you know what? You need to rethink this decision of yours. Because guess what, I'm the one holding the cards here. If you leave, you lose her. End of. You can't support her! You can't support anyone, not even yourself. Have you forgotten the state you were in when I took you in? A complete mess. You don't even have a job!"

"I'm not that person anymore, Myles. I was unwell. I had postnatal depression..."

He shook his head. "No, some people can't handle what life throws at them. You tried to look after her, and you failed. As you will now, if you try to cope without me. You're *nothing* without me, Charlotte! Nothing! No wonder that waste of space left you. He must have known what a terrible mother you'd be, and he didn't want to be stuck with a baby, so he escaped while he could..."

The crack of her palm against his cheek stopped him dead. He stared at her, shellshocked. "Don't you talk about him like that! You know *nothing* about him. *Nothing!*"

"No?" He laughed. "Good slap, by the way. I wouldn't even have thought you were capable of that. I've not seen you actually fight for anything since the day I met you, miserable and alone in that cafe. I know he left you, with Izzy. To rot. You had nobody when you met me, nobody. And nothing! And here you are, about to throw everything away, you're stupid as well as ungrateful! I will take everything from you! Everything! You'll never see that daughter of yours again."

Rage bubbled up inside Charlotte like a pressure cooker. Staring into his cold, hateful eyes, she realised that she couldn't like him any less, let alone love him. Before she knew what she was doing she reached behind her, her hand closing around the cold metal handle of the saucepan she'd filled with water, ready for the spaghetti. Gripping it hard, she used all her strength to swing it in front of her, taking Myles by surprise. She heard the crack of his skull as the hard metal pan hit him. He fell to the floor like a sack of potatoes, still and lifeless on the floor in the cold puddle.

She dropped the pan with a clatter. "M... Myles?"

He didn't move. Trembling, she bent down slowly, holding her breath, barely able to look at him. He was perfectly still. She couldn't see his chest rising and falling at all - he looked like he was made of stone. Reaching to feel the pulse in his neck, she saw blood starting to pool around the back of his head on the tiles, dark red like spilt wine. Hands clamped over her mouth, she let out a little cry, staggering back in horror.

It was too late. He was dead. And she had killed him.

Her whole body now shaking, she edged around the kitchen unit to see her mobile still on the side. She reached for it and was about to call for an ambulance when she saw six missed calls on the screen, all from Jake. She froze. Maybe she should call him back first? What if an ambulance brought the police, and they took her away? What if they thought all this was her fault, and they took Izzy away? Her blood ran cold and she lifted the phone to her ear, willing him to pick up on the first ring when suddenly, something hard contacted with her arm, swiping her phone to the ground, smashing the screen into a thousand pieces. She fell back against the worktop, shocked to find Myles in front of her, his face a picture of absolute fury.

She barely had time to squeal before his hands were around her throat and he pushed her to the floor, squeezing tighter and tighter with every second that passed.

"You'll never win," he muttered to her as she spluttered and kicked, using all her strength to try to flip him over, but despite his recent head injury he was still impossibly strong. She fought with all her strength, the whiteness of the kitchen ceiling above her disappearing into blackness, soon replaced with thousands of technicolour dots as he squeezed the life out of her. Opening her mouth, she tried to beg, but she couldn't get the words out, his grip was too strong. She tried to plead, she tried to beg. She gasped, choked.

She couldn't breathe.

Thrashing about on the floor, a couple of times she almost knocked him off balance, but he was absolutely raging, stuck in a trance, his hands locked around her throat so tightly she knew that it was fruitless.

She was going to die.

On the kitchen floor, with Myles on top of her, her daughter upstairs. Izzy. Tears ran down Charlotte's cheeks as she pictured the look on her daughter's face when she found out her mother was dead. She was going to grow up without either of her real parents, like Charlotte had. Full circle.

Choking, Charlotte used the last of her strength to turn her head, trying to writhe out of Myles's grip, but it was too late. She was too weak. A second before she lost consciousness, her eyes fell on the doorway, which was now open. Their eyes connected for a split second and she knew it was her even though she couldn't see her properly, strange shapes were dancing across her vision and the pressure in her brain was so intense, she felt like it might blow apart at any second. Using the last of her strength to mouth *'I love you'*, she gave up, her limbs still and her eyes closed as she finally allowed him to win.

CHAPTER TWENTY ONE

Charlotte perched on the sofa, the tablet in one hand, a glass of water in the other. It was so tiny. It amazed her how something so minute could be so powerful.

"Charlotte? Are you alright? Are you having second thoughts?"

"No."

Before she could change her mind, she opened her mouth and knocked back the tablet, swallowing it quickly with a couple of gulps of water. Then she set the glass back on the table in front of her firmly. "I hate swallowing tablets, that's all. But it was fine."

The nurse smiled kindly. "Ok. Do you want to talk about anything?"

"No, I'm absolutely fine. Thank you. Can I go now?"

"The doctor would like you to stay here for a little

while, just for half an hour or so. And then I'll get your prescription for the second dose, you'll need to take it tomorrow."

"Right. Thank you."

"If you'd like to take a seat in the waiting area outside, I'll bring the prescription shortly."

Within an hour Charlotte was heading home, the life-changing paper bag perched on the passenger seat next to her. She fastened her grip on her steering wheel, trying not to think about what was currently going on inside her. It was for the best. She'd agonised over this, but she knew it was the best option.

Two weeks ago, Charlotte had discovered that she was pregnant. She hadn't even needed to take a test; she knew, from the dull ache deep in her abdomen and the tender fullness of her breasts. From the way she burst into tears at the end of an animated film Izzy was watching. And she had cried every day since. She had never before understood how any woman could abort their baby. She had never even considered it when she was pregnant with Izzy, even though she was on her own, reeling from the loss of her husband when she found out.

But this time was different. Charlotte had never wanted this baby, she had actively tried to avoid this baby. But it had happened. Myles had got his own way. And Charlotte knew that she had to do something. She couldn't spend every day of the rest of her life looking after a constant reminder of what Myles had done to her in order to create it. Every time she tried to reason with herself, think about the lovely things having a newborn would bring - it was all she could see, and all she could feel. Myles's hand clamped over her mouth as he forced her down on the bed, taking what he wanted. She knew that if she had this baby, that was all she would think about, every time she looked at him or her, for the rest of her life.

After a few minutes, Charlotte pulled into a leafy layby, lined with green trees. She wondered how many weeks it would be before their leaves started to crisp and fall off, littering the ground with an array of autumn colours.

She reached for the bag on the passenger seat, pulling out the box containing the misoprostol together with the box containing three months' worth of contraceptive pills. She was not going to allow herself to get into this situation again. This would buy her a bit of time, until she could talk to Myles rationally about this. She didn't want another child. Not now, and possibly not ever.

After slipping the boxes back into the bag, she reached for her handbag and tucked the bag inside, then retrieved her mobile. She dialled the number she needed, and lifted her phone to her ear. Flicking her hair back, she sighed, relieved that she could get back to all the things she needed to do.

"Amber! Hello, it's Charlotte. How are you?" She smiled. "Ah, that's great to hear. Listen, I need to order a cake. It needs to be extra special..." she paused, waiting for Amber's reply. "Excellent! I need it for Friday, please."

***

Elated from the day's events, Jake was singing along to the radio so loudly, he almost didn't notice his phone when it bleeped on the passenger seat next to him. Glancing at it, his stomach lurched.

He knows.

His blood ran cold. Immediately, he picked up his phone and jabbed at it, trying to keep his eyes on the road as best he could while his index finger scrabbled for the call button. He found it. It went straight to voicemail. Cursing, he slammed his fist against the steering wheel, his elation quickly dissipating, forced out by panic. And he knew. Deep in his gut, that something wasn't right.

Charlotte was in trouble.

Forcing the car off the carriageway and onto the hard shoulder, he slammed the brakes on as he tried to call her again, without success. He jabbed at the screen of his phone, inputting her address, which was now ingrained in his mind, as quickly as he could. Her house was twenty minutes away from his current location. Twenty minutes?! What if he wasn't quick enough? He felt violently sick at the realisation that he might be too late.

Driving twenty or thirty miles an hour over the speed limit, Jake thrashed his car to its limit. It was new, his other one having died just after Christmas, but it was another rust bucket, only marginally better than the last. Still, it did him proud, zipping down the motorway at a touch over ninety, then clunking round the corners of the country roads which approached her house at almost eighty. A couple of times he felt the tyres squeal as the car banked round a corner at speed, but he managed to recover each time, focused only on getting to Charlotte and Izzy. What if he was too late? What if Myles had done something to Charlotte, or Izzy, or both of them? What if he never got the chance to show Charlotte how much he still adored her, or prove to Izzy that he could be a good dad?

Screeching to a stop at the end of their drive, the big electric gates blocked him from entering. He considered ramming them open, but the gates looked stronger than the bumper of his car and he knew that if Charlotte was here and she was in trouble, she might need his help to exit quickly. A car which had lost a fight with an electric gate wouldn't be of any use. Still in his army fatigues, he expertly scaled the wall next to the gates, landing with a thud on the other side. Then he sprinted up the driveway, his heart in his mouth as he passed both cars sitting on the driveway, engines cold. They had been there a while.

The door was locked. For the briefest moment he hesitated - what if Charlotte was sat down with Myles talking properly about this, and he suddenly burst in? Would it make things worse? But deep in his gut, he knew it was far worse than that. She was in danger. And he didn't have time to wait.

He tried to call her again, but it went straight to voicemail, like it had the last twenty times. So he made his decision. There were two stone statues at the bottom of the steps. Using all his strength, he lifted one and staggered up the stairs, then hurled it through one of the ground floor windows, splintering the glass in a perfect bullseye. He used the other statue to push it through, then carefully climbed through the jagged frame, taking care not to impale himself on the shards of glass that remained.

"Charlotte?" He yelled frantically, pounding across the plush living room carpet in his muddy boots. He emerged into a hallway. The house was quiet. He couldn't hear anything apart from the sound of his pulse raging in his ears. "Charlotte?!"

He swung open a couple of doors that led off the hallway, but the rooms were empty. At the far end of the hallway was another door, but this one was open. He turned the corner and reeled back in horror at the sight that greeted him. He was too late.

Swearing, he rushed forwards, ignoring the collapsed heap of the man next to her as he reached Charlotte and cradled her in his arms, a strangled sob escaping his throat. "Charlie, can you hear me? Please open your eyes."

She was unresponsive, her neck all shades of purple and red, all the colour drained out of her face. At first, Jake thought she was dead. But when he lent down, his cheek close to her mouth and nose, he was relieved to feel the faint puff of her slow breath against his skin.

"You're alive. Thank God. I'm so sorry. I should have been here. I'm so sorry."

His eyes travelled to Myles, sprawled on the floor a couple of metres away, his hair matted with blood and his shirt completely bathed in it. What had happened here? Pulling his phone from his pocket, Jake dialled 999. Within seconds he'd requested two ambulances. Whilst talking to the operator, he unfastened his fatigues and pulled off the t-shirt he wore underneath, curling it up into a makeshift pillow to put under Charlotte's head as he rolled her into the recovery position. Then he moved onto Myles. Rolling up his shirt, he found a stab wound at the bottom of his back; the knife lay centimetres away. Jake gulped, wondering how desperate Charlotte must have been to plunge it there.

The man was still alive, but clinging on by a thread. As much as Jake despised him, if there was a chance he might survive and live to face what he'd done, Jake was going to make damn sure he did. Pressing a nearby tea towel to the wound to stem the bleeding with his left hand while firmly holding Charlotte's hand with his right, Jake looked up, his eyes catching movement under the coffee table across the room. He gasped in shock.

There was a fourth person in the room. Tiny and trembling, curled up in a ball, her hands and skirt covered in blood. Jake's eyes travelled to the wound beneath his hands, still seeping even when he held pressure on it. He knew that he couldn't let go; the guy would bleed out in less than a minute if he did. If he'd arrived two minutes later, he'd probably be dead already.

"Hi," Jake said hesitantly, trying his best to force a friendly smile, even though smiling was the last thing he wanted to do right now. "I'm Jake. What's your name?"

Silently, she looked up, her eyes wide and glassy with shock. At that second, her blood and tear-stained face reminded Jake of two things. One, she was the picture of her mother the day he'd sat next to her in the school playground, and given Billy Kemp a fat lip. Two, she looked as petrified as a young lad he'd found hiding in an empty barrel in Afghanistan, lucky to have stayed hidden while his entire family were lined up and shot dead. "It's Izzy, right?"

Slowly, she opened her mouth. "How do you know?"

"I'm... a friend of your mum's."

"Is Mummy dead?"

"No," Jake felt like a knife twisted in his stomach. "No, she's not dead. She's sleeping."

"I tried to wake her up, but she won't."

"I know. Mummy's in a really, really deep sleep right now. But she'll wake up. You'll see."

She stared at his blood stained uniform for a few seconds, then she spoke again. "Are you a soldier?"

"Yes. I am."

"Soldiers kill people, right? Bad guys?"

"Uh..." Jake hesitated, wondering where this was going, but then he nodded. "Yes."

"Have you ever killed someone?"

He frowned. "I er... I don't think this is... where are we going with this?"

"If you kill the bad guy, that doesn't make you bad too, does it? Because you have to stop the bad guy, to stop him hurting others?"

"No, it doesn't make you bad."

She nodded, a flash of relief crossing her eyes. "Ok."

"There's this thing called self defence... it's not the same thing to hurt someone if you're using reasonable and proportionate force to defend yourself, as it is to hurt someone deliberately."

Izzy stared at him blankly.

"So your mum, she had to defend herself, didn't she? Because he was hurting her? Is that what you're trying to say?"

Izzy said nothing, but tucked her knees up to her chest again, hiding behind them like a shield.

"I need someone to help me," Jake said. "An ambulance is coming, but I can't do all this on my own. Can you help me? With your mum?"

Slowly, Izzy nodded. Creeping out from under the table, she crawled across the floor until she was within touching distance.

"Can you hold your mum's hand for me? Talk to her? She can hear you. She'd like to hear you."

Nervously, Izzy clambered off the floor and edged over to Charlotte, then tucked herself in the little gap between her body and the kitchen units. Gently, she stroked the hair off her mum's face and gave her a delicate kiss on the cheek. Then she looked up at Jake and gave him a slight smile. Jake scanned her face - could he see anything of himself in her? He wasn't sure that he could. She was the spitting image of Charlie when she was little. She was wearing the same smile that Charlie flashed at him, that day in the playground. He had been addicted to that smile ever since.

Jake reached for another tea towel, but there wasn't one. The closest thing he could find was an oven glove. He clamped it over the wound, dropping the blood stained towel with a squelch onto the floor. It was dirty, but he'd used worse to stem bleeding in Afghan. With a bit of luck, this abhorrent man would get sepsis and writhe in agony for days. "Was your dad hurting your mum?"

Slowly, Izzy nodded. "He had his hands around her neck. Like this," she placed both her hands around her throat, squeezing gently. "She was crying, she was really scared. I thought she was going to die."

Izzy's eyes filled with tears, and all Jake wanted to do was wrap his arms around his daughter and pull her close to him, hold her tightly and promise that he'd always look out for her, no matter what. But he couldn't. The poor kid was confused and upset enough already.

"She's not. Like I said, she'll be ok. She's brave and strong, your mum. Way stronger than me."

Curiously, Izzy frowned at him. "But you're a soldier?"

He nodded. "Yes."

"Soldiers are brave."

"Not as brave as your mum. Trust me."

The approaching sound of sirens was music to Jake's ears. Help was on the way. After wiping his bloody hand on his fatigues, he reached over to Charlotte's face, relieved to feel the steady puff of her breath against his blood stained fingers. "She's ok. See? If you put your hand here," he placed Izzy's hand gently on Charlotte's back, "you can feel her breathing."

Izzy nodded, but she still looked unsure.

"You're a great helper. I think you could give some of our medics a run for their money."

She grinned at him then, her hand still gently clutching her mother's back. "I'd like to be a soldier. When I'm older."

"Is that right?"

"Yes."

"Do you know how to open the gates?"

Izzy shook her head. "No. I can open the front door, though. Sometimes Daddy lets me."

"Ok. Can you do that, then? I'll see if I can find the button for the gates. We're a good team, hey?"

"Yes, Sir!" She mock saluted before leaving the room, a glimmer of her usual self shining through despite the circumstances.

Scrambling off the floor, Jake glanced quickly back at Charlotte before leaving the room to find the control panel for the gates. It didn't take him long. Within thirty seconds he'd found it. Within another minute, the sirens echoed through the hallway as Izzy opened the front door to greet the paramedics who screeched to a halt on the driveway and jumped out, rushing through to the pair of bodies - Jake shuddered at the thought - patients - sprawled on the floor.

Then, he fell apart.

Jake's head pounded with the echo of the sirens, the flashing lights, the urgent voices of the paramedics who assessed the casualties they found in front of them. The frightened little girl who cowered in the corner, almost unnoticed, as medical packs were unzipped and wounds were examined. Jake's legs wobbled. He collapsed against the wall, realising too late that he had blood all over the backside of his fatigues and had smeared it up the light coloured paint.

He watched them place an oxygen mask on Charlotte, immobilising her neck and carefully edging her onto her back so they could examine her properly. When they cut off her clothing he could see them, all over her body, bruises and cuts, both fresh and old, like a map across her body. A map of all the dark places she'd been over the last five years.

Then someone started to ask him questions. Why was he here, when had he arrived, what had he seen? Had he smashed the window? How did he know Charlotte and Myles?

It took every ounce of strength he had left to answer their questions. He barely noticed an almost hysterical woman stumble into the kitchen and scream, her hands clamped over her mouth, her belly so swollen she looked as though she was about to give birth on the kitchen floor. She was led away by an officer with an arm around her shoulder, then after a few moments he could hear the buzzing of radios in the hallway and upstairs, as officers searched the house. Finally, someone noticed Izzy, still cowering under the table, her knees drawn up to her chest and her forehead resting on her knees, covering her eyes, her hair over her face like a shield.

Jake watched the officer try to get Izzy to talk for a minute or two. He could tell that she was petrified, the officer was making it worse. Opening his mouth, he started to move over to Izzy, but before he could do so he felt a firm grip on his arms and was shoved against the wall, his cheek pressed against the cool plaster.

"Hey! What are you doing?!"

Someone cuffed him. He felt someone else rifling through his pockets. They pulled out his wallet and flipped it open, revealing his photo card driving licence.

"Jake Parsons."

"What... like Corporal Parsons? The disappearing soldier?"

Jake fought back. "Let me go! What are you doing?!"

The officer suddenly recovered from his surprise. "Jake Parsons, I'm arresting you on suspicion of attempted murder. You do not have to say anything. But it may harm your defence if you do not mention when questioned something which you later rely on in court. Anything you do say may be given in evidence."

"What are you talking about?! I haven't done anything, I came here to help... Charlotte!"

His heart was pounding in his chest; it was so tight he could hardly breathe. He fought back, but they were too strong - the more he tried to get to her, the further they pushed him towards the door. He took one desperate glance back at the woman he loved, before he was shoved into the hallway and she disappeared from view.

"I love you," he whispered, so quiet that nobody heard him.

"Wait!"

He heard brisk, desperate footsteps behind him, and they all turned to see a little girl behind them, her hands covered in blood, streaks of blood down her face.

"Where are you going?"

Jake didn't know what to say. Her eyes pleaded up at him, and his eyes pleaded back. The last thing he wanted to do was leave her, right in the middle of all this.

"Time to go," one of the officers said, giving him a shove. But she squeezed past and wrapped her arms tightly around his leg, forcing them all to stop.

"Stop! He didn't do it!"

Jake stared at her, his eyes soft. "Izzy, it's ok. It's all a misunderstanding. You can tell them what you saw. It will be ok."

"It will? You promise?"

"I promise. Tell them the truth, everything will be fine."

Her eyes brimmed with tears; he could see her whole body shaking. She was petrified. But, like her mum, she was also terribly brave.

"I did it," her bottom lip trembled, her voice barely a whisper. "Daddy was hurting Mummy. He had his hands around her neck, she was crying. I walked in and I saw the knife on the floor. I picked it up, and I hit him with it. It was me. I just wanted him to stop."

CHAPTER TWENTY TWO

Shadows danced across the picnic blanket around her as the warm summer breeze whipped through the branches of the willow trees overhead. Charlotte closed her eyes, butterflies dancing in her stomach as she felt the brush of his hand against hers.

"Where do you want to go?"

She said nothing but her lips curved up in a smile, imagining the squawk of seagulls overhead, the clip clop of donkeys hooves steadily travelling down the promenade, the lazy roll of the waves against the sand. She could feel the sand beneath her toes, the warm sun roasting her skin, fresh ice cream resting happily at the bottom of her belly.

The three of them.

She had never needed anyone else. It had taken her a long time to realise it, but Jake and Izzy were all the family she needed. She didn't need her mum. She didn't need money, a posh house, a flash car. All she needed was love. All she needed was...

His lips were soft and gentle against hers, and her stomach lurched with excitement and anticipation. He tasted a little like mint and she could smell a hint of his parents' cigarette smoke in his hair as his body pressed against hers and his palm cupped around her cheek gently. She allowed herself to melt into him until eventually, he broke away and sat back, his eyes glittering adoringly.

"I love you," he whispered.

Her pulse quickened and her heart seemed to skip a beat, like it had all those years before, when she heard those words for the first time. "I love you too."

Then she opened her eyes.

And he was there.

Not in her dream, but right in front of her, close enough for her to touch. She spluttered, gasping for breath until she realised that it was just a plastic mask across her face, and wires trailing her skin, not hands.

"Hey," reaching forwards, he took her hand in his, squeezing it gently, his eyes full of concern. "You're ok."

With her other hand, she pulled the mask off her face. "Izzy... where is she?"

"Izzy's safe. She's with your friend... Essie?"

"Effie..."

Dropping the mask back into place she relaxed slightly, her eyelids heavy. Izzy would be fine with Effie. Suddenly, it hit her. The memories of what she thought were going to be her last moments, the desperation she felt when she thought she was going to leave Izzy all alone, without a mum. Her eyes filled with tears and she pressed her eyelids closed, unable to stop them falling down her cheeks.

"You're safe," he lovingly brushed them away with his thumbs, his eyes intensely fixed on hers. "You're safe. I promise you. He's not going to hurt you again. Not ever."

For a moment, she allowed herself to enjoy the warm safety of his palms against her cheeks, the reassuring pressure of his thumbs against her skin. Their eyes were fixed together like magnets, neither one of them wanting to break the bond they still had, even after all these years.

"I thought I'd lost you..." he muttered, his voice barely a whisper.

"So did I..." she replied, her eyes still welling with tears.

Before either of them could say anything else he pulled her into his arms, holding her tightly against his body, her face against his chest. She closed her eyes and enjoyed the calming beat of his heart against her cheek. For a few minutes they sat together on the bed, their torsos aligned like two pieces of a lost jigsaw puzzle, finally reunited. Charlotte allowed herself to think of nothing else but the steady flutter of his heart, and the warmth and love which radiated from him.

But eventually, reality began to chip its way back in. How had she escaped? The last thing she could remember was seeing her little girl's petrified face, standing in the doorway, watching her mum's last breath being squeezed out of her by the other person Izzy trusted more than anyone in the world. And Effie was his friend, too. What if she took Izzy to him? Where was Myles?

"I need to see Izzy. I want her here."

"Of course. Effie came here this morning, I've got her number. She said she'd bring Izzy whenever you're up to it. I'll give her a ring, if you like?"

Charlotte nodded. "Please. I need to see that she's safe. Where's Myles?"

"He's... not going to be bothering anyone for a long time."

She watched Jake pace across the room whilst he made the phone call. He was wearing a pair of hospital scrubs, too big for him, but she could see the muscles flex in his back as he moved. She wondered what had happened to his clothes. What was he doing here? How had he known she'd be here?

"She's going to bring her in about an hour, they're having lunch. She says Izzy's happy, all things considered. She's been playing with Callum?"

Charlotte sighed with relief. "Her friend."

Jake nodded, taking a seat on the uncomfortable plastic chair by her bed. The same one he'd slept on last night - and his back wasn't thanking him for it now.

"Are you hungry? Thirsty? Can I get you anything-"

"Jake!" Charlotte interrupted, finding her strength. "What are you doing here?"

He clenched his jaw, staring at her intently for a couple of seconds, before opening his mouth. "Where else would I be?"

"I mean, how did you know I was here?"

"You text me, remember? I knew something was wrong. I had a feeling. So I went to the house."

Charlotte inhaled shakily, her chest tight as she momentarily recalled the pressure of Myles's grip around her neck. "And you called an ambulance? The police?"

"Yeah."

"Was he still there?"

"Yes. He was."

"How did you stop him taking Izzy? He said he would. He said he'd take her away from me..."

"He wasn't going anywhere," Jake muttered.

"Did you fight with him?"

"No. I didn't have to. But I would have done anything it took, to keep you safe."

She peered at him curiously. She looked as a fragile as a baby bird. Maybe now wasn't the time. Yet the expression in her eyes told him that she wasn't going to let him leave until he told her everything.

"I need to know what happened. All of it."

"You need to rest. Get yourself better. We can

talk about it when you're stronger."

"I am resting. But I need to know. How I'm alive. I was dying - I took my last breath. It was over. Did you arrive just in time to get him off me?"

Jake raised one eyebrow. "Not exactly. In time for Myles, maybe."

"What do you mean?"

Jake sighed. "Are you sure you're ready to hear this?"

"Yes. Please, tell me. I want to know everything."

His eyes travelled to their clasped hands on the bed. He never, ever wanted to release her. His eyes kept travelling back to the angry bruises around her neck, which were now turning angry purple, red and blue. He could still hear the rasp in her throat, too. Myles had been so close to killing her.

Then suddenly, something clicked in her mind. Something didn't add up. She stared at him, confused. "How did you know where I live?"

He pressed his lips together. "I... I might have had a look at your driving licence before, when we went for a coffee." His cheeks flushed hot with embarrassment as her eyes widened.

"Jake!"

"I know, I know. I'm sorry. But I don't regret it. Because if I hadn't, I'd never have got to you when I did. And who knows how long it would have been before help arrived. I wasn't going to turn up and ruin things for you. I was just... curious."

"I'm glad you did."

He nodded. "When I arrived, I could tell something was up. Everything felt wrong. I broke a window and got in, then I found you and Myles on the kitchen floor. You were unconscious. Myles was next to you, covered in blood."

"What?" Charlotte frowned. This didn't make sense. The last thing she remembered was closing her eyes, the life slowly being squeezed out of her. "I don't understand."

"I thought you were dead."

There it was again, that pang in his chest. The sudden stab of nausea deep in his gut, when he thought about what it would feel like to lose her. What it had felt like when he saw her on the floor, and he was sure that he already had.

"Myles was covered in blood? How?"

He jigged up and down on his seat, the weight of his dilemma firmly on his shoulders. But he had to tell her the truth.

"It was Izzy. She stabbed him."

Charlotte recoiled in horror. "She what?"

"She walked into the kitchen and found him strangling you. She was petrified. She wanted to get him off you, stop him hurting you."

"Is he dead?"

Jake shook his head. "No. He's in HDU, but he'll live. And as soon as he's out of here, he'll be locked up. You don't have to see him again. Izzy told the police everything. How he's been hurting you for months."

Tears were rolling down Charlotte's cheeks now, too fast for her to control them. She choked on her words. Her daughter, her baby, had been forced to do something so drastic to save her.

"She didn't intend to hurt him, she just wanted him to stop. Nothing will happen to her. They'll support her, with psychiatrists, that sort of thing."

She opened her mouth to say something, but tears choked her, rendering her unable to talk - she could hardly breathe.

"This is all my fault," she managed eventually.

"No, none of it is your fault."

"I let him into our lives. I caused all of this. I was so obsessed with wanting the best possible childhood for her."

"Isn't that what most parents want for their children?"

She stared at him. "Most parents don't allow a man like him into their child's life. I should have seen it. But I was blinded by how nice he was... the money, the comfortable home, the private school... I wanted everything for her that I never had. I wanted to teach her that she could have everything. But all I taught her is that people own you if they look after you financially. I've been so stupid."

"You're not even close to stupid."

Again, he cupped her cheek with his palm, causing little butterflies to flutter inside her belly. Leaning his forehead against hers, he took a deep breath of her scent, which was gorgeous even when she had been lying in a hospital bed since the day before.

"I know what I put you through," he said softly. "When I went missing. And I've regretted jumping out of that truck every day since. If only I had followed my orders, none of this would have happened. We'd be happy now, the three of us. Maybe four, or even five. This is all my fault."

He couldn't say anything else, couldn't bear to think of it anymore, so instead he tilted his head and brushed his nose against hers gently, connecting his lips to hers. His lips tingled against hers and she let herself melt against him, finally free to let him in. She had tried so hard to ignore her past, but he had sought her out, and now she knew that whatever happened, he would always be in her life. He kissed her gently and longingly, desperate to show her how much he adored her.

"What am I going to do?" She sighed eventually, leaning back against the pillows.

Jake squeezed her hands. "Everything's going to be ok. You need to get yourself better, then you can come out of here. I've spoken to my mum, she said you can stay for a bit, you and Izzy. You can have James's room, I know it's not massive, but you'll be safe... only for a little while, until you get back on your feet. And I'm back at work now, I'll look after you both. Obviously I don't have as much money as Myles, but I'll have enough..."

"Jake!" She interrupted, shaking her head in

confusion or frustration - he couldn't tell which.

His smile faded into a frown, the sparkle of excitement and love in his eyes quickly replaced with worry and hurt. "What's wrong? She doesn't mind, honestly. She's looking forward to seeing you. And Izzy will love Bee, it's just what she needs to get over-"

"It's not that."

All the hope he had in his body suddenly dropped down to his boots. If it wasn't his mum, then what was it? Was it him?

"I want to look after you. It's all I've ever wanted, ever since the day I met you. I love you, more than anything."

"I know. And you know how I feel about you, Jake. But... I need to put Izzy first. She doesn't even know who you are."

"But she would get to know me. We don't have to tell her, not straight away - she could get to know me first, then we could tell her together. I promise I won't ever let you down again, please give me the chance to prove it..."

"Jake, stop!"

The force in her voice stopped him in his tracks. He closed his mouth, searching her eyes like a lost puppy, his heart dropping like a stone. Had he got this all wrong?

"I need you to listen."

"I am listening. I just don't understand..."

"I do love you, Jake. More than I've ever loved another man. And I want you in my life, so badly it hurts. But I have let my daughter down. And I appreciate the offer, but I need to be the one to fix this. If I whisk her off to a house she's never been to, staying with people she's never met... well, she's going to be more confused than ever. She needs stability. And I need to make sure she gets it."

Suddenly, they could hear brisk footsteps in the corridor outside, light and bouncy, like the sound of skipping feet. Could it be Izzy already? It was. Within ten seconds, the door flung open and Izzy burst through, hurling herself into Charlotte's open arms.

"Mummy!"

"Oh, Izzy!"

Tears of relief streamed down Charlotte's cheeks as she held her daughter tighter than she ever had before. Jake stepped back and stood in the corner of the room, watching them together. Suddenly, he understood. The bond they shared was like nothing he'd ever known before. He was a complete fool for believing that now Myles was out of the way, Charlotte would come back to him, become his again. She no longer had her heart to give him anymore. It had been taken by a four year old. A four year old who was theirs, not hers, but didn't even know who he was.

"Oh, you've been so brave. I'm so, so sorry, sweetheart."

Jake coughed back the lump in his throat, exchanging a small smile with Effie. At least she was no longer staring at him in disgust, like he was a murderer. He took one last look at the love of his life and their daughter together, then quietly ducked out of the room.

He was halfway down the corridor when he heard a door flip open behind him, and she called his name. He stopped in his tracks and looked behind him.

"Jake," she repeated. "Wait."

He waited while she caught him up, her legs buckling slightly under the weight of her heavy bump. "I'm sorry for how I behaved towards you at the house. I assumed... well, I thought you had something to do with what happened. I honestly had no idea what Myles was doing to her. No idea. I mean, I know they'd had their troubles lately, but I thought it was just arguments... I had no idea he was physically hurting her. It's terrifying. You think you know someone. Myles and my husband were best friends, business partners. Connor had no idea either. If we'd have known, we would have done something to help her."

Jake nodded awkwardly.

"I wanted to say thanks. For helping my friend. She'd probably be dead if it wasn't for you."

"My pleasure," he mumbled, although all he felt deep in his gut was sadness.

Turning to leave, his heart broke as he tried to convince himself that this was for the best, that Izzy and Charlotte were better off without him.

"Er, where are you going?!" Effie asked incredulously, her hands on her hips, her brow knitted in a frown.

"I..." he didn't really know what to say.

Effie sighed, exasperated. "You're not going to walk away and leave her now, are you?"

He shoved his hands in his pockets awkwardly. "Her daughter is here... you're here... I thought she'd want some space."

She huffed at him again. Who is this woman, wondered Jake. She'd give any sergeant a run for their money.

"I can't stay long. I'll take Izzy home soon, Charlotte needs to rest. But she doesn't want to be on her own. She thought maybe you could help with that?"

Jake felt a flutter of hope in his chest. "She did?"

"Yes. Now, are you coming, or not? My back's about to break, standing here!"

EPILOGUE

Eight months later

Jake stood with his hands clasped behind his back, ignoring the stares and admiration his uniform often elicited when he was in a public space. Especially when he was surrounded by school mums, like he was now. He pretended not to notice and kept his eyes on target, the metal door in the red brick building, which was due to open in - he glanced at his watch - around thirty seconds.

Right on time, the door swung open and the teachers began to direct the children to their parents and caregivers. She was the sixth one out. As soon as she saw him, her face broke into a huge grin and she ran, waving a picture in her hand, shouting, "Jake! You came!"

She ran at him with such force he took a step back. "Well, I did promise. When did I ever let you down before, hey?"

"Never!" She beamed up at him, her arms

fastened tightly around his waist. "I knew you'd come." Curiously, she peered behind him. "Where's Mummy?"

"She's been held up for an hour, so she said she'd meet us at home. But I thought we might surprise her and pick her up."

"Yay!" Izzy skipped along next to him. It was a relief to see her looking so settled, so content. Both he and Charlotte had worried about this week for months, not knowing how she would copy with yet another transition in her life. And she still had so many more to come, not that she knew it yet.

"How did your first week at school go?"

"Good. I made a friend!"

"Did you? Who?"

"He's called Riley. He was crying in the playground today, so I asked him what was wrong. He said a big, horrible boy called James was being nasty."

"Oh. It's nice to help people who are upset, good girl."

"Yes. So I told him to show me which one was James. And I told him to leave Riley alone, because Riley and me are friends, and my other best friend is a soldier. And if he upsets Riley he'll upset me, and then I'll tell you."

Her hand crept its way into his and she beamed up at him, making his heart swell. It was during moments like these that Jake questioned Charlotte's decision not to tell Izzy that Jake was her dad. Surely she'd be glad? She adored him and proudly showed him off to whoever would listen. Yet there were also times he understood and agreed with Charlotte's decision. The nights when Izzy woke up screaming, her bedsheets drenched, after yet another nightmare. The days when she got upset and confused, because she'd watched her dad turn into someone terrifying and almost kill her mum, but she couldn't understand why deep down, she still loved and missed him.

The nightmares were becoming less regular and her behaviour was stabilising, but she was still having sessions with a psychologist, and both Charlotte and Jake knew that it would be a long time before she was 'back to normal' - in fact, she would probably never be the same innocent little girl ever again. The trauma of what had happened was buried deep inside her, and even if she seemed to get past it, it was likely that it would resurface again in the future.

So for now, Jake was simply Jake, a friend who was around a lot. Myles had recovered from his injury and was in custody, awaiting trial. Hopefully he would go away for a very long time, and Izzy would have long grown up by the time he was released.

"Is Bee at my house?" Izzy asked, breaking Jake from his thoughts as they approached his car.

"Of course she is. She's probably snoring on the sofa right now, waiting for you."

"Yay!" Izzy clapped. "I love it when you bring Bee round. I wish Mummy would let me have a puppy. Then I would have a dog all the time."

"Well, Mummy's busy. It would be difficult for her to find time to look after a dog. And you can see Bee whenever you like, you know that."

They began the drive towards the hospital. It was about half an hour away, and during that time Izzy told him all about her week and the funny things her classmates had done. She loved her new primary school. What a relief. Charlotte had been petrified that she'd hate it, that it wouldn't match up to the private preschool she'd attended when she lived with Charlotte and Myles. But she didn't hate it at all. She'd settled in well, even made friends in the four days she'd been there - just like Jake knew she would. The kid was resilient.

"How are we going to find Mummy? This place is huge!" Izzy gazed up at the vast hospital building in front of them as they pulled up in the car park.

"Er... hm, I didn't really think that far. Hopefully she'll come out of the main entrance and we'll catch her."

"Otherwise we might be following her home!" Izzy laughed. "You're funny, Jake. Don't you ever plan anything?!"

They got out of the car and approached the entrance. Jake's eyes fell on the bench upon which he'd once sat, waiting for visiting hours, when he was visiting Bella and hoping to catch a glimpse of Charlotte. Izzy would like Bella, he thought. Maybe one day they could meet. He still kept in touch with Bella occasionally, and she was doing well, applying to universities to study health and social care.

"Where now?" Izzy asked, as they came to a stop by the entrance.

"Er..."

Honestly, he didn't know. Perhaps this hadn't been such a good plan after all. They should have stuck to the original plan and met Charlotte at her house.

"Shall we sit on this bench? Maybe Mummy will come out of that door and see us?"

"Yeah, good plan."

They sat for a few minutes, waiting. Eventually, Jake began to wonder whether they'd missed her completely. He sighed. "Maybe we'll have to meet your mum at home, after all. I think we might have missed her. We can grab a pizza on the way?"

"Ok. Can we wait for two more minutes? Just in case?"

"Of course we can."

Just as they were about to leave, the double doors opened and two women walked out, deep in conversation.

"Mummy!" Izzy jumped off the bench and sprinted towards her, flinging her arms around her, her eyes squeezed shut.

"Izzy! What are you doing here?"

"Jake brought me! He said we could surprise you."

Jake approached, smiling awkwardly at the nurse she was with. "Hi. Hope you don't mind driving home alone today. I know you normally share lifts, but Izzy wanted to surprise her mum."

"Of course not," she smiled kindly. "You must be Jake. I've heard a lot about you."

The knowing sparkle in her eyes told Jake that she knew a lot more than his name. He grinned awkwardly.

"Well, I'll see you on Sunday, Charlotte?"

"Yep, my turn. I'll pick you up at 5.30."

"Bright and early!"

Then she was gone, and it was just the three of them. Jake and Charlotte's eyes connected and for a moment they stood, bound together like magnets, neither of them wanting to break their connection.

"Did you have a good day at school?" Charlotte asked Izzy.

"Yes, it was good. I made a new friend!"

"Oh, that's lovely. I'm so pleased."

"I love my school."

Izzy took their hands, one in each of hers, and skipped across the forecourt towards the car park. Charlotte sneaked a glance at Jake, and found his eyes were already on her, sparkling with love. These last few months had been the happiest of her life. Izzy had turned a corner, Charlotte and Jake were back at work, doing the jobs they loved, and their relationship was blissful. They were taking things slowly, for Izzy's sake more than anything, but he had spent many a night in Charlotte's bed, making love to her over and over again, until he slipped out first thing in the morning, turning up an hour or two later once Izzy was awake, with breakfast for all of them. They had enjoyed days out, lazy days in and FaceTime calls when he was on base and had to stay for a few days. Finally, Charlotte felt like her life was back on track - she was living again, not simply going through the motions, behaving in the way that others expected her to.

Of course, it had come at a price. Both Charlotte and Izzy were traumatised by what had happened, and they'd given up the lifestyle they had before. They had enough money to live comfortably, but the fast cars and mansion house were gone - not that Charlotte wanted anything from her old life. She had started afresh, keeping in touch with Effie, Connor and Callum, but in a new, smaller house in a new town. Charlotte was proud of how Izzy had taken it in her stride. She didn't seem to miss her old life at all. In fact, when she was having a good day, she seemed happier than she ever had.

"In you get then, Lady Izzy." Jake opened the door for her like she was royalty. Izzy giggled and jumped inside, pulling the door shut behind her.

"Thank you," Charlotte smiled, her body so close that he could feel her warmth radiating into him.

She grabbed his hands and squeezed them, then once she'd checked that Izzy was busy inside the car clipping her seatbelt, she reached forwards and kissed him gently but sensuously on the lips. Jake closed his eyes and melted into her, his heart swelling with love. There was nobody he'd rather be with. When she pulled away, her eyes sparkled with promise for later.

Izzy banged on the window. "Come on, then! I'm hungry! What are you waiting for?!"

Laughing, they climbed into the car, before driving in the direction of home.

BOOKS BY THIS AUTHOR

Battle Cry

Following a catastrophic patrol during the British Army's bloodiest year in Afghanistan, Jess, an army medic, finds herself embroiled in the issues faced by two of her colleagues. Despite her attempts to fight her feelings, she finds herself drawn closer and closer to her Section Commander, Rix, with almost fatal consequences. Can their love survive the almost insurmountable obstacles that they face, and is it stronger than Army regulations and PTSD? Battle Cry tells the story of how love can grow from the most unexpected of places, and how the longest lasting, most life changing battle scars are not always those we can see.

Battle Torn

The sequel to Battle Cry.

Four years after the doomed patrol in Afghanistan

which changed their lives in ways they could never imagine, Jess, Rix and Jase are moving on, both in their professional and personal lives. But when Jess is unexpectedly deployed on a humanitarian mission, resulting in catastrophe, it has far reaching ramifications for all three of them. Is Rix and Jess's relationship strong enough to endure the challenge, and will Jase ever be free from the PTSD which almost destroyed his life?

Battle Torn tells the story of how happiness and stability can be shattered in the blink of an eye, and how even those decisions which, on the face of it, seem straightforward can be the hardest ones to make.